aLL aBOut meN

Bella Pollen was brought up in the USA before moving to England. She lives in London with her husband and three children. *All About Men* is her first novel.

all about men

bella pollen

pan books

For David and for my friend Gerry Beeby.

This is a work of fiction. All names and characters
are either invented or used fictitiously and the events
described are purely imaginary. Any resemblance
to any person living or dead is entirely coincidental.

First published 1997 by Pan Books
an imprint of Macmillan Publishers Ltd
25 Eccleston Place, London SW1W 9NF
and Basingstoke

Associated companies throughout the world

ISBN 0 330 35154 0

9 8 7 6 5 4 3 2 1

A CIP catalogue record for this book is available from
the British Library

Typeset by CentraCet, Cambridge
Printed and bound by Mackays of Chatham plc, Chatham, Kent

With love and gratitude to anybody and
everybody who ever worked at Pollen.

And an XL thank you to
Clare Conville and David Huggins.

Prologue **Paris, 16 October**

Her passport was in her pocket. She stared at the graph on the Metro wall. There it was, the airport at the end of the line. How simple, a red and blue arrow pointing to sanity. She badly wanted the guts to just go, admit everything, plead guilty, ride to the last dot on the map and disappear for ever.

The train screeched past a station. She hung on grimly to the metal rail as the rumble of the wheels shuddered through her body. She squinted again at her watch, willing the hands to whizz backwards; an extra hour she pleaded . . . okay, how about ten fucking lousy minutes then? But it was no good, its happy Swatch face delivered the same bleak message: she was just not going to make it on time.

THE MINUTE SHE'D stepped ouside the flat she'd realized it was hopeless. A storm-cloud lurking overhead had opened up like a pair of bruised lips and spat out another heavy downpour. The roads ahead of her were jammed with angry Parisiens, their windows rolled down, a chorus line of synchronized fists shook in the air, dancing to the tune of honks and oaths.

For a second she'd wavered at the taxi rank, but the drenched man at the top had been waiting twenty minutes, and behind him, the tail end of a long crocodile lashed itself against the rain in frustration. Making a snap decision she ran for the Metro.

Standing in yet another queue to buy the ticket, a quick search in her pocket elicited every scrap of paper she'd hoarded for the last two years . . . except for the one she'd written the address on. Bad karma was playing havoc with her life.

On the seat directly below her an ageing tramp sat guarding his world in a Prisunic shopping bag between his feet. The old man stared up at her with a pair of rheumy bloodshot eyeballs.

—La vie n'est pas toujours si mal, he said and hawked politely onto the floor in front of her sneakers.

Deli look down at him as he wiped his mouth with a frayed cuff.

—You know something, Grandpa, she thought bitterly, —you are absolutely right. So can you please explain to me why mine is so shitty?

part one

Chapter One Show Me Your
Three Best Styles

Early life in the sixties had passed in a haze of good things to eat: Twinkies, Ring-ding donuts, Lucky charms, baloney, Kool Aid, Wonda loaf, and of course, best of all, Jones Hickory Smoked Bacon. The only really bad thing had been junket. Chocolate, vanilla and strawberry junket sitting anaemically on top of the washing machine in china bowls, cold and watery. Instant supper. Yuk.

This meant Mom and Dad were going out. They went out a lot, Mom all sixties and Jackie O in cocktail A-line dresses and a fake-topaz brooch, Dad, full of hip and swagger, hair too long for his job, curling down the back of his neck underneath his shirt collars, suits with cowboy boots, and a huge bear-lined coat with the hem falling down; a legacy from his father.

Theirs wasn't the world of psychedelic twisters, LSD and long stringy hair, they were a decade too old for that. Theirs was a world of squeaky clean TV, Carole King,

Sweet Baby James and the hideous Rita Tushingham hairstyles Mom brought over from London, inspiring her friends to take the chop. Still, they were a beautiful, cool sixties couple.

Sometimes, instead of going out, they had parties at home. Deeply glamorous people came to these parties. Terence Stamp, Jean Shrimpton sitting on the sofa refusing to smile in case of wrinkles, Edward G. Robinson impersonating Jimmy Cagney. M and Deli had junket then too, but at least they got to stay up late to entertain the guests who gurgled fondly over their Vyella pyjamas and cute English accents.

Mom maintained that M was Deli's brother. Deli was reasonably sure this meant M was her own exclusive property, to do with what she would. M on the other hand told Deli she was adopted, and sometimes in weaker moments she believed him. M wasn't the name he was christened with, but due to the premature loss of Deli's teeth from a baseball bat (M's baseball bat as it happens), and the inevitable swelling of her bloodied gums, it was all she could do to close her mouth over a single capital letter let alone enunciate the remaining vowels and consonants that followed and so M it remained.

M did everything Deli said, and if he didn't, she tortured him until he screamed for mercy.

She loved him more than anyone else in the world.

Despite the adoption theory they had apparently both been born in Mount Sinai Hospital on 94th Street. M by

Caesarean, and Deli by gas (too much gas her father was fond of saying). Dad was American and Mom was English but, as far as Deli was concerned, their dual citizenship made them groovily bi-lingual. At home they spoke with exaggerated Bronx accents, but at their aggressively Yankee school they could have been mistaken for Little Lord Fauntleroy and his long lost sister.

Mom's Englishness seemed distant to them, an irrelevance to their lives. They'd only been to London twice when they were small and it had barely made an impression. When Mom had turned twenty she'd got a job working in John Lewis' department store in London selling stockings to embarrassed business men on the third floor. One day a grade-B film actor had strutted in, ostensibly to buy some lingerie but really to throw his weight around for a while. On asking Mom to show him the quickest exit to the street, she had pointed to an open window. (Deli loved this story. Her mother being rude?) After Mom was sacked she'd been seized with the spirit of adventure. She left England for the first time in her life and travelled in a Greyhound bus across the States with her cousin Jean who had fat calves.

They met Dad in Tallahassee, where Jean boasted an obscure friend, and where Dad had been on a fishing holiday. They had both fallen for him at the same time but it was into Mom's ear that Dad had whispered grossly far-fetched stories of wrestling with rattlesnakes in the Florida swamps. Mom whom he had got drunk on Tequila and kissed under a blueberry sky, and it was Mom whom he had followed to England a month later snaffling her up with only minimum force from the protective embrace of her family, and sneaking her back to New York to get married.

While Deli and M played around at school, Dad and Mom went to work. Dad owned a contemporary art gallery with circular staircases and whitewashed walls on which large canvases hung splashed with only the occasional blob of paint.

Mom was a voluntary teacher. She taught fifteen-to eighteen-year-old Harlem kids with leather jackets and attitude how to read. She did this by playing Monopoly with them. Her kids all had names like Jesus, Momo and Jimmy, and the day Mom walked into their classroom with her smooth twang-free voice they couldn't believe their luck. Momo and Jimmy knew jack shit about fractions, were entirely ignorant about George Washington's propensity for the truth, but they were right up there on Real Estate in Park Lane and the Old Kent Road.

Mom adored her boys but she got depressed by their hopelessness, knowing in her heart that by the time she'd got hold of them it was always going to be far too late. But still, she stepped on the uptown bus to Harlem every day, and the presence of the Momos and Jimmys on family visits to Joe's Pizza became part of their lives.

At weekends there was TV to look forward to, *Penelope Pitstop*, *I Dream of Jeannie*, *Batman and Robin*, *Bewitched*. Even the ads were good, 'Let Noxema cream your face', 'Rota Router, the Drain Scooter', and 'Please don't squeeze the Charmen'.

Sunday morning was kept sacred for pillow fights, and the rest of the day reserved for eating. Dad had a macaw called Wilbur, a bad-tempered vodka freak. He would drink the vodka right out of people's glasses at Sunday lunch and get so drunk he'd fall off his perch. This was a frequent party trick.

In winter they drove up to Vermont and skied, the cold air sucked the warmth from their bones and the wind stung their eyes. In spring they drained sap from the trees, made maple syrup and slept in the woods. Dad had a flash white Lincoln Continental with grey leather seats and gleaming silver ashtrays called the Great White Monster, but one day he ran over a skunk, and no matter what he tried to fumigate it with, the smell just got worse and worse, stealing up their nostrils and seeping into their clothes till eventually Dad had to sell the car.

In summer they played baseball in the park, climbed trees, and ate warm roast chicken out of silver foil. Mom's hair grew long again (thank God) and she wore huge round tortoiseshell glasses and knotted denim shirts. Dad got into flares and platform boots in a big way.

Deli didn't remember Kennedy, nor even where she was when he was shot, but she did remember Dad saying Nixon was a slime-ball long before everybody else and on the day of the President's resignation she marvelled at his brilliance in acquiring this information first. Then before too long, Schraft's made way for Baskin and Robbins, Dad fell in love with Joan Baez and Deli developed a crush on Eddie Giacomen, goalie for the New York Rangers.

In 1971 there was the great blizzard and the city froze, then stopped altogether. The Empire State Building gleamed like a giant popsicle. The snow settled so high it blocked the doorways forcing people to ski out of the first-floor windows of their skyscraper. M whimpered when he first looked outside, thinking Bill the doorman must be buried alive but Deli kicked him to shut up, it was the most exciting day of her life. For a week the whole of Park Avenue was closed off to cars and used as a toboggan run. On a really good day, they could get from 98th and Park, where they lived, all the way down to the foot of the Pan Am building without stopping.

Then the thaw came and the slush piled higher and higher in the streets. Every afternoon on the way home from school they counted the dog turds nestling amongst the melting grey mass, grading them for consistency and colour. M told Mom that the particularly runny ones, seeping in brown rivulets down the white pavements, looked just like Dad's paintings.

—Do tell your father, darling, she said vaguely. — He'll be so pleased.

Which they did of course; as they weren't big on irony in those days.

And so life was fab.

★

THEN SOMEHOW, SLOWLY but surely, they became aware of the arguments at night. Rows that Mom and Dad had kept well hidden, closely smothered between the four walls of their bedroom.

One Christmas holiday with the apartment stuffed full of English relations and Deli sleeping on a mattress in her parents' room, she woke every couple of hours to catch drifts of anger from their bed. Very early the next morning she watched puzzled as Dad got dressed in the crack of light from the bathroom door, pulling on his clothes in that short jerky way people reserve for expressing silent fury. She went on watching as he hunted down his wallet, stashed it in his coat pocket and left without saying a word.

—Mom, Deli whispered as the door closed heavily behind him.

—Mom! Panicked, Deli called out to her Mother's shadow crying softly in the bathroom. But she didn't answer and Deli wasn't sure if she had even heard. For the rest of Christmas the atmosphere around the house was gloomy. Dad's face became ever more forbidding, and Mom's increasingly strained.

A couple of months later, one evening after school, Mom and Dad sat M and Deli on the sofa in the sitting room and broke the news. They had been arguing about a deal they had made, a secret and horrifying pact that the children knew nothing about. It turned out that when they had married they had agreed they would live ten years in their respective cities, and Mom's decade was long overdue. Mom hankered terribly after her roots, she told them carefully. Dad didn't want to go but he had made a promise, and honouring his promises was, as he explained somewhat pompously to his children, a big issue for him.

Head down, Deli watched her nails as they steadily raked a hole into the knee of her woolly tights. M sat next to her and asked whether he could take his bicycle with him, but Deli couldn't say a thing, too much in a blue funk of confusion to speak. Their world was coming to an end.

A few days before the boat sailed, M and Deli woke at two in the morning to a flickering sky and black thunder. There was an electric storm over the city. The lightning exploded in yellow flashes over the water tanks and crashed against the neighbouring scrapers bouncing its angry reflections against the glass. They counted a hundred flashes of lightning before they climbed back into M's bed together and swore in the dark silence that followed the storm that they would sneak back as soon as possible and reclaim New York as their home.

Three days later they moved to England. Deli had been thirteen and M eleven.

Chapter Two

Nothing, but nothing could have prepared Deli for the horror of English boarding school; a giant gothic castle in the middle of the countryside. With its turrets, battlements and riotous draining system, it was a piece of real estate of which the Addams Family would have been proud.

As for the countryside, well, wait a minute! This wasn't the country as Deli knew it. Where were the malls? Where were the carefully marked nature trails with the Carmel ice-cream stands, goddammit? Where were the joggers and the twitchers; what had happened to the senior-citizen tennis players in their pink bobble socks? Instead of all these comforting scenes, there were acres of soggy green fields, woods, rivers, countless flowers everywhere, even rock doves cooing away at the crack of dawn. Deli felt hemmed in by so much nature.

Lost, displaced, uprooted, she couldn't get a hang on the rhythm of this new life at all. She yearned for the water tanks, the summer heatwave, the smell of trash and the noise of 98th Street.

M was sent to a boys' prep school where he reported that his headmaster ate dandelions, dressed in a giant schoolboy's outfit and recited large chunks of *Lady Chatterley's Lover* every morning at the breakfast table instead of grace.

On the first day of school Dad delivered her to the front gates three hours late and wearing her washed-out Keds sneakers. Everyone stared at Dad's bear coat. The other girls wore brown Clarks sandals, pixi-shirt collars and laughed at the exaggerated Bronx. They were the daughters of the local gentry, rich Bohemians and politicians. Sunday papers were strictly forbidden due to the frequent exposés of parental scandals. Deli was given the last bed by the curtainless window, and central heating became a far distant memory.

For a while though, she behaved beautifully. She sucked up to all available staff, desperately hoping for parole. She worked hard, ignored everyone and at the end of the first term won every single academic and sports prize going.

—We're sending you to Coventry! shrieked Sarah, whose cabinet minister father (as the tabloids they'd bribed cook to smuggle into school gleefully revealed) enjoyed nothing quite so much as dressing up in an oversized babygro and being spanked by insurance salesmen.

Coventry, Deli thought, hallebloodyllujah. Let's hope it's a good long way from here.

But deeply miserable after only a few weeks in solitary she finally understood what was required to fit in. She stopped studying and began applying herself instead to the systematic destruction of school property and the absolute humiliation of the teachers. Immediately, she became extremely popular and learned her first important lesson in people pleasing.

Everyone despised the staff. Most were an assembled crew of freaks many of whom appeared to have dropped out of teacher training long before their diplomas had been stamped.

Scoring highest marks for the least attractive, Miss Trial (English), had a cat called Felix, a dangerously low bosom, and misshapen legs with black hairs so long they curled underneath her tights like burnt onion rings, squashed down by cheap nylon.

By contrast Mr Connor was a God. He taught Latin and hockey, he was deeply beautiful and had a smooth hairless chest that drove the girls wild. On field he removed his shirt even in the dead of winter to flex his muscles and watch his pupils flush red with longing. In Latin, Deli would hide a packet of crisps between her legs and noisily eat away praying he'd notice. When he did, he'd walk slowly over staring her straight in the eye, and she'd feel the hot prickle of sweat start. Then he'd stick his hand even more slowly between her thighs, still holding her gaze, deliberately, carefully, gently into the packet, rustling it slightly, help himself to a crisp, moving his fingers around softly, lightly pinching her flesh, until she could stand it no longer, and the blood would shoot into her face, breaking the spell, whereupon Connor would dissolve the crisp on his tongue like a religious wafer, smile knowingly and return to the blackboard leaving her faint with longing. Before very long Deli found she'd stopped wearing tights in his classes.

The school had four behaviour groups until a fifth was invented, Deeply Sub Minus, of which Deli became the founder and for some time sole member. She stole from the village shop, excused herself from classes by escaping out of the loo window, learned to lie fluently and smoothly on almost every subject, and bullied the younger girls.

From time to time she heard from M, and to her intense consternation he seemed surprisingly okay. He was playing a frog in his school play's version of Cinderella. He transferred his passion for baseball to cricket. He had a crush on matron, his gym teacher had a crush on him. His headmaster continued to eat whatever shrubs were in season and conducted parental interviews lying flat on his back in a meadow. On the whole M liked boarding school and Deli feared for his future.

Inevitably things went from bad to worse. Deli's group began to hang out with the local VBs (Village Boys of a delinquent nature). The girls gave them detailed instructions and to-scale maps made in geography class on how to get into the dorms at night. The teachers tried valiantly to protect their pupils' honour, putting barbed wire and broken glass on the edge of the turrets, but frankly to no avail.

By the second year Deli had lost control. During the Christmas holiday, she steamed open a letter of final warning to her parents: 'One more incident and she's out' it promised and so, on some flimsy pretext a week into the next spring term, she slapped the headmaster soundly round the face, leaving his jowls flapping wetly against his greying teeth, and found herself expelled on the spot.

ARRIVING AT EUSTON Station she'd felt a momentary qualm as she spotted the hemline of Dad's coat dragging along the platform. He looked at her steadily for about two minutes while she blenched, putty-coloured beneath his gaze.

—Why on earth didn't you tell me how miserable you were? he said finally, and took her to the Great American Disaster for a hamburger. Ah, her father, her hero, her God.

Together they celebrated her freedom in Jean Machine with a pair of mega multi-patch, pre-faded flare at the knee jeans.

Deli's next school, although a less genteel establishment, was not so patient. She lasted only a month before Mom was firmly asked to remove her. Apparently, Mom told Deli through somewhat compressed lips, the glue and cheese and onion crisp collage she'd taken such trouble inciting the other girls to paste onto the walls of the Great Hall had not been appreciated for the contemporary masterpiece her daughter had supposed.

But once installed into the third institution Deli met up with an immediate soulmate, Minna. She threw out her Clarks sandals, moved into Hush Puppies and became a junior hippie.

She learned how to walk with her head sticking forwards and cultivated a bovine facial expression. She rubbed toothpaste into her tits to make them grow and kohled her eyes every morning. She trailed around in embroidered kaftans, Indian tops and drawstring trousers, reeking of incense, and swinging puzzle rings. She did Latin prep cross-legged and swore eternal love for Jethro Tull.

Minna knew boys and the boys Minna knew all smelled of patchouli oil, damp sheets and BO. They had huge quantities of hair and better still, the hairy boyfriends had drugs.

On free weekends they all hung out together stoned and swaying in Leicester Square looking for fights with skinheads. They were the last word in Hip.

By sixteen Deli had become suitably snotty with her parents and acquired a habit of prefixing all statements with 'so':

—So?

—So there.

—So what?
—So who cares?

AFTER O LEVELS she bought three pairs of tie-dyed dungarees, a pair of platform clogs with red leather uppers and metal studs and moved to London. Breathing in the familiar fumes and the smog, hearing the screech of tyres and sirens of the police cars she thanked God for delivering her to a city once again.

So far so good. Now it was just a question of changing continent.

Chapter Three

For A Levels, Deli studied English, Maths, Spanish, Boys and Drugs, not necessarily in that order.

Once back in London, all kinds of new and exciting ways of acquiring brain damage became available. All free time was spent in a coffin-sized bedsit in Earl's Court taking smack with a group of hard-line junkies, all of whom were deliciously wild.

Adam was the meanest, Adam was hers. He had thick wavy black hair and eyes like a spitting cobra. Sexiest of all of course was his double conviction for GBH and aggravated theft.

They shoplifted the whole of the summer together. Having watched *Darling* with Julie Christie where she cruises around Fortnum's stuffing tinned anchovies up her knickers, they copied her slavishly in every store in the West End. For Deli's eighteenth birthday Adam lifted a white leather jacket and for his she filched a pair of red snakeskin cowboy boots with silver stud spurs and toe-caps.

After a while they graduated onto a bit of minor cheque book fraud. They kitted out the Earl's Court flat with an enormously expensive hi-fi, thousands of records, and some squashy designer bean bags on which they lay, silver foil in hand, nattering to themselves about themselves, and listening to King Crimson jumping and scratching on the record player.

Nervous of the ever more vacant expression on her face, and overcome no doubt with the cloying perfume of dirty sheets, Mom and Dad took her to the plush bar of the Europa Hotel for lunch and a pep talk.

—Now, Deli, Dad began. —Let's discuss the question of values . . .

Dad started well but seeing her smile broaden ended up delivering himself of a somewhat half-hearted lecture on the use of condoms.

—And what about looking for a job? said Mom tolerantly. —Surely this afternoon would be a good time to start?

—And what about burgling your parents' flat, suggested Adam later that evening, —and buying a few grams on the proceeds?

Family relationships became somewhat strained.

WHENEVER HE LOOKED back on that summer, M once told his sister, he realized that Deli had done him a monumental favour. It was as if by flicking through the cliché book of malignant teen behaviour, she had pretty much run the spectrum for the both of them. All M really had to do to bypass any rebellious urge of his own was watch the different fads as she played them out and decide to steer absolutely clear.

It had been the last day of the last summer term. M had stood on the platform at Temple Mead and toyed with buying a packet of cigarettes, Marlboro's. At school they were considered the only acceptable brand. He planned to sit in a smoking compartment on the train, preferably opposite a vicar, and openly slaver over *Penthouse* before picking up a nymphomaniac who would crouch on the floor sucking his knee-caps while he designed a strategy for the rest of his life.

In reality, of course, the queue at the newsagents was too long, the most promising nymphomaniac on the platform was all but propped up on a zimmer frame, and the train when it arrived was so full he ended up squatting on his suitcase in the corridor outside a pair of viciously rank loos.

Deli was meeting him at Paddington at four-thirty. At least she had said she would on the telephone the week before. He wasn't sure quite how reliable that was. What he was sure of was that she was going to insist that he stayed at Adam's bedsit. He'd already met Adam at the beginning of the Easter holidays when Deli coerced him round to some seedy Earl's Court address and with a maddening smirk had introduced M to a psychopath on a motorbike outside.

—Hey, brotherfucker! the psychopath had shouted before revving off with Deli laughing like a baboon into the back of his leather jacket. M had experienced an overwhelming urge to smash his face in.

He didn't really want to stay with them, but Mom and Dad were away. Plus he figured the argument wasn't really worth it. Arguing with Deli required patience, a clear-cut strategy planned days in advance and, if all else failed, sheer brute force.

The problem as he saw it was that Deli was not, by most acceptable standards, a normal sister. He knew this because he had spent jealous years comparing notes with his friends; he knew that where other brothers were concerned your normal average sister had various duties to perform, the bottom line of which at the very least included:

1) Doing everything their brothers said (newborn upwards);

2) Providing them with a selection of favourite dolls whose heads they could rip off (four years upwards);

3) Providing them with a selection of girlfriends whose pants they could rip off (fifteen upwards and for the rest of their natural lives).

For some reason, however, these non-negotiable rules hadn't seemed to apply in her case.

As the train had braked to a crawl, M pulled down the window and leaned out to search the crowd for her, narrowing his eyes against the station grit. He guessed they looked pretty much alike really, except of course for their colouring. He had almost black hair and brown eyes whereas Deli had green eyes and blonde hair (regulation bimbo he was inordinately fond of telling her). Mom and Dad also had black hair and brown eyes, hence the adoption gag, but although M's hair colour owed a lot more to his genes than Deli's did it was quite obvious they were related, and if anyone had nothing better to do one afternoon than to lay a book over the heads and eyes of a photograph of the pair of them, they would see that both M and Deli had the same long faces, the same long noses, same fleshy mouths.

He spotted her almost immediately standing on the platform and felt a stab of shock. She was wearing Adam's leather jacket and a pair of dirty torn flares. She looked like a delinquent drug addict, a smeggy runaway who had turned in desperation to prostitution. But perhaps it was simply that she looked cityish and right-on, and he just didn't know the difference.

—Hey, Camelbreath, she said, as he climbed out of the train. She gave him a kiss. He noticed the dark shadows under her eyes.

—Hey, yourself, he muttered over her shoulder, suddenly seeing Adam hovering in the distance. He gave her a hug back.

She smelt of sex and smoke and Adam's dangerous touch.

To call the Earl's Court flat a pigsty would have been grossly complimentary to Deli's housekeeping. M dumped his bags on a mattress in a tiny space no larger than a cupboard, in fact it *was* a cupboard he realized, as he lowered his head and eased himself out the doorway again. He sat down in the sitting room and surreptitiously watched his sister for the rest of the afternoon. In just five months Deli seemed to have undergone a radical transformation. Nervous and hyper, she moved around the flat fetching Adam a drink, changing the record on the surprisingly expensive stereo system and rattling on and on about city life. M kept quiet feeling uptight and out of place.

—Relax, man, you're home and dry, said Adam, sprawling on his stolen bean bag. —No more rules, no more cold showers, no more arsehole teachers telling you what to do.

—Come on, M, said Deli, sitting down next to him. —He's right, let's celebrate your freedom.

They drank a six pack of beer each and Adam rolled joint after joint.

—Christ, what is this? M inhaled cautiously. It was about double strength anything he'd ever tried at school.

—This is super dead head weed, man, boasted Adam. —It'll do you good.

Like hell, M thought. After about half an hour he felt his body detach itself from his head to go and get a drink. He realized he was dribbling.

Adam and Deli disappeared twice during the evening to another room.

The first time they went, Deli had looked back at him and smiled guiltily; the second time, of course, she hadn't bothered.

Chapter Four Doing Zip

After another twenty-four hours looking at her swivelling eyeballs M had
had enough. He dragged her to the
altogether less plush surrounds of the
Bistro in Earl's Court for a bottle of wine, packet of fags,
and a stern lecture. Deli couldn't believe it! M, her
seventeen-year-old brother going on sixty. Stunned she
remained virtually silent throughout. But later as she
tottered in through the peeling front door of the bedsit,
she was secretly flabbergasted to find herself a) caring
hugely what M thought and b) beginning to look at the
Earl's Court set-up through his eyes. The next morning
she woke to find herself sleeping half on and half off the
bed, with Adam, his lungs sawing with phlegm, splayed
out next to her. The stale smell of his breath was
frightening. She got out of bed and went to the kitchen
where the overload of unwashed plates had spilled out
onto the dirty lino and a mashed syringe was lying in the
corner. It began to dawn on her that Adam wasn't sexy

and dangerous at all, he was just sad and squalid. So she gave up drugs, she gave up shoplifting, and reluctantly she gave up bad boys with anti-social habits.

M and Deli moved into a tiny rented flat off the Harrow road. She told her parents she'd got a job in catering; but to be more accurate she worked on an ice-cream van and sold Mr Softy's to unsuspecting Arabs for three pounds each.

Parked outside the Albert Hall on the dusty evening of a hot day, Gerard bought an ice-cream from her.

She'd noticed him particularly because he was wearing velvet jeans, and the temperature was well into the eighties. When she knew him better she realized that Gerard dressed almost exclusively in wing-tip shirts and different coloured velvet pants, but the day he bought the ice-cream (20p for him by the way) he was wearing a pair that were so tight his crotch stuck out like a sledgeham-mer. It was love at first sight.

—Didn't I buy a frankfurter off you this morning, he asked, biting the top off a very stale flake, —in Oxford Circus?

Deli watched mesmerized as his tongue wrapped itself for a second time around the chocolate.

—We have to move along all the time or we get nicked. He was so sexy she could hardly look him in the eye. Blushing she double-wiped the counter instead.

—How many of these things do you eat a day? he asked.

She made a face. —You have no idea what they're made of.

He laughed. —Thanks, but I'd rather not know. He turned to go.

—So how was your hot dog? She glanced up, desperate to keep the conversation going.

—Oh, you know, it looked all right, he shrugged, —but it tasted like a dachsund's penis.

Deli uncharacteristically found herself lost for a reply.

—Or did I mean that the other way round? he said. —Anyway . . . hey, whatever. He waved the ice-cream in the air as a goodbye and she watched him regretfully as he and his velvets meandered off slowly towards the park.

Twenty minutes later he reappeared, poking his head through the counter opening as she was packing away the burger rolls. He leaned against the window and smiled. The edges of his smile almost touched his sideburns.

—Why don't you come for a walk in the park if you're through for the evening?

GERARD WAS AN artist. His creative forte had been the construction of eight-foot long fishes out of papier mâché. Each fish took two months to finish and weighed about a ton, although, after a while, he invented a mould and the entire process became much quicker.

But the best thing about Gerard, apart from his long

sideburns and carved cheeks, was that he had talent, the sort of real God-given talent that Deli would have traded anything to possess.

Gerard was the first really nice boyfriend she'd had, a boy with a beginning, a middle and an end, a boy to have a decent affair with, take home and even meet the parents.

Within a week, he moved his knapsack from a friend's garage in Bromley, where he'd been working on his fish, and into her tiny bedroom in the new flat.

UP UNTIL THAT point being in the clothes business had never so much as crossed her mind. It was hardly as if she'd spent her whole childhood dressing up in Mom's clothes, smearing her face with lipstick and whispering to Barbie dolls. But she did covet clothes and when you can no longer steal them, chances are you have to pay for them. At that point in her life the piece of clothing she had coveted more than anything else was a micro mini pair of fringed suede shorts she'd seen in the window of Elle in Bond Street. They had them in chocolate brown and taupe. Deli liked the chocolate brown and she had tried them on one afternoon, speechless with longing, turning round and round in the changing room craning over her shoulder amazed to see how thin they made her look. They had double stitching on the pockets and they cost £100.

She confessed her fixation to Gerard one evening.

She'd been in a foul mood, fed up with circling non-entity jobs in the paper.

—So make them yourself, Gerard had said.

—Myself? she asked incredulously. She hopped off the sofa and went to the fridge for a couple of beers.

—Get the suede, cut them out, sew them together, use your hands. He held up his own, encrusted with white plaster of Paris.

—My hands? Get real, Gerard. She laughed uneasily and chucked him one of the cans.

—Come on, he smiled as he deftly caught the can with one hand and pulled off the tab with the other, —I'll help you, it'll be easy.

So she had made them, and he was right, it was a cinch. She found a leather warehouse in the directory and bought two skins of beautiful chocolate brown pigskin, which were a bit pigmented, but which Alfie in the factory assured her would wear well.

At home she laid them carefully out on the floor and after taking some scanty measurements, drew what nearly resembled a pair of shorts onto the backs with a thick felt-tip pen. The suede slipped through her old Singer machine like butter. They cost thirteen pounds.

SHE BEGAN TO sift through the markets in London buying up remnants of cheap cloth. On Sundays, getting up at five (a wholly new and extremely unpleasant experience) she headed down to Brick Lane, wending her way round the stalls as she crammed doughnuts into her mouth and bargained for bits of old costumes with red-faced women, a million tiny whisky veins exploding across their cheeks like fireballs, as they breathed into their scalding cups of watery tea to keep warm.

She taught herself how to sew. It wasn't too hard, although generally speaking it required more patience than she had the good luck to be born with. She started making up clothes for friends, and turned on to the fish scene, thanks to Gerard, sending them out dressed as mermaids, staggering to walk in skin-tight silver skirts or scaly dresses with long trailing fins.

Two months later after some deft struggling with a calculator she confronted Gerard furiously.

—I've made a profit of seven pence for Christ's sake, she wailed.

—Single orders aren't lucrative, said Gerard patronizingly. —Think bulk, babe.

Back in Brick Lane, it appeared that every stall owner knew a machinist and every machinist had a friend. After a few months of stockpiling, her cupboard had accumulated metres of cloth, trim, dozens of old patterns and a notebook of contacts. So, with the last of the money from a ring Mom had given her for her eighteenth birthday (which she'd promptly sold) she bought a pair of orange leather boots with fake-fur trim in Kenzo, had every scrap of cloth she'd collected made into clothes, sent out invitations to everyone she knew, posted flyers in the street, and held a sale in the flat.

—This is ridiculously easy, she shouted to M as the front door closed on another customer, and as the sound of tinkling change grew louder, she realized she was gone, addicted, sold.

—We are a nation of shopkeepers, she chanted proudly, and, cash stuffed into a back pocket, tripped off to invest in some heavy-duty machinery, buying an industrial sewing machine and a prehistoric overlocker from a couple of cute Indian brothers in Balham, who soundly ripped her off.

—Deli, the flat's a fucking mess, said M one evening when he got back from work. M had a new waitering and washing-up job in the Asterix pancake restaurant in the King's Road.

But surveying the cyclone of rubbish underfoot, Deli felt only a wave of pleasure at how much work she'd got through that day.

—Did it ever occur to you that I live here too? he said, and Deli felt a tiny twinge of shame.

—Yes, okay, sorry.

—*And* Charlotte.

—Oh, enough about Miss Precious, Deli groaned. M had a new girlfriend he was very into. Charlotte was 'sensitive' and wore small round glasses. She called herself a New Left Sculptor, whatever the hell that was. Still worse, she lived in Edinburgh. Edinburgh? Please!

—On the few occasions she gets down to London, M went on, —she doesn't want to spend her evenings knee-deep in your workroom gunge.

—Frankly, Charlotte doesn't sound very New Left to me, said Deli.

—But why don't you get an office?' said M, looking pained.

—Oh sure, she said sarcastically, —I'll go find myself a sugar daddy, just give me a minute. After all, how hard can it be? She drummed her fingers on the kitchen table. —Let me see, he should be rich, obviously Jewish, he should dote on me like a daughter and give me his credit card to play with at weekends. He should wear finely pressed mohair suits, sharp shoes and a white fur coat draped over his shoulders. He should have much precious metal about his person, preferably a swinging medallion or, failing that, some other ostentatious bit of jewellery will do. His underpants too should be made of spun gold thread and should have his initials tattooed in diamond studs on the inside label.

—He could be into the following businesses: pornography, prostitution, gun running and/or drugs. He must keep wads of fifty pound notes in the deep freeze and . . . she paused . . . —Let me see, what else?

—Okay, okay, said M wearily.

—Oh, yes, I nearly forgot, Deli said, ignoring him, —he must start a business for me and install me into plush offices in the West End. In return for these small services

I will be prepared to dress in a nurse's uniform and spring out of cupboards swinging a selection of leather goods in my rubber-gloved hands. This is my criteria, M, she finished triumphantly. —Know anyone who fits the bill?

Chapter Five

It had been a Saturday afternoon and the sun was shining out of the puddles of rain collected in the corners of the cobblestoned road. Deli sashayed into Revolution, the swanky new store in South Molton street, partly to check out the goods and partly because Charlotte and M had wanted to have lunch in Ma Applebaum's opposite, where they probably served the most sensitive hamburgers and New Left chocolate cake in London.

Inside the shop she immediately felt uncomfortable. The salesgirls in Revolution stared at her with those hard-boiled-egg eyes of theirs, following her every move so closely you'd think she was on heat, making it obvious they believed she was a gifted shoplifter about to course into the street with a six-hundred-dollar jacket under her jumper, laughing like a hyena.

And okay, so they had a point. Had this been a year ago, they would have been absolutely right: but things had changed now.

She wandered into the second room, fingering menswear; the salesgirls were still staring and she was getting a bit paranoid, maybe it was the outfit. She was wearing a black cotton dress with leather trim, she thought she was looking pretty spiffy, but she wasn't entirely sure. Surreptitiously she cast around for a mirror.

Suddenly a door marked Private opened and out came a man with wavy blond hair, rigged up in green trousers and tight black polo. He stared at Deli for a second or two then advanced on her. Involuntarily she took a step backwards.

—This dress, he said, looking her up and down, —whose is it?

—It's mine, she said defensively. Jesus what was this? Did she have ex-shoplifter tattooed on her forehead?

—No, I mean whose label is it, who's the *designer*?

—Oh, it's mine, she mumbled, embarrassed. —I made it.

—It's totally fab, he said putting out his hand. —I'm Jerry Picks, the head buyer here and I'd like to order ten.

Deli giggled nervously. This must be a set-up. Dubiously she looked around to see if Gerard was hiding out somewhere.

—Do you have any other stuff like this, or a portfolio I could look at? Jerry Picks was now expertly pinching the leather on her cuffs.

—Of course, Deli rallied. Actually, she didn't have

anything approaching a portfolio, but she did have some photographs of clothes she had made, which had just been sent back from the Vogue/Cecil Beaton competition, along with their polite but, nonetheless, crushing letter of refusal.

Jerry had been a buyer for Revolution for three years, and had contacts in the fashion world. A month later through a friend of a friend of a friend who worked at the *Sunday Times*, he was taking her to see someone else who might be interested in backing a business.

A sugar daddy, she hoped.

BY THE TIME the day of the meeting had come along Deli had whipped herself into a nervous frenzy. She felt sticky and uncomfortable in a tight cropped tweed jacket over the brown suede hot pants. The jacket was too thick for the weather but she could hardly take it off as the crawl of new sweat was already tickling her armpits.

By contrast Jerry was looking good in a white tab-collared shirt with a woven tie. He looked calm, in control and deeply professional.

They both sat in white leather swivel chairs in front of a gold-leaf coffee table in Zelda Hartebeest's penthouse pad overlooking the Thames.

Despite all Deli's intentions to appear nonchalant and worldly, she was thrown by the vision in front of them. She'd been expecting a genuine wide-boy, a loud besuited card-sharp, but here instead was a glossy female swatched in ochre cashmere with tonally pleasing shoes. At least a vulgar signet ring on her pinkie flashed promisingly.

After initial niceties, Zelda got down to basics.

—What makes you think you can succeed in fashion? she asked. —They say it's a tough business to be in.

Deli, still rendered somewhat inarticulate by surprise, paused, then phased by the ensuing silence, broke into verbal four-wheel drive, opting to send out a message of force of personality in case Zelda didn't believe in her extraordinary talent.

—I'm keen and energetic and determined to succeed, I intend to become a world force in the schmatter business.

Too late she realized the woman wasn't even Jewish. Jerry kicked her to shut up.

—She has great potential, Jerry said calmly, —she's a startling new talent. Revolution is renowned for spotting trends.

—You have no training I understand, said their potential benefactress.

—I'm self-taught, Deli gabbled nervously, —but this has been my dream since I was a little girl, my burning ambition has always been . . . fashion.

The air-conditioning in the flat was on full throttle, inside the tweed jacket the sweat under her armpits was beginning to freeze from the onslaught of icy conditions.

Zelda laid her salon-buffed nails firmly on the portfolio still lying zipped shut on the top of the desk.

—I would like to show this to my husband, she

said. —If he thinks it has business possibilities, I may call
you.

They slunk out.

—Schmatter, said Jerry shaking his head. —Jesus, Deli.

—I'm sorry, I must have been in the throes of gender
confusion. She stared at the pavement.

—Hey, said Jerry resignedly, —aren't we all?

The telephone call had come a week later. Giving
Gerard a quick hug, Deli ran out of the flat. Jerry had
been out when she'd rung with the news, she'd go in
person and surprise him. She skipped into the tube station,
danced through the underground tunnel to the trains on
the other side, Zelda'd said yes, *yes!* She couldn't believe
it. She loved her, she loved Jerry, she loved M, she loved
London.

—My own company, she sang, generously tossing
some change into a busker's hat, —all my very own.

I'D LIKE FIFTY per cent of your half share, demanded
Jerry over lunch in Ma Applebaum's an hour later.

—Wh-aaat, are you kidding? Deli stared at him,
cheeseburger dropping from her mouth.

—Certainly not. You couldn't have done it without
me, I think it's the least I deserve.

—But you said you wanted to help, you said you'd do
it as a friend, she wailed.

Jerry's eyes narrowed as he leaned across the table.
—I'm a buyer, not a fucking Good Samaritan, he snapped.

—If you don't give me fifty per cent I'll make sure the deal doesn't go through and you'll get nothing.

Deli looked at him, and felt a minuscule piece of her heart, before as red and rosy as Snow White's apple, suddenly turn to a slice of hard cold steel.

Enter the first of many lawyers.

—He'll settle for ten per cent, the man said, —and it doesn't matter anyway, you'll be bankrupt before the year's out.

—No bloody way, Deli had vowed, signing the share transfer document. —Absolutely not, you'll see.

The lawyer had smiled thinly as he snapped his briefcase shut.

—Welcome to the fashion business, Sucker, he'd said.

The tramp stared ahead of him. The mustardy ooze of sleep had glued his lashes together into three individual sticky prongs above each eye. Deli turned away in pity. How many wrong turnings must he have taken to end up facing the concrete wall of his own personal cul de sac? And at what point had he noticed? At what point had she? Certainly not at the beginning, that was for sure.

fashion tips nº 1

Sales

A few months into this new career you discover something called THE FASHION TIMETABLE. Apparently it is quite important to stick with it if you want to get along in the Fashion Business. Oh, and by the way, you also have to design a collection, that helps a lot too.

For reasons best kept to themselves fashion people have decreed that winter collections should be shown in spring in an exhibition during something else called FASHION WEEK. In this exhibition you're supposed to show what's known as your merchandise. Before long you elevate yourself to the heady position of Sales Director, so you can indulge in the unparalleled pleasure of ringing shops and asking them for an appointment to buy. You quickly discover, however, that this is quite a frustrating job.

Who did you say? Whose collection? screeches Hymen the buyer.

—Madison, Schmadison, never heard of it, yawns Dovanna, her associate.

The tone of voice here is more or less what you might expect if you walked up to these people on the street and said:

—Hi! Nice to meet you, I've got a cold sore. Would you like to kiss it?

But you feel, you really do, that it is only a matter of time.

Chapter Six

Zelda's husband had been a real-estate man, less glamorous than firearms, but more concrete somehow than porn. Karl Hartebeest was second-generation German but had been brought up in Switzerland before moving to England. He had supposedly made his money clawing lucrative property deals for his compatriots eager to vacate the homeland, their assets freshly laundered into starched and pleasing piles of bank notes.

He had coal-black hair, limpid blue eyes, an unusually straight nose, and three children. Obscurely, Karl and Zelda's children seemed to be named after German recipe dishes. Strudella, Brotundbutta and . . . unfortunately Deli could never pronounce the third. All three were rampant teenage girls with black hair, limpid blue eyes, unusually straight noses and curious skin complaints. They were also in varying, not to say embarrassing, stages of adolescent sexual confusion.

But it had indeed been Zelda who fascinated Deli and

M the most. What was astonishing for three such jet-headed concorde-nosed girls was the fact that their mother had been a Titian bombshell, with a gravity defying beehive and the tightest of spandex clothes. An ex-model from Surrey, she had once nearly decided to paint. But now, at forty-seven, her lack of personality had become increasingly etched into her face in a mask of downwardly mobile wrinkles.

Zelda was bored and rich and had nothing to do. Her ovaries had sucked dry the sperm of her husband on three separate occasions, swallowing and ingesting his genes whole, and ruthlessly spitting out hers, so that no trace of her watery provincial blood had seeped through into her own offspring. Every morning she sat across the breakfast table from her husband, stared at his three replicants, and wondered how the hell it had happened.

So Karl okayed her decision to invest in the business, thrilled to give his spouse something to do with her life in between, of course, her social mountaineering and shopping.

—Fat chance, Deli told Gerard after the first meeting with Zelda in a smart West End restaurant. —You can just see she has this neat little fantasy of sitting in design meetings dressed in beige cashmere casuals, crossing her pale-tighted legs with their tan shoes, quietly making colour choices, maybe even dreaming of a gold and white shop in Beauchamp Place where she can take her friends after lunch in San Lorenzo. Well, over my dead body.

The first time Zelda tried to muscle in on a meeting of any kind Deli accidentally left her in a small enclosed space with Tom the Van, sometime delivery service and the lewdest mouth in London. After fifteen minutes or so, Deli was gratified to see Zelda edging her way around the walls of the office towards the door, Tom in casual pursuit. After listening to Deli's strenuously insincere apologies, Zelda stalked off and was not seen again for two whole seasons.

THREE MONTHS AFTER Deli had set up the business, M decided to leave London to work his way across the States. Tentatively he broke the news one evening in the flat.

—I can't believe you're going without me, M. Deli was determined to pile on the guilt.

—So come. But he knew perfectly well she wouldn't.

—Why don't you stay here, we could work together now then go in the autumn?

—Don't be daft, M said, irritated, —I can't wait around till you decide you need a weekend break.

So M left, and Deli cried, and then M cried a bit too. They both swore they'd write (they both lied) then M got on the plane and for the first time that he could ever remember, he felt free as a fucking bird.

Deli had resolved to follow him as soon as she could but in her new and wholly exciting role of working girl she'd been hard pressed to figure out how.

Chapter Seven **Blow Me I'm Buying**

The exhibition was in three weeks and Deli still had to get most of the garments ready. Plus the really bad news was that M, her brother, her baby, had finally found his way from New York to Los Angeles but instead of coming back as planned, was now headed for South America with his back pack. Deli imagined him dancing along the Copocobana Beach with stubble on his cheeks and a llama for company and she felt jealous, mean-spirited and sour.

Then to really sugar up the news, Gerard decided to disappear from her life as well.

—You know, Deli, I'm leaving London next Tuesday, he announced suddenly one evening over scrambled eggs.

—What do you mean? she asked distractedly, scraping the top of some burnt toast into the sink. In her head she was going over and over the pieces she had still to finish. She was both terrified and elated about the prospect of the exhibition.

—I'm off to Scotland.

—What, for ever? she said idly, thinking he meant for a couple of days. Gerard was always disappearing off here and there to collect driftwood from Brighton or scrap metal from Crouch End.

—I've found an old barnhouse that I can convert into a studio, it will hardly cost a thing. Gerard looked over at her. —I can store all the fish moulds there. His eyes slid guiltily away.

Deli stopped scraping. —Oh my God, you're serious aren't you? She stared at him. —You are going for ever.

—I need the space, he told her. And she was stunned. She put down the knife and went over to sit next to him.

—Have you met someone? she asked him tragically. —Have I ever put pressure on you?

—Come off it, Deli, Gerard said, laughing nervously. —space to work, I can't remotely afford a studio here. Anyway, you're really into your own thing now, and I'm into mine so . . .

Who would have thought that underneath those hot velvet pants, Gerard was a cold pragmatist?

—Five foot eight of me compared to 1,400 square foot of warehousing, she said lightly. —How can I possibly compete? Oh, Miss Flip to the bitter end, she thought.

Later that night she had put out her hand to touch Gerard's back as he lay asleep next to her. She felt miserable at the idea of him leaving. It wasn't that Gerard had ever been a big demonstrative kind of guy and, okay, maybe their relationship wasn't full of black and white movie passion, but Gerard was someone to play with, sleep with and not get too complicated with, he was there and solid and sweet. And anyway, surely nothing at that moment was more important than work? Was that the right way round? Maybe yes, maybe no, but who had the time to stop and think about where everything fitted in?

Gerard had stayed his last night in Deli's flat, setting the alarm for four a.m. the following morning. After he'd loaded all his belongings into his van, and finished securing his turbot tails onto the roof rack, he turned to say goodbye. The sun splashed onto the pavement through the dawn haze as he bent down and gave her a quick hug.

—You can always come up you know, he said cheerfully for the fiftieth time.

Deli had pulled her dressing gown closed again. —I'm strictly a city girl, she'd said sadly, waiting quite naturally for him to beg, but he hadn't begged and as she'd watched the back of the van trundle round the corner leaving her standing alone, unwanted on the street, she remembered promising somewhat overdramatically that if she was to be so ignored by Love then she would instead forge a career that would make the world and all the Gerards in it sit up and take jealous notice.

THE DAY OF the exhibition had loomed and in the last-minute rush she'd realized she hadn't priced anything, shit!

Where to even start? The clothes were already hanging in neat lines on rails as the doorbell sounded.

Tom the Van, who'd been hired for the day, opened the door looking resplendent in what could almost be described as clean clothes. Two guys in matching flasher macs swept in, and behind them an iron lady with stiff hair and an expensive looking handbag swept in too. The flashers didn't speak as they were too important, but the iron lady introduced them as Somebody and Somebody from Boston's most fashionable store. The reason Deli couldn't remember their names was because from the moment she laid eyes on them they were immediately clocked in her mind as Mr Wint and Mr Kidd, those two bad guys in *Diamonds are Forever* who were endlessly putting scorpions down James Bond's Y-Fronts.

They all sat down. The buyers didn't say anything, and Deli didn't say anything, discovering her mouth was suddenly as dry as a hamster's buttock. She soon realized however that silence was probably a mistake.

—Show us your line, rapped the iron lady.

Deli leapt up and lunged for the first garment on the rail.

Mr Wint and Mr Kidd were still totally non-vocal but had taken off their macs to reveal sharp designer suits with complementary natty ties. Deli went into babble overdrive.

Wint interrupted.

—What is the wool content of this fabric? It looks very heavy. We have a lot of central heating in Boston.

Deli assured him confidently, —This fabric is warm in winter and cool in summer. Mr Wint looked doubtful.

—Show us your three best styles, said Mr Kidd.

Mercifully the telephone went in the next-door room, an enormous fictitious order was being taken by Tom the Van. The Iron Lady threw Deli a don't-think-we're-not-onto-you-look that nearly made her pee her pants with fright.

When are you shipping Fall? the Iron Lady demanded.

—Soon? Deli offered, risking a joke.

The three were silent.

—October? she guessed again, sensing disapproval.

The Iron Lady scribbled a few notes and looked up. —Our cancellation date is 30 July *in store*. Deli accepted immediately. Meanwhile Mr Kidd and Mr Wint were actually holding a conversation.

Wint: I like it, it has a look, but it's young.

Kidd: It could go on the third, but it's expensive.

Wint: I'm worried about the fabrication, it looks itchy.

It is itchy, you berk, it itches like fuck, she was dying to say.

Kidd: Have you sold it to anyone in the States?

Aha, so this was it then, this was the crunch.

—No, not yet, she said sadly, rising to open the door.

The Iron Lady nuked her with a glance.

—We'll do a small order just to see what the reaction is, we'd like it in the buying office beginning July ready to ship. We'd prefer it free, but we'll accept a sixty per cent discount and we'd like exclusivity, she finished.

Deli showed them out, slobbering with gratitude, kissing the indentations on the carpet where they had trod. —What talent, what skill, what brilliance, she crowed to Tom the Van. —I'm going to be independently wealthy and successful for the rest of my life. And you, Tom, are privileged to be my witness.

The order had come through five days later. It had been for three pieces.

Deli laughed out loud as the Metro shunted into its first stop. The crone standing in front and whose head was more or less nestling under her armpit twisted around to stare disapprovingly at her with a pair of haddocky eyes. Effortlessly Deli exploded the woman's skull with one of the few remaining imaginary Vulcan Missiles she had in stock. So she'd been a bit disingenuous about her prospects, but then she'd always convinced herself it was better to know less than more because, inevitably, most people, when faced with the map, knowledge and crossroads, were forced by logic to pick the safest road ahead.

Production

And on the road ahead lies Production.

Desperation finds you gravitating towards the East End where eventually you abandon your garments in factories picked more or less at random. Entering one of these places is a real eye-popper. Weaving your way through the corridor of Hades, depression hits you *smack* in the face, invading your head with a dark sulphuric cloud. Through the gloom, rows and rows of bleak-eyed Greek girls swing into focus, rumbling away on heavy-duty industrial machines. The girls glance vacantly at you for a brief moment before getting back down to their crude piece-work. No Andarte here, Ladies, no Mountains of Zeus, this is the nightmare world of sweat shops, this is the guts and belly of the fashion underworld and, believe you me, it stinks.

Before you can get too far through the door, the purveyor

of this hell-hole appraises you skilfully – your particular brand of ethnic minority, your age, your clothes, and, most importantly of all, the degree of desperation with which you are clasping your docket for twenty shirts. By the time you have picked your way across the floor towards him he will either have assessed you as:

a) somebody with whom he is likely to do business,
    or
b) a spring lamb ripe for fleecing.

If you see signs of the latter it is probably best to exit backwards until you are left on the street sucking in the fresh air, shaking the depression out of your clothes and the guilt from your mind but all the time you're thinking:

—Christ alive, they're in there and I'm out here, what kind of luck does it take?

Chapter Eight

Somewhere between Spitalfields and Stoke Newington, Deli had stumbled across a factory owned by a Mr Patel. She still had forty itchy dresses on her hands, and could find no one to accept them. They had been photographed by *Vogue*, were about to appear in next month's issue, and the image of thousands of customers storming the shops, clutching the magazine was keeping her awake at night. To make matters even worse, two had been ordered by her very own beloved Royal Family, bless their good taste and unswerving patriotism.

When she first met Mr Patel he was propriety itself, ushering her inside his spanking cardboard-partitioned offices, hastily switching off the high keening of a Bengali pop star on the radio by his desk.

—Oh, please, come in, Miss Madison. You are so very young, Miss Madison.

Deli instantly warmed to this obsequiousness. Despite the somewhat unpalatable mixture of BO tempered with rancid mutton, his offices really were substantially cleaner than most she'd run out of during the last few months. More to the point, he sounded convincing.

—I am thinking this needs a new pattern, Miss, perhaps even grading. Ah, that's very nice pintucking, Miss, very skilled work. I have good girls who can do this, not very lazy at all.

Deli had asked to check out his factory floor downstairs, but it had been shut for the day.

—We are finishing very big order yesterday, Miss. My many twenty girls are having a jolly fine rest.

She gave him all the dockets, a three-week deadline and left, relief cooling her worries like a blast of air-conditioning.

However, two weeks later, having rung several times for a progress report but failing to raise Patel on the telephone, she began to get a little twitchy, so armed with a box of hangers and a pile of plastic garment bags over one arm, Deli trekked off, naively thinking to come home again with the entire order completed and probably gift-wrapped.

Arriving at the outside of the building, she found the entrance obscured by a half-shut metal grille, a large rusty padlock hanging through a gap near the bottom. She rapped loudly on the grille and then harder on the bottom half of the door inside.

There was no answer. She stepped back, thinking she must have confused the address, but the same faded tin sign was nailed through the bricks above the metal framework. SOOJIR ENTERPRISES. She banged the grille again, this time much more strenuously, still nothing, no sign of life from within, not even the radio.

The fire escape on the outside of the building led to another opening into the factory area. Deli climbed down, the plastic bags still over one arm, and pushed her way through the basement door which thankfully proved to be unlocked.

Remember *Klute*? With Jane Fonda as that hooker who gets to have it away with Donald Sutherland? Remember the scene right at the end in the old man's sweatshop when Jane's just about to be murdered by the whacko business man, and that dippy sixties bird on acid is la-la-laaing away on the soundtrack trying to sound psychotic? Well, that's exactly what Mr Patel's factory looked like. A huge cavernous room, lit by intermittent shafts of sunlight which fought for entrance through the window bars, dust spinning and whirling in the light, and behind, a ghost town of dead and decaying machinery stretching some forty feet back in uneven lines. The legs of their worktables were bolted defiantly to the floor, their thin metal spool holders rising a foot into the air like the swords of a people-less army manning an industrial city under siege.

There was nobody there, nobody at all. The machines were all switched off except for one which was quietly humming away on its own. On the table beside it, a dirty piece of plastic sheeting obscured the fruits of somebody's irresolute labour, and on top of that perched a crumbled, half-eaten packet of custard creams. There was no sign of the cloth she'd left, no finished dresses hanging in neat rows waiting to grace the backs of grateful customers, no sound at all in fact apart from the deserted whirring machine.

Spooky.

Well, spooky for about three seconds, until suddenly Deli heard noises emanating from the L-shaped end of the basement. The sound of strained grunting, the sound of jagged breathing, getting louder, then joined by an insistent scraping noise of something being dragged forwards and backwards, wood against lino, and underlying these, another higher pitched quickening of breath, half murmuring, half sobbing . . .

She knew what it was, of course she knew what it was, it was just that she couldn't believe it. She crept round the corner, and there was Mr Patel, his smooth brown back to her, slicked with sweat, his hairless arse, raised and pumping, his feet balanced precariously on a small wooden stool, scraping against the lino workroom floor, backwards and forwards while he drove himself harder and harder between the legs of the machinist below, her orange nylon skirt rucked up onto the cutting table, her thighs damp with pleasure, her head moving from side to side, like she was being pistol whipped. And clearly visible, moving backwards and forwards as she did, were the crumpled but finished forms of the itchy tweed dresses.

Mr Patel came with a series of short 'oh's' and more scummy throat-clearing. Swaying slightly he took himself off in the direction of the toilets. Snatching the dresses from underneath the surprised girl, Deli edged out backwards, far too cowardly to face the inevitable scene, when Mr Patel, his senses deflating as fast as his erection, came spiralling down to reality and saw her.

All she could really concentrate on during the long drive back through the East London traffic was whether spunk on tweed was dry-cleanable and, if so, whether it would come off before she delivered to the Palace.

Chapter Nine

Just how much romance there was in travelling alone M later admitted he wasn't altogether sure. He'd found himself in the grottiest hostel in the smallest town in the most obscure part of Ecuador, and to round off a really bad day his passport had just been nicked.

Dead place, dead town, dead country. No, not a dead country, he thought, in fact most places had been great up till now, but today for some reason his spirits had slumped. Earlier that morning, when in the grip of excitement of unexplored territory, he'd taken a wander round the town of Quintos. The place had seemed deserted, just a few pale splintered shanty houses leaning against each other for support. Eventually he'd stumbled across the market where it seemed most of the living things were being decapitated in front of his eyes. Oh he'd seen it all before in much the same looking markets all over South America, but now his middle-class fascination with extreme poverty had pretty much worn off. As he walked on he'd heard laughter and watched from the corner of his eye as a knife was plunged deep into the belly of a dead cat; its guts tumbled out onto the dusty ground and he'd felt his stomach turn. He felt depressed, rootless, lifeless, dirty and sweaty, then guilty for all of the above.

Guilty because when you travel alone you're not supposed to get depressed, you're supposed to feel spurred on to embark on more ambitious adventures, you're supposed to lay bare your soul to the open sky, be at one with the spirits of past travellers, scream in the darkness of tunnels with the Indians. You're supposed to have understood and accepted your own mortality, and a whole lot of other philosophical crap, but actually all that M really understood right at that moment was that he wanted a hot bath and to get laid, neither of which looked particularly hopeful. He thought wistfully of the girl he had picked up the month before who had been holiday jobbing as a gas-pump attendant in New Mexico. She'd been a kittenish twenty-year-old with skin the colour of Coca-Cola and a pair of swinging breasts behind loose dungarees and he thought even more wistfully of the brain-curdling sex he'd enjoyed with her for three days.

He finished with his packing, and attempted to restore his map to its former rectangular glory and as he did so an old crumpled letter from Deli dropped out of its creases. He had opened it out and re-read it slowly.

Darling M

Help, go to the nearest exit, take a plane and come back home.

Being family (some say) I'm sure you'll want to know what the problem is. This is the problem. I am running a company of three here, just me, myself and I . . .

I'm pissed off with being Duchess Do It All. The Reigning Princess of No Free Time. Crowned Queen of the Non Existent Social Events.

Spotlight on my love life since Gerard? Well, thank you for asking. Yes, I have a new boyfriend now, he's called TV. He's bright and well informed on world events. On the whole we get along just fine.

Come back soon. You know you're not having a nice time (are you? aren't you? Surely a letter would be reasonable at this point?).

Miss you,
Deli

In England it would be spring. M closed his eyes and smelled the fresh grass. He saw the whites of the cricket players, heard the crack of his old school bat. He realized he had never understood why Deli was so hooked up on America; in spring God was an Englishman. He thought about the cherry blossom snowing in their street, then he thought about TV, running water, he remembered his Velvet Underground albums sitting, dusty, in his bedroom. He experienced an embarrassing urge to listen to Procul Harum's 'Sweaty Dog', and for the first time in eleven months he wondered about going home.

HALLELUJAH. M WAS back. He really was back. Deli felt somewhat uneasy that his sudden return might have had something to do with her endless whinging postcards, but what do you write to someone who you imagine to be riding hell for leather through the Prairie sunshine, gnawing on biltong, and lassooing snakes in bushes?

Dear M – only last week the postman had a small but noticeable pimple on his left cheek. Hey! I wonder if it's still there?

Hardly inspiring.

He'd called her office from Heathrow and left a message. As soon as Deli had got it she'd dumped her bales of cloth and rushed straight home, but now as she turned the key in the door she suddenly felt strange from nearly a year of separation. Would he be harder, taller, wiser? Would his adventures have jellied his soul or would he wear an air of unmistakable cynicism that made his lips curl?

She walked hesitantly into the sitting room and stared down at the familiar face asleep on the sofa until he opened his eyes and saw her. In reality he looked a lot thinner than when he'd left, thinner and hollower, older she supposed.

M SAT IN the office and looked with satisfaction at the stack of black and red Arch Lever files on the shelf in front of him. Each one boasted their name and date in neat printed caps down the side. He stirred his coffee, with three sugars, thoughtfully. Had he found Deli's professional activities in any kind of organized state he realized he would not have picked up the challenge. But order and symmetry appealed to him in almost direct proportion as it repelled his sister, and the sight of hundreds of bills disintegrating unpaid in the back of drawers not to mention realms of paperwork covered in mug rings inspired in him some kind of perverse urge to install systems. Now two months later he was only mildly surprised time had gone so fast.

The telephone rang beside him on the desk. He picked it up. It was a person to person call from the States. Carol, he thought sourly as he waited for the voice to be connected.

Carol had creamed into their lives through a tenuous magazine connection only a week after M got back.

Carol: Christ, the very thought of her made him wince. Thirty-eight D-cup, long hair with swept up edges, and a hand always poised near somebody else's wallet.

She was into a breathtakingly unoriginal combination

of older men, fast cars, free plane tickets and designer clothes. Last week she had left for New York with her fifty-five-year-old American boyfriend, Gene, to promote one of her clients, and as she apparently had nothing to wear, she had offered to take the collection with her. M thought this was a bad plan, but Deli thought it was a swell idea. Suddenly, it seemed, the business had a P. R.

—M, a voice said breathily as the connection came though, —It's Carol!

What a surprise M thought as he went to find his sister.

—You'll never guess what, Deli! Carol had shouted down the line.

—What? Deli put a finger in one ear and tried to avoid M's scowling face.

—We've hit the jackpot, honey. Her voice quivered with excitement.

—What's heppened? Deli felt her heart start to pound.

—We've been offered a free show in Toxic Taste. They want to stage it immediately. They'll pay for everything. Just make sure M agrees to cover for you. She hung up with a triumphant click.

—Toxic Taste. Oh my God, M! Deli shouted. — Probably the most famous nightclub in the world. Plus, it's free, *free*! This could make us.

—It could break us too, Deli, M retorted. —New York isn't going to be the gooey nostalgic place of your dreams. Frankly, it's a terrible idea. I don't think you should go.

   —Oh, for God's sake, M, she'd said exasperated. —Take a risk once in a while.

Chapter Ten Toxic Doodles

There had been only five minutes to go. *Only five goddamn minutes*! Deli had glanced at her watch for the ninth time. Oh, terrific . . . four and a half and counting.

The floor of the club was already packed with hot, cross people – hot, cross and expectant people, from whom noise had escalated from its previous low rumblings to an ugly roar, and they were still coming in. Outside the open doors, the rope strained and groaned under the surge of clubbers squished against each other in a sweaty body sandwich.

—Doesn't this ticket mean *anything*, screamed a tall black man in drag, waving the invitation furiously. His leopard fedora bobbled threateningly towards the bouncers.

Deli put her hands over her ears, shut her eyes and prayed. —Please, God, let them come back. I'll do anything, give up anything, sex, drugs, wrestling in mud.

The technicians had walked out. She couldn't believe it. Nobody, but nobody walks out minutes before a fashion show, but then this was New York and she couldn't have been more wrong.

She'd been trying to get link-up for the stage head-sets, but the cable had been too short; with no link-up there was no way the models could be sent out on time.

There'd been a stand-up row with Andy, the lighting guy. *He* wouldn't give her any more cable. Why wouldn't he? Who knew? Andy had very small eyes, perching in a large blunt head, and looked not unlike a great white shark. The rest of the crew had stood around laughing, pot bellies sticking out of their shrunk T-shirts, long hair twisted behind their ears like a bunch of fat teenage schoolgirls with stubble.

—If you don't give me what I want I'll tell Rob, and he'll bury you, Deli shouted furiously.

Rob Howard, a small balding ex-con from New Jersey, was Toxic's owner.

—You tell Rob, little sister, and we're outta here, said Andy.

—Okay, she said, shrugging. —So go. She'd thought they were bluffing and stalked off to find Rob.

They *knew* she was bluffing and disappeared off to find the nearest flat shiny surface, dollar bills rolled at the ready. Rob was nowhere to be found. Immobilized by fear, Deli sat on the edge of the stage by the speakers.

Backstage there was pandemonium as the models struggled into their first outfits, the crowd was building up under the smoke, people were virtually standing one on top of the other.

Rob had decreed green smog was the look for the evening, so green smog there was ... great clouds of it poured from every direction. Two TV crews, who'd arrived early to set up, were spluttering, coughing and complaining vigorously about the poor light. Almost everyone Deli knew in the whole world seemed to be in town, and what was worse they were all coming to Toxic Taste tonight.

Toxic Taste was where it was at, everything else was tired, dead, finished, over. Sputnik space? Studio 54? Xenon? Where? What? Sorry never heard of them. Oh! Wait, yes! Didn't someone get arrested down at 54 for murder? Yeah, I remember, just before it closed down. Christmas time, wasn't it? Six months was a long time in this city.

Toxic was set up on three floors of a large warehouse a few blocks south of Canal Street. Inside the floors were divided into the following sections:

Dancing and drinking.
Drinking and shagging.
Drug taking and sleeping.

Scary, scary looking people everywhere. In the first five minutes after Deli had sneaked through the back entrance she decided the club was her 1984, but Carol loved it, in fact everyone loved it, but it gave Deli bad vibes.

Carol appeared suddenly by her side, blinking through the green fog, her casualty-coloured eye-shadow had scattered sparkle onto her cheeks.

—What the fuck's going on, Deli? We should be starting.

—No crew, Deli mumbled.

—What? Carol said. —Whaaat! There are a thousand people out there.

—I know.

—This is not a joke, Deli. This is *not* funny.

—*And I'm not laughing*! Deli yelled at her.

Only seconds to go now, a slow clapping had already started and a premonition of collective audience-sneering flashed through Deli's head. She looked at her watch again, it was 10.14.

She reckoned her fifteen minutes of fame were almost up.

—Hi, baby, missed us?

A grubby thumb and forefinger tweaked Deli's ear.

Andy was standing behind her, his pupils receded to microscopic specks in his shark's eyes, a filmy moustache of coke clung to his upper lip.

Behind Andy, the rest of the crew sauntered back in

through the stage door sniggering and beaming, stoned out of their heads. The jeering of the audience pulsated around them.

Crazed with relief, Deli pushed out the first girl. The show went on, staged in the dark. Models bumped into each other, backdrops from previous shows whizzed up and down, and throughout the proceedings she could hear Andy whispering obscenities into her headphones.

—Hey, baby, now you've spun on my finger, why don't ya try my dick?

FOUR HOURS LATER, squashed against the balcony on Drug Taking and Sleeping, Deli gazed out onto the maelstrom below. Every weirdo and fancy dresser in town had surfaced, even several varieties of sexual deviants were throwing up in the toilet bowls.

—At least the party's a success, howled Carol in Deli's ear. Small beads of sweat glistened on her bosom and her eyes were bloodshot.

Later still Deli was swaying around the dance floor, her face pressed into the shoulder of a wildly attractive man, in front of them a lone skinny girl in a gold mini dress spun slowly around, her long blonde hair flashing under the strobes.

Deli focused with difficulty on her date.

—Hello, she said, surprised to find her voice so slurred. —Who are you?

—My name's Pele, he said. —Who are you?

—I'm Deli, this is my party. She shifted in his arms. —What do you do?

—Oh, he said, —nothing much, but I've been known to kick a football on occasion.

She smiled dreamily at him. —That's nice, say, do you know what time it is, please?

—It's five-thirty, he said glancing at his watch. —Morning, I guess.

—Morning, she said, —how lovely, morning – she stopped short. —Oh no. She remembered with horror a photoshoot for *Interview* magazine scheduled for nine o'clock.

As THE CAB rocketed up the west side of the city, unimpeded in the early morning emptiness, Deli's skull had been gripped in the relentless jaws of club headache, only a dull thud remaining, a painful echo of the night's excesses.

Through the open crack in the window, a wet smell of garbage floated off the river and sneaked into her consciousness. She wrinkled her nose in distaste. Oh God, M had been so right, an hour after touching down at Kennedy, she had indeed been in the throes of gooey nostalgia: the whackos, the Wall Street rollerskaters, the chequered cabs, the water tanks, even the Guggenheim, she could have kissed them all. Now, scarcely a few days later, she'd managed to make a complete and public arse of herself, and if she thought the show had been bad, she could only imagine the horror of the reviews.

Chapter Eleven

Why is it, that when you meet the great love of your life, he turns out to be bald? Not only that, but he turns out to be bald, practically middle-aged and living in a country which is not the same as yours. Typical, just typical.

It had been the evening after the *Interview* shoot and unbelievably the Toxic show had been all over the papers that morning, including a page and half in *Fashion! The Bible*, probably the world's most influential daily fashion newspaper. Its publisher, the legendary Mr Don Cataract, had then cemented his approval by taking Carol and Deli out for lunch in La Grenouille earlier that afternoon.

Don, who looked like a benign old football coach for some third-league kids baseball team, was reputed to be the most ruthless man in the business, not to mention the most dangerous. He was apparently equally famous for peeing into his own glass at parties and toasting himself loudly before downing it in one quick gulp.

—*Suck hard on the nipple of success!* he had cried, inching his hand up Carol's skirt. —And remember to advertise.

Later she and Carol had been celebrating in the Noho Star. They had just finished a huge bowl of clam chowder, and were in the middle of sharing a helping of mashed potato of the day, when in walked two guys, one tall and gangly, and the other short and gangly. The point being that Deli had noticed them because they were both balding. They had that peculiar kind of sexy American Jewish baldness, just a bit of curlyish black hair around the sides and back, framing dark, dark eyes.

Personally Deli couldn't get into English Protestant Balds with their few sad follicles huddling together for comfort on self-conscious shiny pates, but she had to say that Jewish American Balds were right up her street. And the tall one she thought was so far up her street she reckoned she might as well open the front door and ask him to move in.

She had just been eyeing them up when she heard Carol shouting, —Hey, Petey, over here!

Carol knew one, what luck! Petey squinted for a second, registered, then came over to sit down with them and immediately started to talk record labels. The tall thin one was called Aaron and for some reason Deli found herself staring at him for the rest of the meal, making stupid small talk during which she discovered he was thirty-eight and worked for Schmeil, Gottfink and Hershey, specializing in Media Law.

The conversation over coffee became sluggish and

awkward. Deli couldn't make out whether it was just her or whether they were both being simultaneously spastic.

—Why don't we go back to my flat and play some billiards? suggested Aaron as he gently eased the bill out of Deli's fingers and handed it to the waitress with his credit card.

AARON'S LOFT WAS on the corner of Broadway and Bleeker, two minutes from the restaurant. It was a gothic building decorated with gargoyles round the top, their swollen tongues directed obscenely towards the pavement below. On the first floor Aaron unlocked a door which led straight into one giant room with the billiard table at one end and a large steel fridge at the other.

By two in the morning, Peter and Carol had mercifully peeled off to one of Gene's obscure night-time hangouts and Deli had cunningly engineered herself next to Aaron on the sofa where she was curled up eating banana ice-cream straight from the tub. Surreptitiously she scanned the room for evidence of a girlfriend. The decoration was scanty but comfortable, furnished with an eclectic mixture of relics from a fifties' furniture graveyard. Deli was relieved to notice however that there weren't any tell-tale happy couple photos perched warningly on side-tables.

—I'm going to give it up though.

—Mm, what? Deli said, colouring. She looked back to find Aaron eyeing her closely.

Aaron was saying something and she realized it was indeed just her and not both of them being utterly pathetic. Aaron was managing to make perfectly normal conversation whereas she was already fantasizing about meeting his parents for Sunday lunch and offering to do the washing up. What was it with her and these instant crushes? Other people met, flirted and sometimes even controversially dated before they decided they liked each other. Oh God, she thought in dismay, she was quite capable of making a fool of herself over someone before they'd been formally introduced.

—Am I boring you? Aaron was looking fairly certain that he wasn't.

—I was just thinking of something, she said, feeling idiotic.

Actually she was thinking that he had crinkle lines when he laughed and dark grey eyes which turned up slightly at the edges. She was thinking that she liked the way his arms were freckled and his face was lined.

—I'm thinking of giving up lawyering, Aaron repeated.

—Is lawyering a word? She pulled her head together.

—I don't think so, but I'm thinking of giving it up anyway. I appear to spend most of my day arguing about things I don't really care about.

—What would you do instead?

—Oh, anything that would be a change. Right now though, I'm bored. He shrugged and smiled. —Or maybe I'm just having an early mid-life crisis.

—I guess you'll just have to find somebody, er, something that really turns you on, Deli said without thinking. There was an immediate post-Freudian slip silence while she bit her tongue, then went puce with humiliation, but either Aaron was too grown-up to recognize the horror of the moment or just too grown-up to mention it.

—Yes, I suppose I will. There was, she thought she could detect, the faintest suggestion of a smile around his eyes.

After a decent interval Deli felt obliged to leave.

—So how long are you in town for? Aaron asked her at the door.

—Oh, a few more days, a week, four more nights maybe. Depends. I don't know.

Quite what it depended on she wasn't sure, but for some inexplicable reason she felt if she managed to confuse him she might regain some ground from earlier gaffs.

—You want to do something, get together maybe? Aaron stood, his hand in the back pocket of his jeans, grey T-shirt slopping over the top. His feet were bare.

—Oh, that would be so lovely, she mimicked to herself as she ran down the street after a cab. —God, he'll never call me, I sounded just like Princess Anne.

AARON HAD CALLED her in the plush surrounds of Gene's apartment the next morning and asked her out to lunch.

The restaurant was a tiny Japanese noodle bar on the west side of town near Aaron's office. She forgot to tip the cab and, oaths flying behind her, climbed out at fifty-eighth street instead of fifty-six, because for some reason, she didn't want him to see her arriving.

Sophisticated really, the things you do when you fancy someone.

She found Aaron sitting at the bar, reading the *New York Times* and drinking a glass of Japanese beer.

—Hi, Deli said cheerily, determined to get a grip on the date right from the start. She sat down awkwardly on the bar stool without kissing him hello.

In a fit of renewed nerves she struggled with the menu and didn't think too hard about what to order, eventually finding herself working through a bowl of steaming soup and dumplings that burned her tongue on the first sip. The bowl was so big she could have dipped her whole head in it and washed her hair at the same time.

They talked and talked and Aaron looked at her with his grey eyes, and her innards turned to peanut butter. After the soup, she jetted off to the loo to regain strength, find control, play for time, and hopefully make a plan. She got up gracefully enough but slapped her thigh hard into a stray chair and had to struggle not to limp the rest of the way down the stairs.

In the mirror, she was horrified to see that the soup had steamed off most of her make-up, leaving two dark smudges of mascara under her eyes. Her hair at the front was damp and had gone stringy and wavy. She looked like a thirteen-year-old refugee recently airlifted out of Vietnam.

Carefully she wound her way back to the table.

—Hi, she laughed nervously. —Sorry I was so long, I had to take a bath.

—You look adorable, said Aaron, —like a refugee. He touched her cheek with his finger and she immediately became his slave.

AARON'S LOFT LOOKED even larger in the daylight, the sun spilled in through the high windows and bounced off the billiard balls, throwing their reflection back up onto the ceiling in shadowy colliding planets.

They left it only once during the next week when, on whim, they decided to take a night-time boat ride round Manhattan. The lights of the city crackled across the water, the moon above them gleamed a silver thumbprint against the inky sky.

—Here, said Aaron. He handed Deli a cigarette. Having just sobbed through Bette Davis in *Now Voyager*, Aaron kept copying it and lighting up two at the same time. Deli thought it was pretty romantic except that Aaron didn't smoke and had to keep throwing the second one overboard.

On Saturday Deli lied to Carol, then waved her off in a cab to the airport. On Sunday she rang M and lied to him, then on Monday she lied to British Airways, changed her ticket and stayed another week.

And Aaron, well, she didn't know what it was all about, but what she did know was that Aaron made it feel to her like she had finally come home again.

★

THE DAY BEFORE her flight back to London, Deli had woken up in tears. Not wanting Aaron to see her scarlet nose and puffy eyes, she hid in the bathroom and took a long shower. She felt moody and claustrophobic and for the rest of the morning drifted around the place fiddling with the books, rolling the billiard balls across the table, trailing over to the fridge for yet more juice, trying in fact to avoid confrontation with Aaron at all costs. Anything to ward off the impending conversation about the future, or, more to the point, the lack of it.

He cornered her eventually by the deep freeze. He stood against her, one arm bent at the elbow, leaning against the wall behind her head.

—Stay, move in with me, live on ice-cream, he said abruptly. —And if you want to be boring and practical, you can even look for a job here. He kissed her.

She didn't say anything, too taken aback to answer.

—This is America, remember? Aaron moved his knee between her legs, holding his hands cupped on either side of her face. —The land of opportunity. Come on, take a risk, better still, take me? He tailed off looking almost apologetic.

—It isn't that simple, Deli said feebly, breaking loose. But she wondered why she'd said it, because it was in some ways exactly that simple.

She took the subway uptown and went for a walk around the city. With a queasy feeling in the pit of her stomach she passed the school, the sweet shop, Joe's Pizza

Parlour, the rest of the beat, finally ending up outside the apartment on 98th. She poked her head inside, it was exactly the same, same marble floors, same elevators, same quiet cold hall.

—Can I do something for you? A strange face was living underneath Bill the doorman's hat.

—Er, no, nothing, she muttered. —I used to live here, I just wanted to see if it had changed.

—Oh, in that case, come on inside. The doorman's suspicious look lit up into a 1000 watt Welcome-to-America smile. —What apartment?

—It's okay, Deli said quickly. —I don't want to go up or anything. The prospect of getting any closer was terrifying, she moved off rapidly.

AND SHE HAD wandered through Central Park that afternoon, hesitating at the entrance to the zoo, breathing in the familiar stench of the crocodile hut. She'd walked slowly past the Alice in Wonderland statue, stopping for a moment, concentrating hard on trying to conjure up a sign, a portent, anything to tip the scales of indecision, but nothing happened and she eventually found her way out of the park into Fifth Avenue down which she walked for the next two hours until she reached Aaron's loft.

The next day, after an uneasy evening during which she could find nothing to say to Aaron, she found herself bolting for the nearest cab, jumping on the plane and sobbing most of the way back home.

Back in London, the land of dull reality, she had wondered why she was there and not in New York, why she had said no, turned Aaron down, why she'd messed her chances so thoroughly. She dreamed of Aaron day and night, of his grey sloppy T-shirts, his laughter lines, his quiet tidy mind. She'd mooned around the office until M had firmly instructed her to get a grip and start doing some work for a change. Aaron rang her every day, then detoured to London a month later on his way to Europe and again on his way back, but he couldn't stay long and so she had been doomed to a love affair by telephone and postcard that had been only just bearable and, as the months had flown by, increasingly hard to sustain.

The brakes of the train screeched to a halt in the underground blackness of no man's land. Somewhere in the distance Deli thought she could hear a siren. Great! At least a bona fide reason for being late – a suicide, a jumper probably twitching and frying on the track ahead, or, if she was really in luck, a terrorist attack even. If she was quick-witted enough she could save the day, blind a passing reactionary with the zip of her backpack. Tonight she would accept the key to the City of Paris, an International Bravery Award, Come Dancing with Mitterand.

After all, anything, let's face it, would be preferable to where she was heading.

fashion tips n° 3

Delivery

So. You have actually manufactured things. And in numbers of more than one each.

Weird, eh?

But what is really sinister, is that these warm winter clothes have to be delivered. Not in winter, you understand, not even in autumn, oh no, but in the middle of July.

Apparently, this is because the kind of people who buy designer clothing are also the kind of people who are prepared to cut short their summer holiday. They are willing to leap over the side of their yachts and swim back to England in order to be the first to purchase this fabulous new look. And if this is true, God forbid, then maybe this is scientific proof that there really is a neurological connection between full wallets and empty heads.

Still, you've made them, delivered them, and soon, amazingly, people might even buy them. But be warned. Only at this point, and at this point alone, might you expect to see a little cash flowing in for all your trouble.

Chapter Twelve Cheap Cuts

Kenneth Sopp was a whole new species of man made up from a dense mass of aqua molecular spodules, each one connected to the other by a complex set of nerve endings with extremely overactive sweat glands. In short he was one hundred per cent liquid and thus able to squelch when he walked and sweat while he talked.

Kenneth Sopp was an accountant. He was a present to Deli from Zelda in celebration of their first anniversary together. Kenneth loathed spending of any description, but the refunding of expenses as a general concept left him feeling morbidly unwell.

—I am here to curb cash flow, he stuttered, when the necessity of signing a cheque became inevitable.

M had complained to Deli, who had complained to Zelda who determinedly ignored both of them.

Post Toxic Taste, Deli was suddenly 'Hot news', 'A fresh new talent' and although Zelda was ecstatic, sunning herself in the first rays of glory that filtered down from the press coverage, Karl on the other hand, was becoming decidedly twitchy. He was nervous it was all heading out of his control. Karl wanted the brakes on, he wanted things small, he wanted a toy for his wife, not another business that required wages, overheads and months of expensive auditing. But Deli, distracted from her blues over Aaron by all the attention she was getting, was becoming impatient. M watched as she immersed herself deeper and deeper in the industry. It seemed to him that with the publication of each new article her appetite for success grew ten fold. Deli wanted things big and she wanted them soon.

M sat in the middle and wondered how long till the oil boiled over.

THE OIL FINALLY boiled over around the end of the summer when, torpedoed with orders from all directions, Zelda Interference suddenly loomed large and menacing again.

—We must increase our turnover, M informed Zelda at their packed shareholders' meeting of three people. —Put the business on a more professional scale.

Having scared Zelda off so successfully once, M had been unprepared for any resistance, but Zelda on the flightpath to menopause, her beehive losing a little of its former height and lustre, had suddenly panicked at the thought of approaching retirement from the nothingness of her life. Fully recovered from her unfortunate experience with Tom the Van she decided in a last ditch attempt that she too would become a tycoon like her beloved Karl. —I agree totally, she cried, thumping her manicured fist smartly down on the table. She reached inside her suit pocket; for a split second M thought she was about to produce a four-inch thick cigar but instead she carefully placed a white envelope on the table.

—A few little drawings of mine, she said. —I was thinking a shop, gold fitments, white leather sofas, somewhere I can take my friends . . . definitely Beauchamp Place . . .

BUT AS LUCK would have it, in the beginning of autumn a strange disease whirled in from nowhere, knocking the leaves from the trees and enveloping London in its cyclone. It was formally identified as the change of career bug, it was highly contagious and hit everyone M knew.

The first to succumb was Kenneth who had met a female accountant called Gloria, who had succeeded in making his mouth dry for the first time in his life. She was the spiritual type, and had talked Kenneth into a speedy marriage and a Kibbutz in Israel for their honeymoon.

The second was M's old flame Charlotte who sent him a surprise postcard in September explaining that she'd decided to give up sculpture and take up crop spraying in Arizona instead and would he like to join her?

But the third and by far the most inspiring was Zelda,

who having partied in the right place at the right time suddenly scored herself a media opportunity, and with the aid of a huge neon autocue, began anchoring a lunch-time news show with an extraordinary degree of success.

In the middle of Zelda's new found fame and euphoria M sidled up to her with a proposition of independence.

Aaron lent them the money, M declined Charlotte's invitation and vowing never, ever, *ever* again to be anything else but one hundred per cent a family-owned business, they paid off the reptilian Jerry and bought Zelda Hartebeest out.

Chapter Thirteen

It had been M who'd stumbled on the perfect new offices.

The Blacknag Trading Complex was a vast red Victorian warehouse perched somewhere between the M40 and the canal. Swinging from a makeshift gallows by the entrance was a skeleton, presumably left by some drunken medical students from the nearby hospital, and in all the years Deli and M were there, even throughout the period when the estate became neo-gentrified, the skeleton remained there too, grinning like a benevolent night-watchman.

The outside of the building's many entrances were fortified with huge steel gates like an airport hangar, the padlocks that secured them as big as frying pans. The buildings themselves had immense loft-like spaces, supported by internal pillars, and arched windows which let in a stream of yellowing light from end to end.

Once inside, a cranky industrial elevator took an unacceptably long time to get from floor to floor and made such agonizing straining noises whilst doing so that it seemed at any minute the cable might snap, and the elevator shaft would plummet down at a thousand miles an hour.

The first time Deli stepped into the lift with M, he said to her, —*Omen 2*, remember?

—Huh?

—When the black doctor discovers it really *is* wolf's blood, and he's hurrying off to find someone to tell, and you know what's going to happen because his assistant has just had her eyeballs pecked out on the road only minutes before by the raven . . . remember?

—No.

—Then the black doctor gets back in the lift, looks up and there's the shaft coming straight down at him, a hundred miles an hour—

—I have no idea what you're talking about, Deli said.

—And slices him in half like a jam roll.

—Oh yeah, said Deli finally, —I remember . . . so?

—Oh, forget it, M said in disgust.

The inside of the elevator walls were a myriad of metal and paint finishes, every millimetre of surface area covered in lewd graffiti scratched out with keys and then Maji-marked in with felt pens; the delivery man's labour of love. The subject matter was mostly about the tenants themselves, the insinuation of canine status for their respective mothers, and the size and appearance of their genitalia. But the most memorable were two of the most obscure. 'Is muffin' the mule an offence?' and the even more cryptic 'Roddy is unhelpful'.

They decided to take 1500 square feet. It was a corner office facing west on the top floor with the arched windows Deli liked so much, and a deluxe view over the canal. It also had, they discovered during the winter, the worst damp and the only lift in the entire complex manned by a poltergeist.

Their immediate neighbour was Terry, who had the 1500 square feet on the other side of the lift. Terry was a photographer of sorts, whose speciality was advertising. His real forte within the industry was food photography, for which he would spend hours creating handsome still lifes of nectarines, strawberries and figs that Archimboldo would have died for.

Terry himself could not be described as a man in the peak of condition, the main feature of his body being his stomach, which veered out from somewhere underneath his chest at an unholy angle, making him look like a cartoon of a man who'd swallowed the python who'd swallowed an elephant. His head was shaped like a guitar without the handle but his sad sagging clown's face totally belied his chirpy nature.

Terry's two great loves were magic and curry. He belonged to every magic club in the country and received dozens of letters every day from like-minded fanatics with whom he kept up an impressive correspondence re the latest tricks.

★

As THEY UNLOADED the last of their stuff from the removal van outside, M and Deli stood in the unit and surveyed the mess.

—Send help now, begged M down the phone to a secretarial agency, and within half an hour a dainty little china figure was picking her way over the packing cases.

Janine. M hired her on the spot.

Janine – terrible twangy accent and nails as long as skewers – had clearly mugged up on all published literature detailing how to be the world's most irritating secretary, and was determined to practise during office hours. She chewed spearmint gum for smokers' breath and on the second day wore a pussy-cat bow and a tight skirt. She lasted forty-eight hours.

There followed a long line of misfits and minor criminals until finally M settled on Tish, an American girl with wavy auburn hair, who pipped the other candidates to the post by virtue of not having a police record.

With studio staff they fared little better. The samples were beginning to make the stock room smell like a third-world supermarket. A pungent aroma of onion bhajis was noticeable on the shirts, while the jackets from Angel reeked of cigarettes. Dresses from a small Chinese unit in Ruislip often had smears of black bean sauce on the plastic coverings. M decided they needed a team.

The industry of pattern cutting was rife with weirdos. Realms upon realms of pallid squashy men trouped out of their basement flats to answer the ad. M sat at his makeshift desk for the interviews drinking scaly coffee after coffee.

—And what are your hobbies, Mr Yardstick? M sighed.

—Oh, let me see, yes, pederasty, bicycle-seat sniffing and wind surfing.

—Indeed, and yours, Mr Cardcut?

—Why now, just give me a minute, yes, I would have to say phone book perversions and gardening.

—We'll have to take Fred, M said finally.

—Which one was he? Carol and Deli wailed in despair.

—You know when you see those deranged men of indeterminate age with wispy hair, pinched faces and tight brown suits wheeling a supermarket trolley around with only a single can of Ambrosia creamed rice, or a frozen pack of faggots in gravy? M said. —And you think, Christ alive! how does a human being get to be like that? What did he look like when he was younger when blood not bile flowed through his veins? Well, that's what he looked like, that was Fred, M finished.

Fortunately, Fred was available immediately.

Fred bought with him two Polish henchwomen, Basia and Goshia, staff machinists, who took it in turns to have sick days off. But, finally, Madison Ltd was a team.

—MINNA JUST CALLED, Deli said, finding M coming out of the studio area grinding his teeth with irritation. After two months of running what seemed like a freak show, they had both been nearing physical violence with their new team. —Minna, my friend from school with the hairy boyfriends, remember her?

—She was gorgeous. M had visibly perked up. —Is she coming to London?

—Her brother Sebastian has just finished a design course, he's looking for a job.

—Deli, you know we can't take anyone else on, M had said dubiously.

—I know, I know, Deli said, —but Minna insisted I see him, what could I say?

—No would have done just fine, said M, stomping off.

DELI EYED SEB'S purple trousers and custard skin-tight T-shirt as she flicked slowly through his portfolio, cursing herself and wondering how to get rid of him.

—I'd never have recognized you, Seb, Deli mumbled, closing the book carefully. —Never in a million years. You had braces and spots last time we met.

—And that doped out glazed look in your eyes has gone too. He grinned back.

Deli laughed ruefully. —Yes, well, it's been replaced by fanaticism. How's Minna these days?

—Oh, she's still burning incense and plastering on the kohl. I guess she thinks moving on is far too energetic an undertaking.

—She's probably right, Deli said, stroking the portfolio absently. —Look, Seb . . . She hesitated. —Your book's great, but we really haven't got enough money to take anyone on –

—And I haven't got the experience to get a proper job, Seb interrupted drily. —Don't think you're the first company I've tried. You're not, you're pretty much my last hope. He pushed a strand of hair back from his eyes. Despite the outward confidence, Deli could see he was nervous. She suddenly remembered sitting in Zelda's penthouse, damp with insecurity.

—But what would you do? she pleaded.

—General dogsbody? he said hopefully.

—That's my job, Deli said, still hedging.

—But I'll do it so much better than you, said Seb, —and then think what fun you can have taking all the credit.

—Yeah, sure, Seb. She laughed.

—Come on, Deli, please, just give me a fucking job.

WITHIN A MONTH Seb had become a fixture, calm, efficient, exceptionally talented, and utterly dedicated. By comparison Carol's behaviour became more and more erratic.

One day they all watched fascinated as Carol sailed in to work after a two-week absence-without-leave, casually slipped a bulky expense-claim form on Tish's desk and, positioning herself next to the petty cash tin, stealthily extracted a tenner.

—Just off for lunch, she announced brassily.

She looked totally gobsmacked when M fired her, as if the idea that doing nothing, and getting paid for it was just fine really, as long as you did it to friends.

—At least that's her salary gone, said M grimly, —but we're going to need a small miracle to get through another season.

Chapter Fourteen

The small miracle had been five foot high and Japanese.

M had just driven through the gates of the Blacknag one morning and was admiring the way the sun mirrored off the oil patches on the ground when he nearly ran over a cowed looking individual wading through the permanent workman's mud outside their office.

Over a cup of coffee, Mr Yono explained that he worked for a broking house in London. He gave them a brochure and an introductory letter from a Tokyo-based company who was interested in licensing their name and who had been fruitlessly trying to contact them at their old office address for weeks.

The brochure was slick and carried a cheesy looking portrait and message of goodwill from the president on the inside front page. The letter asked for a meeting that Friday evening.

Deli telexed Aaron and asked him to get as much information as possible on a company called Mijiyama.

BY FRIDAY AFTERNOON M, Seb and Deli were spinning around the studio like a trio of killer ants, shovelling great piles of Marathon wrappers into the bin.

Outside, council improvements to naff up the estate were still in progress. The air was filled with the smell of tar and a million flecks of hot coal dust were sailing on the breeze making headway up to the third floor. A drill started up, indecently loud, just outside the window. M prayed for sanity.

Deli wandered into the office to change out of her protective clothing and into some swanky executive gear when the telephone rang.

—Deli, I'm in LA. I'm sorry I haven't called you before.

—Aaron! As usual her heart dipped when she heard his voice. —So, what's the score on Mijiyama?

—Not a lot more than that they're a giant licensing company. My advice would be to sit tight and see what they want. This evening is bound to be just an exploratory meeting.

—How big is giant?

—About the second largest in Japan.

—Oh great, just terrific, she moaned. —I've got to get changed.

—Mmmm, indeed, and what are you wearing? Aaron asked.

—Really, Aaron, if you're that desperate why don't you get on over here? She pictured him longingly in his faded T-shirt, one hand stuck into his back pocket as he talked to her.

—I wish, he said. —You've no idea, call me later and, remember, all Japanese arrive early for their meetings, this is a proven fact.

—They're not due for another hour, she protested.

—Don't say I didn't warn you.

As she put the phone down, there was a noise of knocking at the door. M was still half naked, tidying his desk. He glanced over at Deli, almost completely naked, except for a pair of laddered pop socks and some greying knickers. Seb was wiping down the floor under the cutting table.

—It's only 4 o'clock! Seb shouted from the studio. —It can't be them.

The doorbell rang, then the sound of shuffling feet, oddly loud. Deli paled. —M, you didn't leave the front door open, did you, you fucking *idiot*?

They indulged in a moment of irrational horror, giggling like three loonies sharing a spider for lunch, then threw on whatever was handy in a frenzy of clothes, arms and legs.

—Go head them off, Seb! Deli yelled, but it was already too late. She could hear crunching down the other end of the corridor. A line of men in identical suits marched into view, single file. Seb behind them held up his hands in resignation. As the Japanese approached the glass partitioning separating the corridor from the office, Deli sprinted out to intercept them with some hasty breathless gibberish. M, cursing and easing up his trousers, followed suit.

There followed a subtle game of cards in which the Japanese held the unfair advantage of a pack in each breast pocket. They bowed, Deli and M bowed, much nodding and shaking ensued, they bowed again. M became confused, and, as his head veered dizzily towards the floor for what he suspected was the very last time before he passed out, he suddenly realized he hadn't got his shoes or socks on.

AARON HAD BEEN right. This was just an exploratory meeting, the Japanese finally got up to leave.
– Mr Yakisojo from European office arrive Monday, said the interpreter Rikki who had a portrait of Jack Nicklaus cunningly knitted across his torso. —We have meeting to discuss contract.

Deli smiled and smiled till she had face-ache, and off they trooped.
—Pinch me, M, she said.
—My little cash cow, said M fondly and gave her a hug.

AARON, SENSING DEBT repayment time, flew over for the next meeting which was held in the offices of

Mijiyama's shipping company in the city. Having warned M not to get upset if he banged the table a bit, Aaron arrived three quarters of an hour late just as M, who had long since run out of polite conversation, was considering excusing himself for a pee, then disembowelling himself with a biro. Aaron sat down, laughed derisively at the Japanese's opening offer, demanded five times as much, banged the table and walked out.

After three more similar meetings, it was Mijiyama who banged the table, walked out and stomped back to Tokyo in a bait.

—Fuck it, Aaron, you've blown it, said M.

—They'll be back, promised Aaron. —Believe me, they're hooked.

Aaron left for New York. After a three week silence the telexes started again and before long, another eight or so executives filed back into the office.

Rikki carefully layed out a his and hers purple and green Wimbledon outfit on the cutting table as a goodwill gift. Deli and M in turn, having agonized over a suitable present, resorted to handing each of the executives a small gift-wrapped Wedgwood ashtray, which they later discovered could be bought on special offer in Narita Airport.

For the three-day bonding session that followed M put Deli in charge of the catering. For Friday lunch she gave them the local Texan Chicken in a Bun which the Japanese ate, a look of unparalleled disgust on their faces.

The next day she offered them a dose of British fish and chips wrapped up in page three of the *Daily Mirror* which gave them heart palpitations. By Sunday the suggestion of steak and kidney pie reduced them to tears and bowing deeply they insisted on taking M and Deli to an ultra-traditional Japanese restaurant in the City.

DINNER WAS SERVED on the floor.

A giggling Geisha crawled in with bowl after bowl of inedible delicacies, then crawled out backwards again, still giggling and pointing at M.

—She thinks you are a very big man, said Rikki. —She has not seen such a big man before.

M had the grace to blush.

Meanwhile Deli stared into the baleful accusing pupil of what looked like an eyeball. Plucking up courage, she prodded it lightly with her chopstick, there was a thin milky film over the black circle, but the membrane of the eye was too thick to cut with blunt wood. She'd have to manage it whole, she glanced over at M, he raised his eyebrows and picked up his looking competitive.

Deli glared at him. Fuck, she popped it in her mouth, and nearly spat it out again immediately. It was stone bloody cold.

She rolled it around with her tongue, weighing up the feasibility of swallowing it in one gulp, *impossible – too big*. The others were watching, and now it was making her gag. Quickly she savaged it with her teeth and split it apart, a thick jellied gunk ran out onto her tongue, and trickled down the back of her throat. Deli got rid of the carcass with some sake, looked up, smiled and nodded.

—Delicious, she croaked.

M was looking sympathetic, but faint with nausea. Deli could only pray that pudding would be nothing worse than a live baby white mouse dipped in hot sugar.

THE CONTRACT WAS to be signed with the President himself. He of the cheesy brochure smile.

Deli and M stood in the Mijiyama London office clutching their 1000 year old bottle of whisky which they'd been assured was the ideal present.

—Give him whisky, said Aaron. —Give them all whisky, they love it, they can't get enough of it, Jesus, they even take baths in it.

After a few sweaty moments the door was opened, and they were led through to the President's office.

And there he was, a man so old he'd clearly been dead for the last fifteen years, but had somehow been beautifully preserved in a combination of pickled whisky and Tama-goyaki. He bestowed on M the latest model Yashica and on Deli a neat looking Walkman. Another set of more updated winter-wear Stella Artois outfits were carefully folded on the table.

Deli in turn presented him with the Glenfiddich as if it were the Holy Fucking Grail and a T-shirt from the last show. The President told them he was teetotal but kindly said he'd give the T-shirt to his wife when he got back to Japan.

After an unfathomable speech lasting no more than an hour, he'd held a solid gold Parker pen out towards them. And as they signed the contract Deli had succeeded, but really only just, in repressing a shriek of joy as she handed the pen back.

Chapter Fifteen Gum On My Shoe

Darling Aaron   **3 November 1984**

Since the Japs, you've been really off the air. So where are you holed up?

My heart bleeds, my mind is in turmoil, and I need to know which brand of aftershave you use. Can this be love or is it just stomach cramps?

Delixxxxxxxxxxxxx

Thursday's post was delivered to the office. Hovering, Deli had made a snatch at the familiar airmail envelope, but M was too quick for her.

—Tish, come and help me, Deli pleaded, pinning M's hands behind his back.

—Are you crazy? Tish said. —He's your brother. You have sex with him.

Deli snatched it out of his hand. Thank God, she'd been beginning to get uneasy. It was so unlike Aaron not to keep in touch. She took the letter into the loo and shut the door.

Dear Deli,

I'm sorry. . . . one of the letters you so often write but can't send . . . please understand . . . since I've spent a great deal of time and effort in my life ensuring I wouldn't be this vulnerable with anyone . . .
. . . Adelaide is moving in with me . . .
. . . want you to be happy too . . .

She scanned the single piece of paper. Scraps of sentences fired through her head. Shrapnel of betrayal. Aaron had fallen in love with someone else. He'd fallen in love with some girl who'd started to work for him, some girl who was there for him. Some girl who wasn't her. The unimaginative cowardly shit. He could have fucking phoned.

She managed to get out of the loo, past Fred, his doughy features kneaded into a concerned look, past Seb, signing out work dockets and even past M, who was now on the telephone and making frantic beckoning gestures at her to come and talk, down the stairs and outside.

She walked along the canal for a while. The green water swirled groggily with the murky decay of North London. *What should she have done? Given everything up? Moved there?*

A couple of people were squatting on the bank, fishing. Surely nothing could possibly be alive in there? She wanted to push them into the canal and watch as their heads slid under the mud. She walked on down the path, squeezed through a couple of bent iron railings up into the cemetery, and found Terry sitting on a bench forking yet another curry into his mouth, guzzling a beer and having a cigarette all at the same time.

—How does your wife stand you? Deli asked bitterly, squatting down next to him.

—Blimey, you're scratchy. Terry turned to look at her.

She glared at him.

—What's the matter, love?

—Nothing.

—Come on, spit it out.

—Oh fuck, I don't know, nothing ever seems to go right . . . She crumpled the damp letter in her hand.

—Aaron upped and off has he? said Terry. He didn't seem too surprised.

—He's getting married, to his assistant, can you believe it? I didn't even know he had one. Bitch. Deli stared stonily at the ground.

—You'll never get a decent boyfriend. Terry licked the underside of his plastic fork.

—What's that supposed to mean? Deli said furiously.

—You're too ambitious, too obsessed with your work.

—I am not, she retorted. —It's just that there's always so much to do.

—At the end of the day when you get home what

have you got left to give anyone? I see you in the office night after night . . .

—Whose side are you on? Deli was indignant.

—When's the last time you saw a movie? When's the last time you had a free weekend? Made love?

—Go to hell, Terry.

—Aaron was all in your head, that was all crap nostalgia stuff, you wanting to be back in America, etc. I've told you before. You can't hanker after the past and plan for the future at the same time, love, it doesn't work.

—Thank you very much, Dr Fucking Freud, Deli said quietly. She started to cry.

—Come on, darling, give us a kiss.

Terry smelt of chicken korma, beer, cigarettes and his wife's scent.

Deli felt isolated by his cosiness.

He wasn't right, of course he wasn't right. She was having a great time, a ball. Everything was there now for M and her to take. There was no way she could let it go. Aaron was just selfish and short-sighted, and if he didn't want her, well, fuck him. One day in the not too distant future he would discover that his stinking assistant had quit her job and instead would be sitting around the loft all day sewing frilly blinds and languishing in the garden of ironing death. And one evening not too long after that, she would open her mouth to speak to her husband when he got home from work but would find she had nothing left to say. Aaron, too late, would realize that in dumping

Deli, he had, quite simply, made the biggest mistake of his whole life . . .

PERHAPS IT WAS true what people said; that you can never really turn your back on the first real love of your life. Aaron's role was to be that person, the one she would never quite get over, that person whom she would always look for a tiny bit of in everyone else afterwards.

Of course at the time, she didn't know that.

—Get over him as soon as possible, advised Seb.

—Wipe him clean from your mind, urged M.

—Cut him out of your heart, said Terry, —or, if you prefer I'll break his legs.

But her own favoured cure had been to adopt the throwing-yourself-into-your-work cliché, and it had to be said that in this respect the money from Japan had helped a lot.

Suddenly their bank manager, a body double for Mr Creosote, had begun smiling like a slice of watermelon and sending out statements printed in black. They no longer had to trade illegally, they'd been solvent, they'd pretended less and less that the cheque was in the post, they didn't kneel by the window at the end of every month with semi-automatics picking off their creditors arriving with writs.

They had felt the weight of dollars, the rustle of lire, and the clanking of yen in their pockets. Creepier than that, they had actually been making a profit.

They had even begun experiencing a new phenomenon, a phenomenon called weekends; or at least M had been experiencing them, and M had been experiencing them with Tish.

—Yes, that's right! Deli shouted furiously at Seb. —Tish from The Office, Tish of the 'You have sex with him, he's your brother' comments. *Ha*, bloody *ha*.

—Nothing like shitting in your own back yard, she had told M.

—Shagging the secretary, that's original.

—What did you do? she sniped. —Bend her backwards over the photocopier one evening?

—What on earth are you getting so snarky about Deli? Seb asked, bewildered. —Is this some kind of sick incestuous thing?

It had been ten days before the start of the next collections and everyone had been working late except for M and Tish who had sneaked out of the office for a hot date looking shifty and first flush of love-ish.

—No. Wrong. Deli held up her hands. —I'm not jealous that M's got Tish, that you've got Kevin. It's nothing to do with the fact that I've got no boyfriend, a date, or even a stupid crush to look forward to, thank you.

—So, what then, you don't like her?

—No, I do like her, she's great, she's ... Deli shrugged, unsure herself why she felt so upset. —She's pretty, tough, funny even, in a wisecracking kind of way.

—You're just pissed off because you were the last to

know, Seb said shrewdly. He shut the windows and tested the locks.

—Well, wouldn't you be?' Deli said indignantly. —Everyone else in the whole world seemed to know. Fred, Basia, Goshia, Terry, Mr Creosote, most of the delivery men probably. Oh yes, and of course you, Seb. Thanks for telling me by the way. Fine friend you are.

—As you know, said Seb loftily as they walked to the front door together, —my first loyalty is always to other men.

—Fucking fags. She laughed and punched him. —Anyway I don't care because, you know what? I've got much more important things to think about.

Which had been that Madison Ltd was suddenly establishment. The Japanese money allowed them to give fashion shows, exhibit in trade fairs. Suddenly they had found themselves attending worthy fashion functions and Deli smiled strenuously at all the right people in many of the right places.

She sat on the board of the Exhibition Panel, belonged even to special designer committees; hand-picked groups of highly talented individuals who lobbied their peers energetically on key issues.

These had not simply been spurious exercises for stroking their creative egos, no, certainly not. These had been decisions of the utmost importance like, um . . . the spirit of the floral arrangements for the forthcoming exhibition, er . . . the mood of the sandwiches, the colour coding for the tickets. The spraying of dozens of sheaves of golden wheat and even the commissioning of a replica Taj Mahal for the exhibition entrance . . .

Oh happy days.

The metro crunched yet again to a stop throwing Deli momentarily off balance. There was an ominous heaving of bodies as the passengers shuffled claustrophobically around her, still damp and steaming from the rain as they waited, shoulders tense, for the doors to open. As more and more people pushed on, Deli stretched her head upwards trying to snatch some air into her lungs. She looked at her watch again: 7.46. She was now officially one minute late for the meeting. She tried to imagine M's face as the seconds ticked by without her. For his sake, she should at least be prepared, get her brain jump started. But her brain seemed to be suffering from some kind of priority amnesia. Instead of preparing for the fight ahead, it kept crowding over with the images of the past, of Gerard, Aaron, and now even Seb's tight face was pushing in. If only Seb could be here she thought . . . Oh God, if only.

fashion tips nº 4

Buyers

So through the Taj Mahal entrance spews forth the guts of the fashion world. Amongst the sheaves of golden wheat the designers stand, grovelling obsequiously, trying to look busy, happy, trying not to appear desperate, but they're all on the lookout for one thing and for one thing alone.

Buyers.

The quality of buyers falls into several categories.

a) The suburban English boutique owner invariably arrives with their husband who, for the bargain price of a bi-annual blow job, has dizzily agreed to accompany his wife to the show, where he sits in a state of catatonia, induced by the occasional glimpse of a model's breast through the changing-room curtain.

b) Major Department Store Buyers. These women, almost without exception, need a hard rhino shagging from behind.

They are anal, they are mean. They've hacked it through from counter girl to sales assistant to head buyer. Now they're too old and bitter to remember what it was like to enjoy the impulse purchase. They hate the young and glamorous, they can't even get through the first-floor make-up and beauty department without wearing garlic around their withered necks and carrying crosses. Worse if they are American, these hags are religiously mumbling Chapter Eleven under their breath, haunted by the knowledge that one bad sell-through, just one, and they will join that endangered Seventh Avenue species relegated to handing out hairdressing flyers on street corners.

You want to shake them till their teeth rattle, put your face close and shout: Hey! get a life. Have sex, take your hair off, melt your earrings down and feed Africa.

But, of course, you don't. You smile and smile and smile till your stupid face drops off.

Chapter Sixteen Hag city

Two days after the spring show had found Deli sitting in the sales room waiting for Bergdorf Goodman to arrive for their buying appointment.

They'd had all the American stores fighting over them this season, how fab it was to be no longer the smallest fry. Ha ha, tee, hee, she thought smugly. She glanced at their review in the *New York Times* that Aaron had sent over. Why she was suddenly speaking to Aaron again she had no idea but it was such a relief not to be angry with him any more.

As she obsessed happily over the review for the eighth time the double doors to the sale room suddenly flew open and in marched Judy Schmackerliptz, the first-floor buyer from Bloomingdales, flanked by females in high heels. Deli's mouth dropped open. Bergdorf's were due in two minutes.

Panic . . .

Only a year earlier Deli had been in New York on a

pre-sell with the Fall sketches, and the very first person she had gone to see was Judy Schmackerliptz.

She'd heard rumours about her that made Medusa sound like Mother Theresa and, indeed, every time she tried to confirm her appointment from Aaron's loft, the woman had been out.

—Judy's not in staw right now. She's at the market, said one nasal Brooklyn voice.

—Weya very sawry, Judy's down at the market said another. —She's not on the flaw right now.

There was a time when she'd been confused by the phrase, 'Down at the market.' She really used to think it meant that these winsome women were browsing through a little bric a brac, or purchasing old Pan Am aeroplane stickers from some hobo in a tweed jacket, rather than terrorizing their suppliers on Seventh Avenue. Now, of course, she knew better.

Finally, one of the Brooklyn's gave her an appointment.

—Miss Schmackerliptz will see you at twelve-fifty. Please be sure to be on time, as she has a lunch appointment uptown at one o'clock.

FIRST OF ALL the hag kept her waiting an hour. The central heating was turned up to about 300 degrees and still climbing. Deli began to get paranoid that she had a personal hygiene problem. She rummaged in her bag where she was sure an old bottle of Quick Dry was secreted away. Glancing around to make sure no one was watching, she surreptitiously rubbed it up and down her armpit underneath her cotton shirt. It was a bit dried up but eventually a medicinal looking slime of blue liquid reluctantly oozed forth smelling of floor-cleaner. As she popped it back into her bag she heard a slight coughing noise at the door, and discovered a thin female watching her.

Deli smiled in an English Eccentric way. Pityingly, the female pointed to an office door with a single sharpened red talon.

Behind her desk, locked on to her telephone and not bothering to look up, sat Judy. Instead an incredible corkscrew cone of a hairstyle was levelled in Deli's direction. Briefly, Deli imagined the gruelling routine of training it upwards each morning like a prize vine, then ruthlessly spraying it into shape, and shuddered. Judy was shoe-horned into a red suit with white silk T underneath and appeared to be a strange dark-brown bottle-tan colour all over.

Yup, your basic twentieth-century liberated New York woman.

Eventually she unglued herself from the telephone.

—Who are you and where is your merchandise? she had rapped.

—I just wanted to leave my portfolio with you as arranged, stammered Deli.

Judy looked at her like she had a new-born slug crawling out of a boil on her cheek.

—You can leave it, but I won't look at it, you'll just be wasting my time.

Deli's brain caught fire with rage: *slam her head into the ground, her nostrils smushed against the earth, her scarf taut around her throat, her eyes beginning to bulge nicely* . . .

—Okay, Deli said politely. —Thank you so very much.

And suddenly, there she was, Judy herself, in Deli's London showroom, uninvited and like an Olympic vaulter, leaping onto the bandwagon, flicking through the racks accompanied by an entire entourage of women, computing colour, style and commercial viability at a terrifying pace.

Jesus the nerve!

Deli had offered her a cup of coffee and a biscuit, hating herself while Judy advanced on her relentlessly.

Deli cringed.

—We know you're selling to Bergdorf's, have they been in yet? Judy's mouth was so close Deli could see the bright red lipstick creeping slowly down from her lips in tiny Mississippi tributaries.

Deli shook her head, glancing nervously at the door, her brain temporarily impaired by great mists of scratch'n'sniff Calvin Klein.

—Bloomingdales is a much better store for women, it's hipper, it's cooler, it's more upbeat. Bergdorf's is on the way down, it's lost its fashion credibility.

Deli attempted steeliness. —Actually, I'm afraid we've given Bergdorf's a two-season exclusive.

—Let me tell you something, Judy spat. —We have a major opening on the first floor now . . . She paused for dramatic effect. —And I mean major. Babe Owen, our hottest exclusive, has Aids, he won't be around much longer. The store has decided to put advertising money only into female designers, men are just too risky.

Deli began to feel glazed and insecure. She tried not to look into Judy's eyes which were glowing like a creature from a sci-fi comic. Small multi-coloured lines were circling around her pupils.

—Listen to me, Judy snarled, her cone quivering. —You *will* sell to us exclusively. You *will* break your contract with Bergdorfs, because, if you do not, your career will be *over*.

Deli felt her head flicking from side to side, her hands gripped the arms of the leather chair, she knew it was only a matter of time before she gave in.

My God, What did these women do in their spare time? Collect debts for the mob? Hack up children?

Just then Bergdorf Goodman arrived. Thank God. Deli snapped out of her space world, and jumped on them with relief.

Judy sneered.

The designer buyer, Mernadeen, was a sweetheart. All blonde cropped hair, squashy legs and A-line dresses. She had good eyes, a straight little nose, and a mouth that ran in a gentle slope to her neck, uninterrupted by even a hint of chinbone; but she was earnest and genuine, and truly *into* fashion . . . Deli just knew that when all the rest of Mernadeen's generation, those college kids in the sixties, were protesting the war and banning the bomb, Mernadeen had been proudly marching around campus carrying billboards:

DE–BOOST CHOLESTEROL LEVELS
FEEL FABULOUS 365 DAYS OF THE YEAR
PRO DESIGNER SMILES
IT'S ABOUT BARE SKIN

Mernadeen scowled, and Judy scowled, but temporarily subjugated, Judy had been forced to leave, her hairspray army clicking out on their suede pumps after her.

No money into advertising male designers?

What? It was true, apparently. Sick, but true.

The Aids time bomb had hit the world, and, boy oh boy, was fashion ever in the line of fallout. Rob Howard from Toxic was dead and his lover dying. Seb's boyfriend Kevin was HIV positive as were a lot of others, all in varying stages of the disease. Deli looked at Seb, then she looked at Kevin and wondered if Seb saw his future in the increasingly wasted frame of his lover. Sometimes she searched for misery and self pity written into friends faces as they waited for the ashes to drift over the city, but she found none, just acceptance, patience and courage. She felt guilty and bewildered. Guilty that she was relieved it wasn't her and scared by the knowledge that however hard you hold on to it, life was never within your control.

Everyone was looking over their shoulder now, everyone was busy composing intricate family trees of previous lovers – and it wasn't just men and wasn't just gays. All her girlfriends were at it too.

Deli had hardly ever slept with someone who wasn't at one time or other an intravenous drug user, and she'd certainly slept with several people she'd suspected of being bisexual. That was her era. She was born into a pocket of time set aside for smack, the pink liberation movement, gender bending and the *Rocky Horror Show*. Those who weren't, all those who believed they were in a position to feel really safe, were busy discriminating – writing smug and moralistic articles on the wrath of God, counselling repentance, predicting doom.

Oh, sure – it would all calm down. Of course everyone would get things back into perspective soon enough. The sceptics would rule again, Aids would become just another financial disease, a question of higher health insurance, a spanking good opportunity for charity. The first half-way decent drug through the FDA would clean up, and for the fashion industry? Ha! Well, for the fashion industry it would just mean a change in the department store's budget allocation . . .

Chapter Seventeen

Darling Aaron   22 December 1986

Greetings from the land of the Make–Believe! So you
want to keep this writing thing up? Fine, but I bet you
crack before I do.

So where to start?

Well, most importantly, I'm off next week to
Jamaica for my jetty holiday with my new jetty
friends.

Meantime, I'm becoming rich and famous.

How do I know? I know this is true for several
reasons. Firstly, I have appeared on a programme
actually called *Lifestyles of the Rich and Famous*, where I
have been seen doing things that only other like-
minded celebrities can do, and only then by
hobnobbing with each other.

Secondly, *People* magazine have reported that I
earn over £150,000 a year before bonuses. M is
astounded.

—Please can I have some? he begs, looking hurt.
—I need a new pair of underpants.

Thirdly, I'm learning to be a prima donna now. I feel it's no more than my due . . .

Only the other day Seb and I were off to the Annual Designers Convention, a shindig invented to boost the image of the faltering fabric trade in Great Britain (mild laughter) so I decided to practise on Seb.

—I'd like you to dress in livery and call me ma'am, I said to him the day before departure.

—Give me a break, Cruella, he said smirking.

Furious, I went downstairs to find M. —I'd like you to phone through my dietary requirements to the hotel staff, I said with authority.

—Fuck off, overweight bitch, he said without even looking up.

Aaron, it's not easy being a star, I can tell you.

So – the heavy dating? Uh yup, well, memory's a little sketchy of late, maybe if I get bored in Jamaica I'll swing by NY so you can set me up with some hairless acquaintance of yours, but don't hold your breath.

Love you, miss you, tell Adelaide to go fuck herself.

Big kiss, Deli xx

P.S. In response to your unnecessarily sarcastic question, it's not so much that I'd like to rule the world, it's just that I'd like to keep it in the fridge and take a slice of it whenever I'm hungry.

Handy the butler picked Deli up from the airport at Montego Bay. She was staying with Al Plezzi, art collector, control freak, jazz-playing industrialist and womanizer. Physically, Al was a phenomenon: over six foot tall with hands like a slab of spare ribs and an ugly sexy face which looked like some down-and-out had parked bags and slept on it for a week. He was wickedly funny and not to be trusted.

The villa was near Lucy, right on the sea. Handy gained entry through a series of ever more complicated gates and barked codes until he drew up at the front door where Al was waiting in baseball cap and towel wrapped around his gargantuan stomach.

Outside on the front lawn, an assorted group were still snacking on breakfast: jugs of fresh orange juice, gouged out paw paws and mangoes were upended invitingly, thin slices of toast and marmalade littered the table.

Deli heaved a sigh of relief, thank God her friends Katy and Jim were there. She hugged them both quickly. Actually Jim wasn't really a friend, although Deli often pretended he was on account of his extreme fame. He was, however, the boyfriend of one of her few fashion pals, Katy, who was herself something of a Supermodel. Jim was the lead singer of the group Ghetto Posse, a rap rock group breaking new ground in the States with the usual line-up of nihilistic songs (yawn). Jim had long straggly hair, and a goatee beard, underneath which you could see the almost obligatory delinquent hero features.

Everyone else was lounging around the table in dressing gowns, reading what remained of the papers.

Across the lawn from the direction of the sea, a man with dark hair was making his way slowly towards the group; he was bare-footed and bare-chested, a pair of faded shorts belted around his waist.

—Ned Harrison, said Al as he joined the group. —Ned, Deli.

Deli looked at him. His name rang a bell, but God only knew from where.

Ned nodded briefly and stuck out his hand.

Mental age of five years and a mother problem she thought immediately as Ned threw himself sourly down on the sofa by the table and rammed his nose deep into a newspaper, but, still, reasonably attractive with a hard stocky body and dark-brown eyes.

She smelt the torpor in the air and settled in for a week's stint.

Ned Harrison turned out to be 'the writer'. Deli knew she'd recognized his name. She'd read *The Chocolate Drop*, a short novel on urban doom, gloom and drugs, written by Ned at the precocious age of twenty-five. As far as she remembered it had been a huge hit, but subsequently made into a mediocre movie. His second book had been a collection of short stories on pretty much the same subjects with a bit of pseudo political content thrown in.

—He's a pretentious git, said Deli as she and Katy lolled around the pool that evening.

—Al says he's having major girl trouble.

—Well, maybe he should go have it someplace else. I'm trying to have a good time. Ned's bad mood had already got up her nose.

—Do we think he's attractive? Katy was painting her toenails a dried blood colour. She admired them thoughtfully.

—Yes, Deli mused. —We think he's quite sexy in a dirty sort of way, but he's too arrogant.

—He's got a bad reputation, doesn't treat women very well apparently. He's very intense, very controlling. You've only got to look at his eyes. Katy shook her head – Thank God Jim's not like that.

Deli laughed. Jim was so stoned most of the time, his pupils didn't even move. —Well, he's beginning to sound much like my perfect man.

—He fancies you. Katy threw her a sly look.

—He's only spoken to me once since I arrived, Deli protested, thrilled.

—There you go. Katy realized she'd never seen Deli twice with the same guy since Aaron. —You could probably do with a little man trouble right now.

—Oh God, and how, said Deli wistfully.

IT WAS ANOTHER glorious morning, and the usual tough duty round the swimming pool. Deli watched, slowly turning the pages of her book as Handy ambled down with the third tray of drinks.

She'd finally started to wind down, her bones were

hot and her skin was turning brown, even her nerves had begun to melt and evaporate.

Idly she wondered what was for lunch.

—Demanding regime this, she said to Ned, as Handy offered her another rum and ginger ale.

Ned smiled lazily. He was sexy when he smiled, which had been about three times that she'd noticed, but he'd definitely warmed up a little, in fact, when he wasn't trying to be bolshy, he was almost charming. Katy was right though, he was trouble. But he was the kind of trouble you could reach out and touch, then tangle yourself up in knots with.

—What are you reading? he asked.

Deli folded the book over to its front cover to show him. —*Dalva*, Jim Harrison.

He nodded. —No relation.

—Huh? Oh, of course. She twigged. —Harrison, I didn't make the connection.

—Good?

—Yeah. She shrugged. I will not show interest, she thought – I will remain calm, aloof, bored even.

Ned stared intently at her. —I'm trying to make polite conversation you know, you're not exactly co-operating.

She looked at the cover again. —It says, I quote from the *New York Times* book review: 'a raunchy, funny, swaggering, angry, cocksure book'.

—Sounds more like my ideal woman than a work of fiction, Ned said.

—Every man's ideal woman *is* a work of fiction, Deli answered deftly.

Just then a yacht the size of a small peninsula bobbed into sight, and appeared to be approaching their general direction.

—Goody, another millionaire. Deli yawned.

Before long a man emerged from the dinghy at the pier, shiny, fit and tanned like a much loved and polished briefcase. He shrugged himself into a spanking white towelling dressing gown and combed his hair before venturing up to the pool.

—Good God, who's that? asked Ned, shielding his eyes against the glare.

—Singer Bottleman, oil, art, land, horses and lunch, said Al arriving down from the house. —In fact one of America's more affluent sons. You'll like him, Ned, his meanness is legendary. He can feed a party of eight on the remains of his dental floss. Al padded off to meet him.

Close-up Singer looked the part, fiftyish, but well preserved with smoothed out skin and an almost day-glo tan, a body toned and honed and hard green eyes. All in all a superior specimen of west-coast refinement.

The four of them tooled out through the water to the yacht, Singer, swimming up front, sleek as a porpoise.

SITTING AT A game of poker on deck, two women smoking in heavy concentration gave them a cursory hi before returning to their cards. The younger of the two perched resplendent in a kaleidoscopic bikini, her feet encased in low mules, their uppers printed with some unidentifiable, possibly extinct, animal species.

—Singer's wife, whispered Al. —The Miracle.

—Why is she called that? Deli asked.

—The miracle of slash and cut, said Al. —See for yourself.

On closer inspection, the Miracle was indeed a vision of tiny tucks and picks, her skin stretched thinly over her cheekbones and eyes, all puffiness ruthlessly hoovered out. God only knew what it looked like around her ears where the hundreds of tiny lanes and by-roads of the knife must have met in a huge motorway junction. But all this was concealed by a strategic haircut.

Her cards adversary, Ruthie, looked fifteen years older, and no amount of vitamin E was going to help her complexion at this stage. Her skin had just come to the end of its career as a beauty aid and had slumped over her face in happy retirement.

—Is getting through lunch some kind of friendship test? Deli whispered to Al.

Singer reappeared from the bowels of the yacht freshly laundered in a pair of crisp white shorts and hat. He strolled off to steer the yacht in a hands on, Fletcher Christian sort of a way.

★

—WHO WOULD YOU rather shag, Deli whispered to Ned, looking up from the backgammon board, —the Miracle or Ruthie?

—I'd rather have both my legs amputated.

—Uh uh, you *have* to have one or the other.

—Ruthie probably.

—You can't be serious, she'd chat all the way through.

—Yes, but I'd probably have to have my dick animal-tattooed before the Miracle would allow it inside her, and even then, I'd have a hard time getting it back out again.

—Imagine if you got too rough with her. Deli glanced over her shoulder. —All the stitches might become loose at the same time and her face would fall apart like an old baseball. She cleared the board with double sixes.— Ha! Another?

—No. Ned put the pieces back in the box as Deli considered him. He seemed to have lost interest and was about to withdraw again.

—Do you get neurotic when you start on a new book? She tried to rev him back up, idly wondering what made him reverse mood so quickly.

—Angry more than neurotic. I find it difficult to concentrate.

—What do you do? Hang around the word processor, waiting for your brain to spew up something interesting? Deli realized with a start that sometime in the last hour she had decided to fancy him badly.

—I seesaw between the fridge and typewriter. Whenever I get an idea I go get a beer to celebrate. The expectation of being creative makes me thirsty.

—It's the other way around for me, she said. —I sit in the bottom shelf of the biscuit cupboard working my way through the contents until I get an idea.

—What happens if you don't get one?

—Well, you always get one, it's just that sometimes they're not very good.

—Do you like what you do? he asked curiously.

—Most of the time. Occasionally though, I think I'm a fake, trespassing, living somebody else's career by accident. Somewhere out there there's probably this great fashion designer conducting Greyhound tours around America feeling confused and unfulfilled.

—Well, I've wanted to write ever since I can remember. Whoah. Ned grabbed his glass. The sea was becoming choppy. The Miracle lolled back against her cushions, eyes closed, her face turning greener with every roll and swell. —Not a pretty sight, said Ned.

Deli glanced back at him. He was looking at her and smiling slightly, a disturbing smile. His eyes changed colour. And suddenly with one smile, she thought, we jump levels.

—So, drown or burn? Ned demanded, looking anxiously at the swelling sea.

—Drown. And you?

—Drown, but only if they're no sea-things involved.

—Knifed or shot? Deli asked.

—Knifed for sure.

—Why for sure?

—Because you're much more likely to survive a knife wound than a gunshot wound.

—Slightly depends where it is, doesn't it? She grinned idiotically at him.

—It's far more romantic to be knifed, said Ned.

—It's only romantic if it's in the left shoulder, and then only if you're John Wayne. I'd much rather be shot.

—Well, at this rate, said Ned glancing down the hatch to where lunch was reportedly being prepared, —we're more likely to starve to death.

Singer, stern-side, could be heard regaling the rest of the party with an example of the average LA workman's inefficiency. Deli hadn't the faintest idea what he was talking about, watching instead a line of smaller boats making their way precariously around the coastline through waves of spray.

—So, of course I made them break up all the marble . . . company went under . . . still suing . . .

Suddenly a motorboat roared by very close, and seconds later there was a god almighty bang.

Everyone jumped up. Singer called for his binoculars.

Five hundred yards away, the motorboat had crashed almost on the stone pier on the corner of Al's property. Legs and arms were flailing in the water, thrashing impotently against the high waves. A crowd of spectators was beginning to gather on the other side of the barbed-wire fence which marked Al's privacy, shrieking and pointing with excitement.

Singer stood, binoculars raised, interestedly surveying the mayhem.

Lashed to the side of the yacht were several sturdy looking life-boats. The musclepower of the crew stood by on deck, summoned up by the commotion.

—It looks like a man and a woman, and, oh yes, there's something else in the water. It could be either a small child or a dog. Singer twiddled his focus with dispassionate interest. —You know, they won't be able to get up the steps by the pier, the waves are much too high. By the way, did you have those built, Al? They're very attractive. Singer waved the binoculars around. —Anyone else want a look?

—Are they black? demanded the Miracle, miraculously revitalized by the misfortune of others. She lit a cigarette not moving from the table.

—For Christ's sake can't you send out one of the boats or something? You can't just ignore them. Deli couldn't keep quiet any longer as she watched the agonized thrashings.

—Oh no, I don't think that will be necessary, Singer said, like she was being really uncool or something.

Now the onlookers were making desperate efforts to help, reaching through the barbed wire, and stretching down arms and even towels.

—Jesus, what kind of people are you! Deli shouted, hysterical with nerves.

But, of course, Singer was right, as their struggles grew less and less energetic, a small figure in white was spotted hurrying to the scene of the accident from the direction of Al's pool.

—Oh look, Al, here comes your man. Singer pointed with his glasses. —And he's got a rope, what a guy.

And indeed there was Handy, valiantly roping in the joyless couple, although the child/dog was nowhere to be seen.

The next day, the rocks were covered in the debris from the boat, planks of wood, bits of engine, a pair of sailing shoes, even a first-aid kit, still protected by its envelope of clear plastic, had been salvaged. Handy had kindly hauled everything he could from the calm of the morning's sea and arranged them artistically on the rocks to dry. A still-life of a tragedy.

The anguished couple who, according to the local papers, turned out to have one of the houses further round the coast, had driven over, and were now picking through the remains of their belongings in mute misery.

The wife had broken her arm and it was encased in a turquoise-blue silk scarf printed with sea-urchins. She looked pale and drawn despite the heat.

Deli and Katy got out of the pool and went over.

—I'm sorry about your, er, dog, Deli mumbled. Her heart was still roasting with guilt at the memory of the previous day's performance when suddenly Ned came up behind them and put his arms round Deli's waist. She felt the rasp of his stubble grate against her neck. It was so unexpected she started to blush.

—You must be heartbroken, added Katy who indulged in every model's hobby of animal rescue.

—Was he very old? stammered Deli. Ned still had hold of her, he dug his chin into her shoulder and rocked her slightly.

The woman dragged her griefstricken eyes to Deli's hot face.

—We have another dog at home, older you know, but same pure pedigree. But my earrings were Palomo Picasso originals and they're not even insured, she wailed.

Fresh tears sprung to her eyes, her husband, looking supportive, took her good arm and, heads bowed with the dignity of the bereaved, they walked off to their waiting car.

Ned howled and howled and howled.

NED FLEW BACK to London three days later, and by that time Deli had nearly convinced herself to leave early and go with him. After the arms round the waist incident she was aware of him every minute of the day. Suddenly their every conversation became charged, loaded. Every look fired off a potential blush. Convinced he was toying with her, she waited for him to make a move; to touch, to kiss her, but he didn't. Then, once, when he put his hand on the back of her neck, she had felt it there, sparking and burning hot on her skin, she realized too late she was in trouble, because when he took it away she felt cold and couldn't work out how to get it back again,

By the morning he left, he was difficult and moody, he climbed into the car, barely saying goodbye.

—Fuck you too, she thought miserably, furious that she minded so much.

NED DIDN'T CALL her the very second she arrived back in London, nor did he call the next day or even the day after that. For five days she looked forward to getting home to check her messages, on the sixth day she threw the machine across the room.

Back in the office Seb asked her why she was so preoccupied.

—I'm not, I'm fine, all right? she snapped. Even now she could still feel Ned's hands, hot as Raljax on her skin.

—You sound ecstatic, he said, and went off to make a cup of tea,

—I'm sorry, Seb, Deli said contritely when he came back. Odd really, the way you turn on good friends enquiring solicitously after your well-being as if they were perfect strangers and have no right to speak, and yet you hope and pray that the perfect stranger you've only just met (and who is obviously a complete shit) will be ringing you up enquiring solicitously after a date.

Happens every time.

★

The train swung sharply round a corner and into a tunnel. Deli felt her shoulders tense, and just at the point when the light exploded to black, she found she could see Ned's face grinning at her, Ned with his familiar expression of confident arrogance. She'd fallen in love with him with the violent energy of rebound passion, and been blinded to the probable consequences.

fashion tips n° 5

Image

—Hi. (*kiss*) Did you enjoy the show? Didn't the girls look great? (*hope*) Yes, of course, it's selling marvellously well. (*exaggeration*) You want to know to who? (*gulp*) Oh well, everyone's just left paper so far. *Oh*, excuse me one minute. Hi there, how are you? Great to see you. (*kiss, kiss*) Did you like the show? Oh, you didn't come? (*despair*) Seat not good last season? (*horror*) Oh, I'm so sorry. Hello there, hi! (*handshake, fixed smile*) Yes, thank you, I saw the article. *No*, not at all! Constructive criticism, right? (*fake laugh*) And I loved the pictures. So, (*squirm*) can I get you some lunch? Champagne? Hamper from Harrods? Holiday home in the Canaries? I'll be right back. (*run*) Oops. Hey! Nice to see you. (*handshake*) Great, business is great. Why, yes, our sell-through has been really solid. (*huge lie*) Where? (*panic*) Um, oh, like in . . . um . . . *I've got it* . . . Patagonia, (*relief*) we're really building there . . .

Chapter Eighteen Giving Good Lip

It had been the following Friday. Deli found herself in yet another crisis meeting about the state of British Fashion. Forget fucking shopkeepers she thought yawning – they were a nation of ditherers.

She'd been doodling mindlessly on her agenda when the door opened quietly and the receptionist sidled in carrying a little folded fix-it note which to Deli's surprise she put down in front of her.

—Telephone message for you, hissed the woman. —They said it was urgent.

Deli opened the note on top of the table. The chairman of the Council was looking out of the corner of his eye, quickly she put it in her lap.

There is a screening of *Sid & Nancy* on the 11th.
20 Soho Square, W1.
7.00 p.m. sharp.
Meet you there.
Ned

By five-thirty Seb couldn't take the strain any longer. —I can't take the strain any longer, he shouted, laying out a roll of fake leatherette on the cutting table. —Go, go on, get out, go home.

—Am I having a bad skin day? Deli asked dreamily, peering into the mirror. —Do I look difficult, mysterious, luscious, slightly psychotic but completely wild in bed?

—You look like you've been embalmed, Seb grimaced. —As for the rest, for obvious reasons I can't help you, Miss Self-obsession Run Riot.

—Try a little harder to be supportive, Seb. It doesn't cost anything, you know, like they say about a smile a day. You could be supportive once a day and it would cost you nothing.

—Please go home, he begged. —And then you can be neurotic in the privacy of your own padded cell.

—Would you fancy me if you were straight? she demanded.

—With your legs, no, frankly. Seb looked at his watch pointedly.

—Do I get to sleep with him?

—Make sure he's rich, make sure he's got no spots on his back and make sure he's domiciled in this country.

—A little something for yourself maybe? Deli said sarcastically.

—You've got to be more business-like in your approach to your love life, Seb insisted.

—You're not shagging my brother are you? Deli asked suspiciously.

—No, why? Has he gone pink? Seb raised his eyebrows hopefully looking across at M who was photocopying some papers.

—Not that I know of, she sighed. —But you're becoming alarmingly alike.

She was late for the screening, knee-deep in the middle of a what-to-wear panic. One of the really bad ones, the kind that leaves you crouched, naked, desperate and miserable on the bed after an hour of tearing on and off thousands of clothes. She settled for getting her hair, which looked like it had been deep-fried, to flop in smouldering sex appeal across her face.

On the way out the door, the phone went. Deli toyed with the idea of leaving it, then, worrying it might be work, picked it up on the fifth ring. It wasn't work. It was Ned, calling to cancel. No real explanation, no proper apology for that matter, just a cold clammy cancellation.

She was dead cool on the telephone, dead dead cool. Something had come up he said, something really important.

—Sure, that's fine, Deli told him. It was tough for me to get away too.

—Can we do it another time? he asked.

Some other time, she repeated. —Sure, why not? But something in his voice told her there wouldn't be any other time. —Thank you, goodbye.

She slammed the receiver down and sat on the sofa. —Why me? Why? she asked the telephone babyishly and burst into tears.

Chapter Nineteen

Two months later Deli had almost forgotten he'd existed. Almost, but not quite.

She had been due to leave the next day on a trip to Frankfurt with M when Tish buzzed up a call on the intercom.

Deli, it's a Ned Harrison, line two for you.

Seb looked over at her from the stand where he was pinning a shoulder pad into a toile and arched his eyebrows. Deli's stomach somersaulted. Yes, yes, yes. She picked up the phone, hesitated, and then pressed the extension number.

—Deli?

—Yes?

—It's Ned.

—Ned? she repeated, sounding puzzled, feigning memory loss. Playing for time.

—Yes. He clearly wasn't fooled. —Ned.

—Oh, *Ned*, sorry. She gave in. She felt a knot of

nerves, and pushed it away. *Where the fuck have you been all this time?* she wanted to shout. *How come you haven't called? How could you have resisted? Who have you been with, and why wasn't it me?* — Ah, Ned, of course, how are you? She kept her voice light. Her I'm-a-busy professional, please-don't-bother-me-unnecessarily kind of voice.

—Can you have supper with me tonight? As usual Ned sounded annoyingly confident.

—What, tonight? She immediately felt her high ground slipping.

Ned waited in silence.

—But I can't, she protested. —I'm going away tomorrow. I have to pack, and I've got a bunch of stuff to do here still.

—I'd like to see you, he cut in. —I'd like to see you a lot.

—Ned, I really don't think so.

—Please, I want to talk to you.

Deli hesitated, feeling hopelessly intimidated. Okay, what were the rules here? She desperately wanted to see him, she knew she shouldn't. She knew if she fell under his thumb this easily, she was in danger of being flattened.

Seb was wagging his finger backwards and forwards at her and mouthing, no, no, *no*.

—Deli! Ned's voice sounded impatient. —Are you still there?

—Okay, she said, ignoring Seb. —All right, but not till later, after supper.

Seb crossed himself dramatically. Deli frowned at him.

—You sound angry, Ned said.

—I'm not angry.

—You sound furious. Are you still annoyed I stood you up?

Yes, of course I am, you arrogant bastard. —Well, you're definitely on probation, she mumbled unconvincingly.

—Look, I have to drop in on a friend's party later, just for a while, he's moving to California. Why don't you meet me there whenever you can get away.

Ned spelled out the address and hung up triumphantly.

Oh shit, oh shit, shit, shit. Deli stared at the piece of paper in front of her.

—Hey, all those feelings you try so hard to squash, said Seb, shaking his head, —just when you *have* in fact squashed and stowed them away, just when you've managed to stop praying that every time the phone goes it's him, *bam*. That's all it takes, just one call to bring them frothing to the surface again. Am I right as usual?

—Yes, you and your huge love IQ are right again, she growled.

—Big mistake, said Seb. Big, enormous, huge, gigantic error of judgement.

—Don't be silly. Deli found herself grinning broadly.

—Deli, put your dented ego straight down the loo then go and flush it. This guy is trouble, this guy is not good news. Seb had his annoying wise face on.

—I'm only going to a stupid party with him. It's not like I've agreed to marry him or anything.

—You should've at least made him suffer. Seb relented slightly.

—Oh, there's still time, Deli said happily.

SHE HEARD THE steady hum of the party from half-way down the street. As she walked up the steps, two people came out of the front door and brushed past her without a glance, hands stuck into the pockets of their overcoats. She climbed up to the fourth floor and felt a sudden flash of annoyance with herself for agreeing to come. Her feelings towards Ned were too ambivalent to be trusted, hovering as they did somewhere between dislike and obsession. That tried and tested formula for disaster.

On the top floor she hesitated, thumb against the doorbell. The volume of party noise had extended to include the thud of nondescript music and the clunk of beer glasses. Just as she plucked up courage to push the bell, the door opened and three more people clattered past her, talking and laughing. The party was spilling out into the hallway. A fattish man wearing corduroys and maroon polo neck was talking politics to a flaky-lipped woman with a crew cut almost by Deli's elbow.

—I'm a part-time communist, she heard the woman saying. —And of course I'm still working on my thesis on Pygmies.

—Sorry. Deli eased through the middle, stepped

through the door and into the dimly lit hall of the flat where, needless to say, absolutely the first person she saw was Ned.

This really threw her plan.

Which was to leave immediately if he hadn't been there, not to wait, not even for a second, to just go straight home, let the phone ring without answering, ignore the doorbell, burn the mail. This way she would at least feel like she had tried. But it was already too late. He was standing at the far end of the hall, his back against the wall while a man with glasses and a Bloomsbury-style intellectual face talked intently at him.

Suddenly Ned looked up and saw her staring. He frowned, grinned, unlocked his arms from his chest and beckoned her over mouthing something unintelligible. Deli found herself pushing her way through to him. Ned kissed her hard on the lips, mouth closed.

She felt slightly giddy.

Shit . . . obsession.

—You made it! he shouted. He pulled her closer. —This man bores for Britain, he hissed into her ear, — plus has terrible breath, we're going to have to escape. Right now.

Deli smiled encouragingly at the Bloomsbury bore.

—Have you eaten yet? shouted Ned, his eyes were smiling wickedly at her.

She shook her head obediently, feeling the thud of the stereo competing with her heart.

—I'm afraid my date needs feeding up, Ned said. The man with the glasses was still hovering. —Word of advice, Ned added over his shoulder as he pushed Deli in front of him straight back out the door, —try Bactiwash.

THEY FOUND A restaurant still serving on the corner of Camden High Street. The remaining diners seemed oddly out of focus, the decoration and staff slightly soiled and ugly but at least the food when it finally arrived was better than the ambience. A waitress with a pair of energetic tits kept apologizing for the delay.

Deli had already made up her mind not to ask but he told her anyway.

He'd disappeared abroad for the last eight weeks to work out his life, to finish his book. He'd stood her up to resolve some personal stuff over there.

—What kind of personal stuff? she asked.

—Just personal stuff.

—Girl personal stuff?

—Yes. Deli was dying to know, but Ned was not being exactly forthcoming.

—Like serious-relationship girl personal stuff? she pressed, abandoning all cool detachment.

—Like serious she-was-married stuff.

—But, unfortunately, not to you, Deli said, giving a stupid tinkling laugh. She felt irrationally jealous already.

—You know, said Ned, —someone like you could drive me a little crazy.

—What do you mean? she said, immediately flattered.

—I'm not sure when you're being flippant, when you're being cynical and when you're being honest.

—Most of the time I'm flippant, some of the time I'm cynical, and I'm hardly ever honest.

—I see, and which category does that comment fall in then?

—Oh, that was just a cover-up, Deli mumbled. *Hey, the door to my head is marked Private, buster*, she was tempted to say, —*and no one gets to come up here.*

—Okay, Ned said evenly. He leant forward over the table and touched the tip of Deli's hand with his fingers. She jumped as if she'd been brushed by a couple of electric eels. —Okay, Ned said again, —I'll take the cover-up quip for now, but it won't work forever.

Affairs always begin in restaurants. Not parties, not cars, not strange bedrooms, but restaurants. Because in the couple of hours it takes to have that first meal, you can learn a lot about someone, almost everything you need to know in fact, and this is vital for getting beyond the preliminaries. In most other circumstances if you fancy someone, you don't get to look directly at them, it would be considered uncool, you shouldn't even be in the same side of the room as them, that's much too dangerous, a dead give-away.

But in a restaurant, the beauty is that you *have* to stare at them right smack in the face for all three courses. To do anything else would be downright anti-social and they'd only think you were weird. So, at your leisure, you can watch their dichromatic pupils dilating, you're free to check out the symmetry of their face, the thickness of hair on their forearms. As they're reading out the menu you can conduct expeditious affairs in your head whilst pretending to decide on your potatoes, mashed or fried, all in all, you can decide one way or another whether it's going nowhere or whether it's going somewhere . . .

Sometime during dinner, Deli had decided it was going somewhere. She decided she would sleep with Ned. In between the second course and coffee she managed to convince herself that this would be a good thing to do. Not that night of course, but sometime soon.

And the thought had dismayed and excited her.

Her foot was swinging wildly to and fro. Ned's hand shot out and gripped her knee, holding her leg still.

—Sorry, hereditary family twitch, she apologized nervously.

—Why are you nervous? he asked.

—Huh? Why should I be nervous? Ned released her leg.

—No reason that I can think of, Ned said. He was playing with her now. Deli was irritated that he was able to do so.

—You like to needle me, don't you? she asked him.

—I don't think so. Ned's eyes ran lazily over her face. He had picked up his knife off the table and his thumb was running up and down the serrated edge.

—You do, you're always trying to catch me unawares, make me feel just a little off tilt.

—I'm just trying to crack through your skin a bit.

—Why?

—Just to see if what I think's there, is in fact there, Ned said.

—What do you think's in there? She looked challengingly at him. Smug oaf.

—Ah well, he said, laying the knife carefully down by the side of his plate, —hopefully you're in there somewhere.

There was an awkward silence. God forbid he should find her, Deli thought.

Somewhere in between the coffee and the bill, she decided not to sleep with him. She decided it would be a very dangerous idea indeed.

THE STREETS WERE quiet and empty. They walked slowly towards Deli's car. The lights were still on in the window of the party.

Deli shivered with the cold and pushed her hands further into her pockets. Ned took her arm in an iron grip just above the elbow.

—I've still got to pack, said Deli, more to herself than anything.

Ned pulled her round to face him. —Come home with me, Deli.

—No.

—Why?

—I can't.

—Why not?

—Because . . . Deli twisted away and started walking ahead.

Ned caught her up and took her arm again. —Because what?

—Just because.

—What kind of because, because you don't want to, or because you don't think you should?

—Neither . . . I don't know, both.

They reached the car, Deli felt gloomy. She went round to the driver's side and wrenched open the door.

Ned followed her, putting his hand on the metal edge to keep it from swinging shut.

—Come home with me, Deli, you know you want to.

She turned back to face him. He was dangerously close. She suddenly had the image of his chest, brown and tight in Jamaica and nearly put her hand inside his shirt.

—Ned, she pulled herself together and took a deep breath, —My flight's early, I don't know where my passport is, I can't remember what country I'm going to, it's not a good idea, let me go.

She leant forward to kiss him goodbye, as if to finalize her new-found sensible stance but he pulled her out of the door with one hand, firmly shutting it with the other and pinned her back against the car, kissing her again hard, harder than before.

Okay, she thought vaguely, well, I'll just kiss him back then.

Her hands moved through his jacket round to his back, pulling his shirt up, untucking, releasing it from his trousers, she found his back, his bare skin, warm. Cold hands against warm skin.

She kissed him and the icy wind blew disapprovingly against her cheek.

THEY DROVE TO Deli's flat in silence. She found her passport on the floor behind the television and packed, still without speaking. High on anticipation, she had no idea what she was flinging into her suitcase. Ned sat on the corner of her bed and watched her, smiling disconcertingly to himself and flicking through an old copy of *Private Eye*.

—We're going to my flat now, he said when she had finished. —Give me your suitcase and your car keys. Deli wondered why she was doing exactly as she was told.

He took her suitcase, grabbed her hand and pulled her down the steps.

In his bedroom they circled a foot apart, looking at each other warily for a minute. Ned yanked his shirt over his head, and emerged, hair shooting upwards with static, his eyes wild and glittering. He came closer and unbuttoned her shirt, pulled off her clothes piece by piece. He knelt on the floor and tugged down her jeans, burying his face into her, hands tight on her hips. He backed her onto the bed in the dim light, ripped off her watch and threw it onto the floor. He moved on top of her, skin, breath and touch, lips and hands everywhere. She didn't know for how long, but till she couldn't wait any longer and pulled him inside angrily, deeper and deeper, because it could never be deep enough; but she felt an ache filled for the first time since Aaron.

When she woke her brain was jumbled. She touched the top of her head cautiously. It felt like some hippie activist had trepanned it during the night. She looked at the clock, it was late.

Ned drove her to the airport, another trip in silence, both in a floating stupor; her hand wedged between his legs. M was already there, waiting by the check-in desk, eyebrows raised as they walked in through the electronic doors.

—Don't get waylaid by oversized frankfurters, said Ned. He nodded at M and left without looking back.

Chapter Twenty

Deli! 11 May 1987

How sad I was to hear of your sudden illness, your
unexpected retreat from life and your untimely death.
I'm guessing of course, but my life has become
spectacularly dull without your letters.

So – where are you hiding out? My pen bleeds
with unspent ink, my address book is in therapy. Why
haven't you written for so goddamn long?

Could it be that love has finally hit? If so – is M
taking it well, and how is the little sod anyway?

Aaron

P.S. Go right ahead, treat our friendship with the
respect it deserves, i.e. walk all over it in high heels
and take a year or more to answer.

P.P.S. Keep this letter, it may become a rarity.

Aaron (remember me?)

Ned's flat was in Soho, the attic apartment of a creaky Victorian building whose ground floor had been turned into a Chinese supermarket stocking two hundred kinds of noodles and some of the most sinister cuts of meat Deli had ever seen, sold frozen, squashed, bloodied and vacuum-packed in thick body-bag wrappings.

The previous owner of the flat was an old queen called Victor Moreton and the apartment itself was high camp, the walls painted in varying tones of reds, except for the bathroom which was a dark-brown gloss.

—Shit colour bathroom, Deli said as they lay submerged in soapy water together, her toes tickling Ned's armpits. —How novel is your hovel.

The bathroom window looked out high onto a small alley, through which London Life wound its shoddy way backwards and forwards in its never ending quest for a moment's sleaze.

Other than the bathroom, the flat had four rooms; sitting room, bedroom, a small kitchen and a second bedroom which Ned used as an office. The sitting room was painted a dark red colour and had circular mouldings and extravagant cornices covering the ceiling. The bedroom, a pinker shade of the same red, had a ceiling which boasted a shoal of moulded cupids swimming around its perimeter. Frankly the place was hideous.

ONE SUNDAY NIGHT, two months after the Frankfurt trip, Deli managed to poison herself on a batch of

Heat'n'Serve dim sum from the supermarket below and woke suddenly at three-ish in the morning feeling the inevitable swirl of vomit rise up through her stomach.

The brown bathroom didn't help a lot.

Ned, who had a plane to catch early the next morning mumbled encouragement wearily from the bedroom, his head locked firmly under a pillow.

By morning she was feeling shell-shocked and wretched and watched Ned dressing through gluey eyes.

—Just stay there till you feel better, Ned said. —I'll call. He waved from the door and disappeared.

She climbed out of bed gingerly, and padded to the bathroom.

In the mirror her face looked wan and sickly, her eyes sad with suffering. She stuck out her tongue, then hastily retracted it. She had just been diagnosed with a glamorous but incurable blood thinning type of illness, she would get weaker and weaker and eventually die in Ned's arms. She would still look pretty on her deathbed, and her ankles would be slim. Ned's life would be blighted for ever, thousands would mourn.

Feeling better, she crept back to bed and called M at home, and then Seb who was neither at home nor at Kevin's flat. Eight-thirty and still out on the town? She made a mental note to grill him about his social life then fell back into a doze till early afternoon.

★

It's always strange being in night-time places in the middle of the afternoon Deli thought. Ned's flat looked completely different by day, the red walls only really working with artificial light. Now they just looked dark, casting depressing half shadows across the bed.

It was quiet inside the flat. Deli could hear the intermittent drip, drip of the tap in the bathroom. Outside, sounds of city life rode lazily up on the afternoon breeze and floated through the window; a couple of irate traffic honks, people clattering up and down the street, the noise of a market barrow being pushed along, the occasional shriek of a passing child.

Still feeling queasy, she switched on the television to catch the last ten minutes of the afternoon movie. After the credits finished, she picked up the channel changer and scouted through, stopping on *Catwalk Chic*. Donna Chubb was at the Milan shows reporting on the couture collections.

There was a show on, she could see the name Vernon Skeeter, in polystyrene at the top of the stage. A tall thin girl swayed dizzily onto the catwalk. Her long hair was hanging in semi-greased tails on either side of her ears which protruded like two huge pale slices of potato. Her skin looked mottled under the fierce lights, and around the corners of her nose, vivid red marks stood out.

God, she's so victimy. Deli stared at the screen intently.

A second girl stumbled out, scratching her arms. She

looked round wildly with two huge bruised eyes. She kept sniffing, surreptitiously putting her arm up to her face to blot the overflow of her cold. A tight criss-cross top of silver foil wrap made her tits look as if they'd been flattened in a road accident and subjected to an emergency mastectomy.

Just as it occurred to Deli that this was a spoof, the camera cut to the audience. But, no! There was Noleen Banjax of *The Times*, pencil flying over her note pad and next to her sat Gawdy Wolff from the *Herald Tribune*, his lips forming a perfect prune.

Suddenly the girl on the catwalk stopped, reeled and spiralled slowly to the floor. The audience gasped. The girl lay motionless until two stagehands ran out and carried her off semi-conscious. The audience breathed an audible sigh of relief, then clapped wildly. A standing ovation.

Of course, of course, Deli twigged suddenly. They weren't models at all. They were real-life addicts. *What a brilliant press coup* and, realizing that the girl would get Vernon the front page of every newspaper in the country the next day, Deli felt a stab of jealousy and sank into an immediate and furious depression at her own creative inadequacy.

She switched off the television and decided to have a bath, soaking for a while in some unidentifiable green herb relaxant, staring at the brown walls and planning artistic oneuppance. When her skin had puckered to the consistency of a loofah she climbed out feeling dizzy and stole one of Ned's T-shirts to put on. She wandered aimlessly round the flat looking for something to do.

It was only a matter of time before she started snooping. After all, she reasoned, she was a chick. And chicks were notoriously nosy. It wasn't like it was a major decision or anything, but meandering round someone else's territory, turning over a bit of paper here and there, eventually something is bound to catch your eye, and the next thing you know, you're prising open their diary with a crowbar.

Ned, in fact, didn't have a crowbar handy, nor could she find a diary for that matter, but there was a lot of paperwork lying around: some research, a couple of book synopses he was obviously toying with. An old packet of Silk Cut, with a single cigarette left broken inside, lay on the floor where it had missed the bin, and next to it, under the table, a whole pile of articles pulled out of newspapers and hoarded.

Underneath them, a large yellow Kodak envelope caught her eye. Deli leafed through the stack of photographs idly. Ned on holiday, somewhere hot, standing on sand, eyes squinting from the glare of the sun. Ah, he looked adorable. Where was it though? Egypt maybe? Africa? She tried to remember if he had talked about this trip, realizing she was dangerously hooked on someone about whom she knew nothing. As she slipped them back into the pack, a white envelope dropped out and landed on the carpet at her feet. She turned it over. The writing on the front was looped and girlie. A tiny minor sensation of guilt pricked playfully. She hesitated for a second but snoop instinct easily won through.

Inside the envelope, the letter was folded neatly in two, a couple of photographs lodged inside, more snaps of Ned, but this time Ned with a ravishing, sexy, dark-haired girl with a fabulous body and fuck-me-at-once eyes.

Deli scrutinized the photos with a jealousy that tee-tered on the threshold of total paranoia. The girl was Mohican looking with black hair, divided by a clean white centre parting. Her legs were long and brown, her ankles were thin. She had no serious physical defects to speak of. Deli felt pale and powerless. She wanted to kill her.

The date on the letter was the previous week's. But the date printed on the photographs was the same date as the Frankfurt trip. Now Deli wanted to kill Ned. The letter was flowery and rosy. Deli could almost smell her through the paper. She'd gone back to her husband, she said, but she wanted him to have these photos, because they had such a great time together, didn't they? The letter continued, 'such a fabulous time'. She missed him, the letter taunted her, 'so so much'.

Deli got dressed and went home. Broken glass rained down on her head.

—STOP DOODLING, SEB. Deli thumped him on the back. —I need your full attention on my love life.

Seb ran his hand over his head. His hair, which had

been getting shorter and shorter over the last year, now looked like burnt corn-stubble.

—Okay, so she's mad for him, he reasoned patiently. —He's crazy for her, they are waltzing around this very second having a fabulous time. I don't get it. Why is he seeing you? And excuse me, *when* is he seeing her?

—How should I know? Deli wailed.

—When has he had the time? You've practically been living in Shag Palace these last couple of months, Seb went on.

Deli shrugged and blew her nose.

—You know why I'm not sympathetic? Seb asked.

—Because you're a lousy friend, she said crossly.

—Because I don't think he's for you.

—I thought you'd come round to him. Deli hated that Seb and M were so dubious about Ned.

—He's a control freak, and he's got you exactly where he wants you. I've seen you, Deli. You have plenty of nice guys falling over you all the time, then you let go of them all for the first guy who's too slippery to hold. You know what that makes you?

—What?

—A bona fide *Cosmopolitan* agony-column stereotype. Seb picked up his pencil and sharpened it with a professional wrist flick.

—Actually, the problem isn't me, Seb, it's her, Deli said through another nose-blow.

—Look, she's probably the kind of girl that threatens

to throw herself under a tube train if her man's late home from dinner. I bet she just won't let him go, you'll have to talk to him.

—How can I if he hasn't called me, Deli said miserably.

—He's probably upset you weren't there when he got back. He's not to know you've been leafing through all his private correspondence for God's sake.

—What if I left some fingerprints? I didn't wipe anything. What if he has hidden cameras?

—Sweetheart, Seb said sternly – you are becoming one very sick chick.

—Okay, okay, she sighed, —I'll work out a plan.

So this was her plan. She wasn't going to call him . . . just yet that was, she was going to wait till he called her. Then, if he didn't call her, she reasoned, it would be because he was still away, so she could safely call him then. Of course, if his answering machine was on, she would hang up immediately because there was no sense in losing cool points, but if he *was* there – she would hang up anyway, because she'd be so surprised to hear his voice that she'd probably go all fluffy if she spoke to him. But also because if he *was* back and he *hadn't* called her then she didn't see why she should call him . . . but then again . . .

Oh hell. There was nothing like that two-timing thing to make you really keen on a guy.

Ned had called her in the office at six o'clock that

evening. Deli demanded an explanation . . . at least, she skirted around the issue for ten minutes then casually mentioned tripping over the photographs by total accident. There was a pause down the other end of the line. Her mouth went dry.

—She's back with her husband in Paris but she still won't accept it's over, Ned said. —She rings me all the time, tries a new ploy every week. Why? Ned went on and his voice sounded strangely far away. —What on earth did you think?

—Nothing, Deli protested. —It's just that . . .

—Look, Deli, Ned interrupted, his voice sounded harsh, —it's you I'm in love with, not her – you. Do you understand?

Deli held the phone, her mind felt frozen, her chest tight, she had absolutely no idea what to say next. Ned asked her to meet him in Soho at nine. At nine-thirty he asked her to marry him.

Chapter Twenty-One The Unbearable Lightness of Me-ing

Dear Deli   2 March 1988

Thank you for the photographs, I particularly liked a)
which we call 'just a hint of a smile', also b) the
windswept look, and the charming c) entitled, 'All
will be well as soon as you folks leave.'

By the way, who is this scowling man you've
shacked up with? What do we know about him? Does
he pay his taxes, does he like baloney? Has he ever
had a sex operation in Mexico?

Don't get me wrong, you say he's a writer, and I
know you have occasionally read a book, so at least
you are ideally suited. However, I have taken the
precaution of sending both your details along with a
video of your husband (or at least a very good likeness
of him) making love to an under-age goat, to my
friends in the Federal Bureau. Don't be surprised if
you get a visit soon.

I liked M and Seb as bridesmaids, I think they
looked very cute in their mauve acetate frilly dresses
and dark glasses.

Do I sound in any way pissed off to you? It might be because I would have liked to have been asked to this event. After all, I am one of your oldest boyfriends, and I have no hair to prove it.

Enclosed your wedding present from Dino's Deli. Open soon, it's perishable.

Aaron xxxxxx
P.S. Adelaide says, Who's the sucker?

It had been a Thursday, she remembered, early in October. The year of the right-angle pads and the crop-bouff skirts. Deli had looked over at the clock. It was midnight, and the show was the next day. Another season, another show. How life revolved totally around these shows. It was as though nothing else mattered, nothing else was important, everyday stuff was just obliterated. You didn't open mail, you didn't get petrol, you barely remembered to eat. If a light bulb just happened to explode, well, that was it for at least five months, you lived in darkness and you didn't even notice – much less care. No, when there was a collection to finish and a show to put on, it was all your mind could focus on, night and day – day and night.

Deli had been waddling around the office like a giant wind-up toy. Her stomach had got so large M had suggested knocking through the office partitioning to accommodate it.

The reason that she was so fat, was that she was having a love affair with a Chinese restaurant, and the reason that she was having an affair with a Chinese restaurant was because she was pregnant. Nine months and one week pregnant to be exact.

She counted herself lucky with her cravings so far, none of them had been too bizarre. Only Chinese food and tangerines. She ate pounds of each every day. Other people wanted milkshakes made of paint stripper, or worm soufflé. In fact, only last week Aaron had thoughtfully sent her the *National Enquirer*, whose headline had read 'Woman eats stove', so she guessed, all in all, she had got off lightly. Having said that, however, pregnancy was not exactly a blast.

She'd been married for almost a year now. Oh yes, she'd accepted him in the end, not when he first asked her of course. Naturally she tortured him a bit, but about five minutes later, after she'd really made him sweat for a while, she'd agreed.

Her friends thought she'd gone mad.

—You're stark fucking staring mad, they said.

—He's too difficult, they said. —And now you're pregnant too! Jesus! Get rid of it. At once.

But the truth was, she didn't want to get rid of it at all. She'd never wanted anything more in her life . . .

—It'll never work, they jibed. —Kids and a job. You can't have it all. You'll be a steamed pudding for the rest of eternity.

But she was crazy for Ned, crazy crazy crazy for him, crazy for his unbrushed hair, for his quirky scowling face, crazy about his flashes of temper and sparks of madness, and she reckoned it would work, she could *make* it work.

Ned had just finished another of his doom books, *Social Surgery*. He didn't think it was very good, and to be truthful Deli didn't either.

—It's just a temporary blip, she told him sympathetically, which for some reason made him furious with her, but then a lot of things made Ned furious. He wasn't exactly what you might call a relaxed laid-back kind of guy, she thought fondly. Living with Ned was like living permanently in the last nine red seconds before the bomb exploded, sometimes it would be difused, and sometimes it would be detonated. But that's what made it interesting.

At that moment Ned was in Canada promoting *Social Surgery* at a book fair. She didn't mind at all if he wasn't there for the birth, in fact she'd almost rather he wasn't. First because she knew he would just get twitchy and difficult, and she would spend all her time calming him down, instead of heavy breathing, riding the waves, or whatever it was you were supposed to do, and secondly, because, you know, all that blood and gore. *Yich*. She didn't want him having a flashback to all that *gunge* every time they made love.

M was a boy, so he'd just be squeamish and hopeless. He'd peer up the midwives' skirts and take them out for a hamburger if they were pretty enough. So Seb was coming instead. Seb she definitely wanted to be there. Actually, if Seb hadn't been around these past few months, Deli conceded, she would genuinely have been a fruitcake.

The sales started tomorrow too. Deli prayed they were going to go well. She hung the last of the 'Press' pieces on the rail. These were the *key* pieces, the ones that looked the dumbest but scored the front pages. God forbid your whole collection should look like them though. Oh no, you could not afford to ignore commercial realism. You could not allow yourself, for instance, to be inspired by German kitchen appliances, and in a fever of anticipation of the fabulous press notices you were about to receive, send out all your models in shiny clothes made out of Formica, because, if you did, a cheeky picture of the supermodel Origami might well appear on the front page of *The Times* and you'd be simply *euphoric*, the darling of the press, until, that is, you began to choke on the dust kicked up by the buyers as they galloped off in droves to your rivals saying things like:

—What on earth is that? Oh yes, I see now, it's a skirt that turns into a washing machine, how inspired, what an interesting look, and it's certainly *original*. Goodbyeee!

Over at the other end of the office M was pulling down the security grilles on the window. Seb was sitting smoking nearby, dumbly watching the price lists ejaculate out of the top of the computer. Everyone else had just gone home, trudging through the door like zombies.

As usual Deli had felt bad watching them go. Late nights played havoc with people's private lives. They were a company of twenty now, but oddly the workload never got easier and the stress factor just seemed to get higher. Recently she had found herself waking in the mornings, uneasily aware of a hard lump of new emotions living somewhere in her stomach. This lump operated under a variety of aliases too elusive to name. Dormant at night, it woke when she did, speeding through her body like a rocket, causing instant cramp and paralysing panic, and the only cure, it seemed, was to put in more hours.

Ned was twitchy about it though. He didn't understand and, truth be told, he wasn't interested. It's not like it was a big issue or anything, it's just that he used the word *delegate* alarmingly often. Deli had tried explaining it to him, if you weren't prepared to do it yourself, blah, blah, but he didn't really appreciate the problem. The problem was they were all on the same drug. They were all hooked, addicted, chronically co-dependent on the juice that raced round their bodies for that six-month build-up. They were all fashion addicts. God help them, and there was no cure for this kind of abuse.

Also (and it was controversial she knew) being stressed out was, secretly, a lot of fun. Deli pulled on her coat. Tomorrow morning the van would arrive at five a.m. but till then sleep, or at least what passed for sleep when a small human being was camping out on your bladder playing Nick Nack Paddy Whack, was basically a seven-hour-long peeing session punctuated by the occasional doze.

Seb locked up the heavy front doors and as the lift was inevitably somewhere else, the three of them walked slowly down the concrete steps. M ahead, and Seb holding onto Deli's arm.

—Easy there, fatty, Seb said. —Grace of a young gazelle, bless her, he shouted to M.

She pinched him. —Fucking subordinate.

Outside it was pitch dark and eerie, the noosed skeleton swayed backwards and forwards, spiralling round in its perpetual death throes.

—God, I hate this place at night, she said to Seb, shivering. —It scares me witless, it's all shadows and whispers. She was so tired, she felt disconnected, floaty. Reality must be out there somewhere, it was just happening to someone else. She crunched carefully over the builder's rubble clutching onto Seb's hand.

—*Oh no!*

Startled, she looked up hearing M's cry from up ahead.

In the car park Deli's car had been vandalized. Both front side-windows had been smashed, the mirror yanked off and someone had scratched metal keys in thin white aeroplane lines against the sky blue paint.

—Bloody hell, said M shaking his head as they came up behind him. —Not again. He looked around at Deli helplessly.

For a minute she felt like giving in to a calming bout

of sobbing, but this was not the first time that the incredible glamour of working in the fashion industry really hit home. Anyway she was too tired and too fat to get upset. She pulled herself together and opened the door.

—Will you be all right, Hon, want me to drive you? M brushed the fragments of broken glass from the driver's seat.

—If they'd really wanted to be helpful they could have taken the whole door off, she joked weakly as she tried to squish her bulk behind the steering wheel.

—Why don't you come and stay with me as Ned's away? said Seb.

—I'll be fine. Really. She started the engine, feeling absurdly depressed. The house she and Ned had finally bought in the Talbot Road had only just been finished by the builders. But it was still virgin territory, antiseptic and untouched, there were no comforting stains on the carpet to come home to, no familiar piles of ageing mags, yellowing newspapers and half-opened mail. She wished to God that Ned was back.

Fifteen minutes later she had felt a soft popping in her ears and her waters had broken just before turning left down the Westbourne Park Road.

Chapter Twenty-Two

—All undressed are we now, dearie?

A tiny starched hat came into view and underneath, the fat face of the West Indian midwife smiled encouragingly as she popped a stick of Wrigley's into her mouth and worked it round with her tongue to soften it up before she began chewing loudly. Her breath smelled of fermented fruit salad and just a hint of dental decay.

—Please can I have some? Deli begged, eyeing the woman's powerful masticating jaws.

—You're not to have any food in case of anaesthetic, girl. Didn't the doctor tell you that?

—No, Deli lied furiously. —He didn't and I haven't eaten all day.

—Here, the midwife said kindly, suddenly whooshing a jet of water up Deli's backside. —This'll make you feel better. She belched quietly and ambled off leaving Deli stranded in the bathroom.

—It's a potential Caesarean! Deli shouted proudly

down the telephone to M. —So I might be a bit late in the morning – apparently my hips are too small.

—You must be joking, he said. —Have they seen the size of your ass?

Deli pleaded with them for the snip, then and there.

—Oh no, we must give it a chance to come naturally, said the midwife, packing a large beef sandwich down her throat.

But all Deli could think of was food: Lucky charms, Jell-O, Cheese Doodles, Oreos, oh God, for some Oreos.

Nurses traipsed in all night still chewing, crumbs stuck fresh to their lips.

—Dilating nicely, are we?

When the doctor told her it was going to come naturally, Deli was almost disappointed.

But they were wrong of course. Highlight of the night came when the baby's heart stopped and after some consideration, the midwife decided to cease guzzling and panic instead. Moving like lightning despite her bulk, she set off a red flashing fire alarm above the door which brought an obstetrician running down the corridor from where he'd clearly been playing tiddlywinks for pickled placentas with his colleagues.

Going under anaesthetic Deli started to hyperventilate.

—What if they mess up? she shouted at the anaesthetist.

—Don't worry, he said calmly, stroking her vein with a hypodermic, —they've done this a million times before.

—Not them, idiot, she wailed. —What if the models don't show, what if the press snore and the buyers vomit into their handbags, what if . . . what if . . . but as the happy drug started to take effect she could hear far off somewhere in the distance, a clapping of hands, the beating from the flightpath of a thousand baby-bearing storks coming towards her, then a surprised voice from somewhere close by crying: Why, it's a . . . no surely not . . . yes, it is! It's a *jacket* . . . and the voice was growing stronger and stronger now . . . yes, Mrs Harrison . . . you have a lovely little fitted jacket and it weighs . . . £128.99 plus V.A.T.

ACTUALLY, IT WAS a boy, and so unspeakably ugly that M gagged when he looked into the cot, dropping his present of flowers, press cuttings, show video and copy of *Playgirl*.

—*Jee-sus!* he shouted. —Do you think those looks are hereditary? Are mine going to look like that too?

—Only if you're fucking Ned as well, Deli said, pretending not to be hurt.

—And why is he sleeping in a giant butter dish? M said, settling down in a kidney-coloured plastic chair whilst Deli fed the deviant. Its tiny head smelled like a scorched ironing board. Deli wanted to tell someone, anyone, every minute detail of her ordeal, but Ned was on the way back from Canada and Seb was stuck at the exhibition brown-nosing buyers. Instead she bombarded M for a post-mortem on the show about which she suddenly discovered she couldn't care less, while he unfolded the centre spread featuring the well-oiled biceps of Mark, a plumber from Hounslow, and good with his tools.

—Why don't we just have sex now, if you're so deprived, she said to him, frustrated by his lack of interest in her offspring.

—I'm afraid you'll never be able to have sex again, M said calmly, frowning at a picture of a window-cleaner apparently dressed in a leather oven glove.

—Why not?

—Well, you're married, you've got a career, and now you've had a child. Stands to reason, doesn't it?

SEB CAME ROUND later on.

—Are you sure he's yours? Seb asked.

—What are you talking about? Deli said.

—Nothing, just asking that's all. Seb was looking cagey.

—Okay, okay, Deli said, irritated. —I know he's ugly.

—Ye-es, but you can't know what he really looks like.

—What do you mean? Deli said anxiously.

—Because God throws magic dust in a mother's eyes, to make them think their baby is really beautiful, whatever kind of King Troll it is.

—So?

—So if you're looking at it through the magic dust,

imagine what the reality's like for the rest of us. Seb sniggered.

—Oh, very funny, Deli said crossly, wondering why everyone imagined she wanted to play at being offhand. —And since you're so expert on children, you'd better be godfather.

—HE LOOKS LIKE my publisher, said Ned, holding the baby gingerly. —Look at his ears, are those normal? Look at his hands, they're enormous. I can't believe I wasn't here. Oh, Deli, he's beautiful. I'm so proud of you. Ned looked gratifyingly moist around the eyes, he sat for a minute looking at his son, but then he became restless and as soon as the baby began to cry, he handed him back to Deli.

—What's wrong with it, Deli? Why is it screaming? Ned looked terrified.

—I don't know, he's just being a baby, I guess. Deli buried her nose into the soft neck.

Ned got up and looked out of the window of the room.

—You know the heating isn't working yet in the house, Deli, it was really cold when I got back.

—Oh? She wondered why he was telling her this.

—It was freezing in Canada, then cold when I got home, Ned went on. —I know it's been difficult for you, but you'll have to be a bit more organized now you've had the baby.

—Oh. Of course. Deli leaned her head back against the plastic pillow. Ned hadn't said it nastily, but for some reason she felt like crying, and had to turn her head to the wall so he didn't see.

THERE WAS LITTLE doubt about it, M thought, as he leant over his nephew – Rubin was a mutant baby: lying in its basket near Deli's desk, podgy little hands coated in goo, gripping its blanket, and emitting bloodcurdling screams. Once or twice in the past couple of months M had dared to look in its mouth midhowl, down, down, deep into the hellish red cavity of its throat, trying in vain to look for the puzzle of its soul, but so far he'd found nothing.

Physically there hadn't been much improvement. Rubin's head had remained the same size since birth but his ears appeared to have stretched and hung down almost to the full length of his face. Even a dose of milk spots threatened to turn into angry early acne, and now, come to think of it, Rubin's whole demeanour was that of a sullen fourteen-year-old told to tidy his room. When he wasn't roaring with rage, he lay back on his blanket, arms crossed, watching the world through his half-slit eyes as he headbutted the cot with his bald cranium and plotted adult overthrow.

The only person who wasn't fazed by him was Seb who'd embraced the mantle of his godfatherhood with surprising fortitude. Rubin acted like a normal baby with

Seb, he gooed and cooed and, according to Deli, at least once he smiled. What somehow made it worse was that Aaron had issued forth from his loins what sounded from his description like an almost perfect child. From the photograph, Deli could only appreciate the baby's curly cowlick of hair and marvel at his beaming smile. According to Aaron, his nose never ever needed hoovering, Adelaide had never had to take him to casualty and the brat spoke in almost perfect syntax.

—HE'S GETTING QUITE cute now isn't he? Deli kept asking hopefully whenever she brought Rubin into the office. M presumed his sister was still in the throes of milk haze. He reckoned he'd never seen her so happy. She drifted around the studio trailing goodwill and threatening the staff with imminent baby-kissing duties. Not a lot of work was getting done.

Deli, in fact, was well out of the milk haze and into the final stages of exhaustion. At night Rubin wailed and howled forlornly from the moment she and Ned tried to go to bed. She'd put him in the kitchen, the furthest room away, it made little difference. Eventually she put him in the linen cupboard where he was forced to compete with the thudding of the boiler, but the challenge only served to spur him on. It wasn't so much that she minded him crying, in fact she was so immune she could have almost slept through it, but Ned couldn't take it, complaining vigorously at every mewl and growl. So she lay in bed, shoulders rigid, head hunched, a neurotic turtle, waiting for the slightest noise from the baby. And once she was awake in the night, she stayed that way, watching the inert form of Ned sleeping beside her. By day she tripped up and down the studio in a catatonic state, the lump of nerves residing in her stomach twitching at the thought of another sleepless night to come and another matchstick-eye day to get through.

SOON RUBIN BEGAN to crawl and at the same time became flatteringly clingy. He took to following Deli round the studio looking lovelorn, picking up pins with his mouth and swallowing them three or four at a go, just to impress her. Luckily this seemed to have no apparent ill-effects as Rubin's throat was always covered in a thick stream of mucus from the overflow of his nose, and the pins slipped down a treat.

Next he discovered the whereabouts of the fridge and before long, with the stealth of a cat burglar, he'd shimmy across the floorboards right down to the kitchen, pulling open the door with no trouble at all and immersing his head with its enormous earlobes into somebody's lunch.

—I've got a nanny! shouted Deli finally, coming into the office with no baby one morning. Her milk had dried up and her breastfeeding duties were finally over. —She's sensible, she's knowing, she's a vegetarian and she makes Ned's coffee while he's slavering over his typewriter. Jane's a marvel and I'm free again.

Chapter Twenty-Three

There is never enough brown bread or yoghurt in this house. I am leaving.

Jane

Deli produced the crumpled bit of paper from her pocket and shoved it across the aisle.

—So, she was a whacko, Seb had said, looking at the note. —Surely that's normal? He caught sight of a weedy Jal airsteward approaching with a sushi lunchbox, his eyes fixed lustfully towards him.

—Probably. But we came back from the movies and she was gone. The note was pinned onto a carton of soya milk on the kitchen table. Deli stowed Rubin between her knee and the seat arm where he wriggled strenuously before slumping back into a deep Calpol-induced coma.

—Had Ned been shouting at her? asked Seb. He took the lunchbox and unclipped his tray. —Thanks. The steward smiled goofily and swayed back up the aisle.

—Not that I know of, Deli said. —But, get this: she'd been playing hide and seek in her room with about a dozen empty gin bottles. Deli shook her head. —Can you believe it? One was hidden under the mattress, another in the video. Ned found two more stuffed into the soil of the window box.

—What I *can't* believe is that she left Rubin on his own, Seb said. —Ned must have gone spare. He opened the lunchbox and prodded the white square of beancurd doubtfully.

—*I* went spare, forget Ned, Deli said, irritated. Why was it that everyone was so concerned with Ned's reaction all the time? She continued to massacre the nail on her thumb distractedly. —The thing was, I didn't feel horrified that I'd employed a deranged vegetarian drunk to look after our first-born child, I just felt relieved she'd left without harming anyone. This is okay, I managed to convince myself, this is the penalty of working mothers; you are forced to trust the person who's done the best job faking their references. Try not to feel so bad, try not to feel guilty and inadequate. But Ned was furious with me, he shouted all last night about it being my fault. She paused. —Now, of course, I feel bad, guilty and inadequate. She cursed herself for giving them the added problem of Rubin just to keep Ned quiet. Rubin was only a year old, it was unfair to subject him to this kind of crap. She was angry with Ned for making her so paranoid. She was angry with herself too. All her lines of decisions recently seemed smudged and confused. But, somehow, whenever Ned criticized her these days she felt like she needed a lawyer to argue her previous good character and beg for bail. —I'm sorry, Seb, she added contritely. —I had to bring him.

—It's okay, we'll manage. Seb took a deep breath. —Look, Deli, the guy's being a pig. It's like he's drained your confidence, you've got to deal with this. He faltered. Deli hated anybody criticizing Ned.

—You've no idea what's in store for us, Deli was saying fretfully as if she hadn't heard him. —This is Japan, not fucking Disneyland, we're supposed at least to pretend we're serious professional people. What happens if Rubin screams for the whole week?

—I'm a godfather and you're a Superwoman, said Seb soothingly. —He'll have to listen to one of us.

But even Seb couldn't prevent Rubin from thundering with rage as his ears popped on landing. As they were about to get off the aeroplane the crone who was sitting behind them, and who had been sighing furiously for the last eighteen hours every time Rubin let out a squeak, leaned her head through the grey leather seats.

—A slap wouldn't go amiss, you know, she said cattily.

—So slap her, said Seb loudly, and put his arm protectively around Deli.

DELI LAY ON the bed wrapped in her sterile white dressing-gown eating a prawn cocktail from the Okura Room Service Menu. Rubin lay unconscious beside her, his inner clock having finally come full circle.

Seb sprawled next to Rubin watching *Vice-Girls in Isetan* on the 'pay as you masturbate' hotel channel, his hair steaming from the shower. In his dressing-gown Deli thought he looked like one of those hot complimentary flannels they give you on the aeroplane.

Darling Ned [she wrote]   **January 1989**

Then she stopped. *Where are you?* she thought. *How am I to make peace, how am I supposed not to sound chippy, defensive, angry?* She hadn't heard from Ned in the whole six days they'd been in Tokyo, no message of apology, no phone call, no nothing. What's more she had failed to raise him at home, either he was always out, or he was ignoring her messages on the ansaphone. She wondered what the hell was going on.

Why is it that you haven't called? Could it be that Gibbon's secretary is too busy grinding away on your lap removing her glasses to dial my number? Get with it or I'll be forced to sleep with Seb.

Seb looked over her shoulder – Hey, give me that. He grabbed the pen out of her hand.

Dear Ned, Don't worry, the only member of your family I am prepared to interfere with sexually is your son. X Seb XX

We're having a really swell time here, Ned [Deli scribbled]. This afternoon numerous discussions about the bubble economy were thoughtfully laid on for our entertainment. I behaved very well, giving good eye contact, but Seb giggled a lot.

Your son and heir however can only fart in the face of the ailing Japanese market. Tomorrow a meeting with the President again, I'm telling you, if the man tries to give me more hi-fi he's toast.

Deli XXXXXX
Your adorable wife.
P.S. Call me, fax me, anything will do.

But Ned hadn't called or faxed or done any such thing. Instead his silence seemed to mark a turning point and from the moment she and Rubin returned from Tokyo, Ned withdrew into a shell of irritation from which, try as she might, she simply couldn't prise him.

Chapter Twenty–Four The Quick and The Uptight

Seb had watched Deli as she searched for something on the desk, picking up bits of filing and slamming them down again furiously. —What's wrong? he asked eventually.

Deli slumped down into her seat and rested her chin on the palm of her hand. —Ned missed his fucking deadline.

—Oooh, shit, said Seb, his heart sinking. —I thought this was his last chance.

—It was, she said. —They've cancelled his contract.

Seb came across the room and perched on the stool in front of Deli's desk. —What is his problem? The deadline has been on the boil for a year now.

—He says he can't concentrate with Rubin in the house.

And he did have a point she supposed. Rubin was now marauding around in his baby walker, fists clenched, hair still a stunted stubble. Seb had given him some tattoos for Easter and took great trouble pressing snakes, daggers and bleeding roses all over his solid little arms. In his white sleeveless vest, and with the perpetual furious expression he'd inherited from Ned, he looked like a Puerto Rican cruising Alphabet City for a street fight . . . come to think of it, Ned looked a bit like that too, just without the tattoos.

—So what's the state of play at home then? Seb asked her warily.

—Well, Deli shrugged, —he's just a bit moody sometimes, you know, Ned. She shuffled the nomination papers on the desk and stood up restlessly. She didn't want to go into it.

The state of play was that they were fighting a lot. In fact they seemed to be on orange alert for war. It had been the matches incident that had pushed them so close to the edge.

The matches had fallen out of Ned's trousers as she'd taken them out of the cupboard while they were packing to go away for the weekend. She'd looked at them idly for a second.

—Where did these come from? She'd been about to bin them when she noticed they were from the Hotel Raphael in Paris.

—Where did you put my checked shirt? Ned was searching through his clothes in the chest of drawers, his back to her.

—Were you in Paris recently? She didn't remember him ever going.

—I can never fucking find anything in this house. Ned shut the drawer with a snap.

—Ned?

—How should I know? Maybe, he answered impatiently. But there was something in his voice.

—But when? Deli was genuinely puzzled.

—I can't remember, said Ned. —Why on earth does it matter? Sometime. He turned his back again and flicked through a pile of papers on top of the bedside table knocking half of them on the floor. —Oh, for God's sake, I can't stand all this junk everywhere, he said exasperated and stalked into the bathroom.

Deli had stood stupidly, looking at the small square of cardboard in her hand. Her brain clicked over and over. Something was wrong.

—Ned, she raised her voice so he could hear, —I said I don't remember you going.

—I went for a night, you were probably away. He came back into the bedroom and stood with his arms crossed. —Satisfied?

—You never mentioned it. She felt a sick feeling start in her stomach.

—I had to see someone about the European rights to the book.

—And you stayed in the Raphael Hotel?

—Mmm, yes. He walked over to the window and turned the key on either side of the frame.

—When I was in Japan. Her brain stopped clicking

suddenly and locked into place. Ned not calling her, not being able to get in touch with him for six days.

—Can't remember. Ned shrugged.

—Well, that's the only time I've been away, Ned, so it must have been. She knew she was beginning to sound shirty. But she remembered perfectly where he said he'd been. Nowhere, he'd said. He'd just been working and had been lazy about picking up his messages. —Why didn't you tell me? she asked.

—I don't have to account to you, Deli. Ned came close and put his face into hers. —I am not chained to you, do you see? You were away on business, and I was too. You're not the only one who's got a fucking career, right?

—But I did ask and you didn't say anything about Paris. She was going on and on and on now, the same question, too cowardly to get to the next stage, the accusation stage, the potential wronged-wife stage. She had a brief but potent image of herself in a stained counterpane dressing-robe and fluffy slippers hurling abuse from the doorway as her husband coursed down the street with his suitcase.

Ned looked at her, his mouth set. —Drop it, Deli, he said, and his beautiful brown eyes were as hard as mahogany.

SEB BROUGHT HER over a cup of coffee. —Why don't you wait till the Design Awards are over, Deli? Things

won't be so hectic, then you've got to sit down and talk
to Ned. You can't go on pushing this away for ever.

She took the cup of coffee from him gratefully. The
Awards had been right at the back of her mind, so many
other things seemed to be crowding in on her. Still . . . to
win would be amazing, she thought wistfully. She put the
nomination papers back in the envelope but as she did so
she caught sight of M through the glass partitioning,
laughing on the telephone, and immediately felt low
again. His life was so entangled into hers, they were so
like each other, yet his seemed so stable. He had Tish, a
relationship that just got better and stronger. It was as if
he had a lock on his life and the key in his pocket.

Her life on the other hand had become one long
relentless duty. There was no time to breathe, no time to
think, no time to live . . . Keeping up with work, keeping
up with home and Rubin, and especially keeping Rubin
away from Ned. Jesus, it was like juggling daggers.

*The train emerged from the tunnel, the flash of light startling her
out of her reverie. As the tube people came back into focus, Deli
noticed a schoolboy perching on the seat at the other end of the
carriage. The boy's head bobbed gormlessly above his chest while
his torso moved continuously, as though seething with angry
teenage hormones bopping to an internal disco. He was using a
knife to halve a gigantic cheese sandwich on which he began
chewing desultorily. Deli turned her attention to the map on the
wall.*

Two stops to go. Christ.

She hardly ever thought about the early days with Ned, the memories mostly wiped out by the relentless antagonism of their present relationship. But still, for a while, for a very short while, she really had believed she could have it all.

fashion tips n° 6

Stress Control

Now the lump of nerves at the bottom of your stomach refuses to consign itself to day-time activity only. It begins to wake at night. Just as you get into bed, just as you turn out the light, just as you collapse onto the pillow where sleep used to come so easy; it starts messing around with your head.

Now when you close your eyes, a stealthy hand reaches out and switches on the light in your brain. *Pow*. Your eyes snap open with a start, and your body becomes a playground for emotions.

At first it is only the odd one or two, but soon the sleepless nights happen more and more until, too late, you realize it isn't just a lump at all, but an active growth, some kind of nasty little personal devil feeding greedily off the diet of anxiety you are supplying him with.

—It's just stress, says the doctor on whose shoulder you are blubbing. —Lighten up, babe, and have a Valium.

Chapter Twenty-Five Dancing in Disney

A smile had been frozen to her face. Smiles were also frozen to the face of at least twenty other people in the room. She was sitting at a table in the Dorchester Hotel. It was the Annual Design Awards night and Deli reckoned she was going to be sick.

This was it then, the night of a thousand exploding stars if she won or, if not, the night of sobbing ten watery litres of pent-up self-pity into her pillow.

—I'm useless . . . (*sniff*).

—Hopeless . . . (*whimper*).

—I'm—I'm . . . less than an ant. WWWAAAAAA-AAAAAAAAAAAAAA!

Win or lose, it was going to be an evening of excruciating horror for all concerned.

On Deli's table had been the following guests; Donna Chubb, from Cable Chic, a woman the world could safely call a doyenne of fashion. Sitting on Hymen's left, and keeping up a tireless flow of fashion patter was Judy

Schmackerliptz, now one of their chief and most prized customers.

Judy was no longer a cone head. This was because she had deemed it unfashionable this season. Now her hair had been allowed to drop naturally, or as naturally as was possible with half a litre of hair products nestling in between every follicle. Judy sported Pucci this evening. Her legs were encircled in silk jersey leggings, of a peach and violet swirl'n'splatter pattern, and, although she wasn't a lady who could be accurately described as being in the first flush of youth, her brave heralding of the sixties re-explosion had given her a certain fashion credibility. Now she'd got to know her, Judy wasn't so bad, Deli thought. She just needed . . . say to be stripped of her clothes, dipped into an icy pond, beaten with tufts of grass and maybe a baseball bat, and then finally squeezed through a wringing machine. Deli's guess was she'd be just fine after that.

Next to her and looking pretty spiffy tonight in a canary-coloured maxi coatdress was Hymen, one half of the dynamic buying duo from The Loft, their stockists from Chicago. Hymen's partner, Dovanna, had been recovering from a chin tuck and sadly hadn't been able to attend.

Still travelling round the table, next door to Judy, in a piece of really inspired placement, was Katy's boyfriend Jim. The placement was inspired because Judy was hyper verbal, whilst Jim, slumped in his chair and smoking what looked suspiciously like a roach, was so laid-back, it was difficult to know whether or not he was conscious. Next to Jim was their old favourite, Mernadeen from Bergdorf and next to her, Seb, who had drunk so much vodka earlier this evening that he was now, amazingly enough, genuinely enjoying himself.

Then there was Katy. Miss Gorgeous herself, with her unbelievable red brown hair, and those slanted green eyes, those legs! The Stairways to Heaven, M called them. Next to Deli was M who was wearing his, Gee! that's interesting expression to conceal his unutterable boredom, while Judy opposite hypnotized him with her captivating personality.

Ned hadn't come.

Oh, he'd made some excuse about having a business dinner, but Deli knew he could have come if he'd wanted to. Her chest tightened angrily. She didn't care, fuck him, fuck him.

Mernadeen kept asking her if she was nervous in the same tone of voice people use when they've just heard you've got cancer. Deli was pretending to be a block of ice, but the truth was that the devil had gone berserk inside her stomach, giggling and tossing petrol onto a bonfire of nerves.

—And the nominees for the Technical Achievement Award are . . . as the names were being read out, five models burst out on stage in a mass of gangly limbs and gallumphed along the catwalk trying to look tough. They were all New Faces, still raw and hopeful of stardom.

Dream on kids.

The announcement was made and Sarah Scabiena, the leader of the we-say-sucks-to-dry-cleaning brigade, allowed her refrigerated smile to unthaw into a more appropriate expression and stepped up to receive her statuette.

—Are you nervous, sweetie? asked Mernadéen, for perhaps the fifteenth time.

—Yes.

—You'll be just fine. She patted Deli's hand. Deli felt a great rush of love for her.

The other half of Seb's vodka that she'd downed getting dressed earlier had now run through her system. Swaying slightly she meandered through the space between the tables to the loo. There was a huge queue in the ladies, she nipped into the men's.

Vernon Skeeter was inside, zipping the lower half of his hulking six foot frame into a pair of black leather trousers whose seams struggled to remain closed over the undulations of his thigh muscles.

—Hi, cutesie, he said.

—Hi, Vernon. She kissed him. Vernon's hair was now two inches long all over, and dyed cream to match his collection.

—Can you do up my dress for me?

—What's in it for me? he asked.

—Sexual arousal, she said grimly.

—Whose the new Friend of Dorothy on your table? Vernon asked.

—Which one?

—The one sitting next to whatsername, the Bergdorf buyer.

—Oh, that's Seb, haven't you met him before?

—No, darling, and he's gorgeous. Vernon pulled the chiffon at the back of her dress into a knot. —Available?

—He's going out with Kevin Hobson.

—The photographer? Vernon whistled. —Ooh, classy.

—He's not your type anyway, Deli said quickly.

—Darling, everybody's my type these days.

Back at the table, Mernadeen and Judy were hotly debating facial hair.

Up at the podium Dawn French was giving a statuette to Futon, the Japanese designer.

Here we go, Deli thought. Dear God, this was the big one. The Chairman of the Fashion Council was introducing the presenter. Katy had disappeared backstage. And suddenly everyone at the table was watching her. A huge screen flashed up at the back of the stage with the pictures of the nominees and a short video clip of interviews with them. Shit, Deli sank lower into her chair, her hands were damp and sweaty, she stuffed them underneath her legs, quickly pulling them out in case they made wet patches. She strived but failed to remember what expression was on her face. *Don't look sad, but don't look happy, don't look scared*.

She tried out a slight grimace. *If I win, I'll get Ned back*.

Right at the front table she could see Vernon, his lips

were pursed, one arm leant casually on the back of his gold chair, but the muscles in his neck were rigid as a dead man's fingers.

—Nervous, sweetie? asked Mernadeen. Deli only just refrained from punching her.

M was mouthing her a kiss. *No, wait, if I lose, I'll get Ned back . . .*

The models came out, Futon's outfits first, no dancing, giggling and tripping here, these were the big names, the world's top models. Then Vernon's girls, to a high screechy dance tune. Deli knew from the rehearsal she was last. *It's a bad sign, I know that's a bad sign . . .* she obsessed inwardly . . . *but just in case I do win I swear I'll try really hard with Ned anyway.*

She rubbed her sweat-slicked hands on a napkin, but they were shaking so hard it dropped to the floor. As she bent to pick it up, she could hear the familiar beat of Jimmy Hendrix, their show music, and out came Katy, wearing a tungsten pants suit, a pink velcro jacket over frilly faux pony-skin shorts . . . out came the other girls. Oh, cringe cringe cringe, the changes had got faster and faster, the last two girls looked dishevelled and one even had her shorts on back to front. Deli could see the zip snaking up her crotch like an over libidinous centipede. Overcome with humiliation, she looked away. The girls slid off, the audience craned forward. The presenter, a C-grade movie star, came out with the envelope. Deli thought of Mom and Dad watching from home. In her mind's eye she saw Ned's face hard and angry, but still . . . *Oh, damn you, Ned, why aren't you here?*

The chairman, beaming sepulchrally up on stage, looked hot and sweaty under the lights. The movie star read out the name. The floor began to spin.

Everyone started to clap wildly. Seb whooped and kicked her hard under the table, Mernadeen gripped her elbow.

Jesus-H-Christ, she hadn't cottoned on until the winner's photograph flashed back up onto the screen and she'd seen her own face grinning soupily down at them.

Chapter Twenty-Six

She couldn't forgive Ned for not turning up to the Awards. Somehow it had poisoned the stupid object for her, so instead of finding a mantelpiece to put it on, a shelf in the loo, a frame, she had locked it in a drawer at the office along with her fantasy of winning Ned back, because apart from a half-hearted acknowledgment the day after, Ned had never mentioned it again. Not that he mentioned very much really, in fact conversation as a general concept, other than the daily rowing of course, had become a thing of the past.

So after a while she found herself having a new fantasy. Ned and her were in a plane bound for—? Somewhere. She didn't know where, but they were with two friends and they were going on holiday. She fancied the Male Friend, and his name, just for the record, was Danny. He was very funny and smart but he had sad eyes. His wife was okay, but a bit of a ball breaker. She was not worthy of him. He was not happy with his wife, but he was in denial.

The plane crashed. They were all in the water, and Ned and the ball-breaker didn't make it. In fact no one in the plane seemed to make it except for her and Danny. They got to this rock someplace just out of the water. It was dark, and there was no hope of rescue. She and Danny huddled together, muttering things about shared bodily warmth. Danny gave her his coat and put his arm around her. Both of them got over the death of their respective partners within half an hour.

During the night Danny fell in love with her (she was already crazy about him). Just before dawn he kissed her as the sun rose over the flat sea and they both lived happily ever after.

This was a recurring fantasy. That is to say it reoccurred whenever she went home.

SOON IT SEEMED as if Ned had been swallowed by his bad mood. It had become bigger and stronger than he was. They fought continually and Deli hated to fight. She remembered a time when she was still able to come home and at least test the mood: if Ned was depressed she'd try to cheer him up, if he was hot and angry, she'd cool him down. She'd had a semblance of control. It didn't work any longer. Now the boot seemed to be firmly on the other foot and boy was it kicking hard. If she came back feeling happy, Ned succeeded in depressing her. He'd stick in his verbal skewer, twisting it hard till she lashed out at him, then he would shake his head and smile as if he'd won some kind of major victory.

Now as she walked up the steps, as she put the key in the door, she was already dreading the possibility of an attack and as she closed the door behind her she felt the bad vibes whizzing round the house. A flock of black crows settled on her shoulder.

—Hi! she shouted. —Ned, Rubin!

Rubin, she knew, would be upstairs in the bath, sucking the enamel and licking the hot tap. He wouldn't hear her till she got to the first floor. There was no answer from Ned.

—Ned, where are you? She heard a newspaper rustling.

There was still no answer. She walked into the sitting room. Ned was reading the paper. He didn't look up.

—Hi, how's everything? Deli asked brightly.

—Lousy. Ned scowled.

—Why?

—I'm tired and fed up.

Deli's mood started a slow plunge. —Is Rubin upstairs?

—I don't know. Ned went back to reading the paper.

—I got the tickets for the movie, she said, still hovering.

—I don't want to go.

—Ned, she said tentatively, —you wanted to go this afternoon.

—Well, guess what? I don't feel like it now.

Depressed, she turned to leave the room. —I'm going up to see Rubin then.

—No, Ned said, —come in here.

—What is it? She hesitated, still at the door.

—Why haven't you had the kitchen cupboards mended yet?

—They're coming next week.

Finally Ned looked up. —Next week, oh really. Next week. He sounded triumphant. He shut the paper and slapped it down on the sofa.

—Yes, I spoke to them yesterday, Deli said. She made a move for the door again.

—Just what the hell's wrong with you these days? Ned demanded aggressively.

—Nothing, she said. But inside her head she sighed. Pick up the same old tape she thought, put it into the same machine, rewind, and start the same old argument all over again.

—You're so distracted. You can't even get one simple thing organized.

—I said they were coming.

—And you've been like this for some time. Ned ignored her, warming to his theme.

Deli knew she should stop at this point, while the going was good, because Ned wanted to have a row, to let off steam, he wanted her as his personal punchball. But to stop it, she would have to abandon logic, fair play, and ultimately pride. So she paused, her hand on the door-knob. Her stomach shrivelled.

—What do you mean – for some time? She repeated his words trying to keep her voice even. But in spite of her resolve she found herself casting her mind back, just in case she could think of an example.

—You're not worrying about your family, or the kitchen cupboard that's for sure. What the fuck are you thinking all the time? Your fucking work I suppose.

Ned's voice was rising now, anger was pulling his mouth down in a hard set curve. Deli thought how ugly he looked.

—Sometimes, I just switch off in the evenings, she said. —When I'm tired, that's all.

—Well, if you're tired, that's your own fucking fault, not mine.

They were back in the danger zone. She knew where they were; this was a war-torn country they'd visited often. She knew she should evacuate while the going was still good.

—Ned, let's not argue, we're supposed to be going out. I've got the tickets . . .

—I don't want to go to a movie, he interrupted. He got up and paced moodily. —I told you. I'm depressed.

—We don't have to go to the movie, let's just go out for supper? Come on, Ned. *Ned, it's me, look, it's me, Deli*, she thought desperately. She moved to give him a hug. —What would cheer you up?

He thrust her away. She let her hands drop, stung.

—Nothing you could do could cheer me up, he said bitterly. —I just want you to admit that there's something wrong with you.

—This conversation is what's beginning to be wrong with me. The pattern of her own anger started.

Ned picked up on the change immediately. He gripped her wrist. —You're so bloody stubborn, it's never your fault is it? You think you're just perfect. Miss Bloody Perfect of the Year Award, he mimicked. —You can do no wrong. He put his face close to hers. —You just say the opposite to make me angry.

—It's so arrogant to think that every word I say is designed to affect you, Ned. Why do I have to agree with you? Deli was beginning to shout now, losing control of her anger. *Fuck him, why does he have to do this all the time?*

—Because you owe me some respect! he shouted.

—Why should I respect you when you behave like this! she screamed back.

—You should see someone, Deli, he hissed. —You've got a real problem.

—What is it exactly that's bothering you? Be specific, she demanded. —Tell me, then I can try to make it better, you can't just generalize and shout all the time, it's hopeless.

—It's hopeless anyway, I can't fucking work like this. *You've* fucked up my work. You and Rubin.

—Don't put your finger up my nose, Ned, and *Don't shout at me!*

But he was. He was yelling again with his face only inches from hers. There were droplets of white saliva collecting at the corner of his mouth. Deli badly wanted to slap him.

—If this goes on, you'll drive me away. I'll leave you! yelled Ned.

—Go, I couldn't care less! Deli screeched. Even in her rage she was aware she just looked a clichéd fishwife with her hands on her hips.

—You're sick, you know. Ned's face blazed triumphantly. —Look at you, out of control, Christ, get help, Deli, he said with disgust.

—Get your finger away from my face! she screamed.

—And if I go, I can take Rubin with me, you know.

—Shut up, Ned, fuck off, don't you dare threaten . . .

—You're an unfit fucking wife, and an unfit fucking mother. His finger was shaking, so close to her skin, she wanted to grab it, crack it, break his bones. Cripple his writing hand.

There was a noise from the hall.

—Ma-ma. They both turned. Rubin was by the door, face beetroot from the bath.

—Ma-ma, he repeated authoritatively.

—Out! bellowed Ned, pointing his arm.

—Don't say anything else, Deli warned him in a whisper, although she'd been about to say the same.

—Not another word, don't you dare threaten me with my child. And don't you dare shout at Rubin either, she finished, and her eyes were like slits. She stalked to the door, scooped up Rubin, and ran upstairs, where they squatted together in his bedroom: door closed, her crying, and Rubin happily mutilating his Duplo men.

At night she had lain awake after the rows, trying too hard to sleep, dreading the moment when she heard the stinking sparrows start chirping away, the point of no return, the insomnia hour, watching Ned, his back turned to her, drifting off so easily, and hating him for it.

—It's just insomnia, said the GP whose couch she was chewing. —Here, try to relax a bit, and have another thousand Diazepam.

She wondered whether she should have known. From the first moment she had felt the heat of Ned's temper, watched it turn on her, saw the infinitesimal depth of his black hole she should have guessed that he was going to use her to stop it up. Oh, at first she had believed she could handle it, and indeed she had, but after a while she had begun to realize that instead of her stopping it up for him and making him feel better, he was just digging a black hole big enough for the both of them to get lost in, and the truth was that she had started running scared . . .

She began to see her and Ned's relationship as a glass bottle full of sand; one minute particle for every fight and she knew that the day the glass bottle filled up to the top would be the day that their marriage would be over. Still, there had always been room for one little grain more, and another and another.

It had been Christmas before she finally realized the bottle had shattered. She'd been sitting in 192 staring out the window. The wire lines of pixie lights strung across Kensington Park Road blinked their seasonal goodwill at tipsy drivers negotiating their way home through the double-parked cars. It was late. The restaurant was practically empty. Earlier someone had breathed on the icy window by their table and sketched out a fat heart with a quick finger. The outline of the heart had begun to melt and bleed in tiny lines of condensation. Deli put the palm of her hand against it.

—Vandal, M said. —Heartbreaker.

Deli frowned at him. —You're a wag all right, aren't you.

—Deli, said M impatiently. —How about we stop discussing every other subject, except for you.

—Mmm.

—It's just talking, you know. That thing where your lips move and your mouth opens? It's not so hard, some people even manage it every day.

Deli ran her hands over her face and rubbed her eyes. It's just that it's every day, M, she said wearily, —every bloody night. My marriage is a furious monologue interrupted by angry bouts of silence. She pushed a bit of bread around her plate. —I feel like I'm living in a bed of nettles and whichever way I move I get stung.

—He's obviously not very happy.

—Of course he's not, she said miserably. —I don't know what would make him happy, I just know it's not me.

—Can't you talk to him?

—We talk, we argue, but it's like we're digging a tunnel from two different ends that has no hope of meeting in the middle.

—Is his work still going badly?

—He left his old publishers after they cancelled his contract, remember? Of course they want him back now, but he's too proud. He's nervous he can't perform to deadline again. He says he can't concentrate, all the extra responsibility, Rubin and stuff, and he lays that whole guilt trip on me . . . he says having a family has wrecked his work . . .

—Well, he's jealous, said M simply.

—Maybe, I don't know. I'm sorry, M. She lit a cigarette. —I didn't mean to dump this on you.

—Oh, for God's sake, he said, exasperated with her.

—I feel like one of those stupid couples who sit around and bicker about which sit-com to watch, she protested. —It's so fucking mediocre.

The waiter fussed around them trying to clear the table.

—Do you still love him? M demanded.

—And then there's Rubin, Deli said, ignoring the question. —I don't want him to grow up believing that to continually wage war on another human being is an okay state of affairs. She paused. —You know a while back on the radio, they replayed an old interview with someone like Joyce Grenfell. Anyway she said there were only two different types of men, and the test was this: If you were liquidizing carrot soup in your brand new kitchen which he has just decorated, and the lid of the blender flies off and sprays orange gunk all over the ceiling, one type would laugh till his sides split open, but the other would be furious, not speak to you for a year, and wasn't she lucky that she had the first type of man, the right kind, blah, blah. And I remember thinking, fuck, fuck, fuck, but Ned is the other kind, the *wrong* kind . . .

—You didn't answer the question, M said.

Deli ground her cigarette out in the remains of her mashed potato, wondering as she did, why it felt so satisfying. —No, she said softly, —I don't love him any more.

Opera, the sign said. This was finally the stop. She could get out, or she could say to hell with it right now. She hesitated. The doors were temporarily stuck closed. In front of her the tramp's head was bowed, his hand rummaging round and round in his bag. The vinegar pungency of his smell was so strong it had virtually cleared her sinuses. He seemed to find what he was looking for, and pulled out a newspaper which he balanced on one knee. *Turning the pages rapidly he tsked wetly through his teeth before ringing several items with a ball Pentel which had mysteriously materialized in his hand. Deli peered closer, transfixed as she realized he was marking the financial section of* Le Monde. *She gaped then chuckled to herself.*

A minute later, back in the night drizzle, and despite a vague recollection of the street name, she had to admit she was completely lost. Standing in the middle of the roundabout, the rain blurred the headlights of the cars whizzing round into a continuous hula hoop of light. She took stock and ran down a side street, thundering past hundreds of Chinese and Vietnamese restaurants. The bottom of her skirt slapped wetly against her ankles.

A taxi, its light turned off, stood stationary by the side of the road. Inside through the window its bewildered driver stared at a map of the city, and behind, in the back seat, his furious passenger was hitting him with a rolled up newspaper.

The rain was torrential now. In desperation, Deli yanked open the door and jumped into the cab, throwing herself on the mercy of its occupants. The angry passenger turned out to be a charming American industrialist, on his way to the theatre, and as hopelessly late and lost as she was. The driver was just plain hopeless. They snatched the map back from him and pored over it, searching for their respective destinations, triumphantly discovering they were reasonably close to one another. The industrialist proved deeply chivalrous and dropped her outside the restaurant. He gave her his card, wished her luck and, waving away the hundred franc note she'd proffered, kissed her on the cheek.

Finally, Deli stood outside the door of Le Moule Debonair. Through the diamond-patterned glass she could see the heavy velvet drag of the curtains framing the entrance to tables piled high with plates of fruit de mer. She had made it. Only twenty minutes late. Despite her histrionics over the last hour, it was not necessarily a tragedy. Why then did she have such a sense of foreboding about the future?

Ned had once said during a particularly vitriolic row that she had wrecked their future because of her inability to commit her heart to anything for more than a six-month period, and the accusation had remained, a tiny malignant lump lodged under her skin, a sore and itchy post-divorce memento that rose to the surface occasionally to remind her that, although she'd convinced herself it had been Ned's fault, maybe it had indeed been her in the first place who had forced his hand. Now as she hesitated outside the restaurant, the thought that she might have got everything the wrong way around terrified her.

fashion tips n° 7

Accounting

So the 90s have come round and Times-are-a-Changing. Suddenly here you are into a decade dominated by the likes of the new-found Buddhists with their karma chanting; of fashion intellectuals with their minimalist whitey white houses. Suddenly you're surrounded by the anti-meat squaddies, assaulted daily by the patronizing ecstasy of health freaks. Nobody wants designer clothes any more, and so for the industry that means the we-can-sell-anything-as-long-as-it's-expensive ethos of the 80s begins to look just a tad optimistic.

– *Yich*, gasps Dovanna, as the plastic cover of the new season's produce is removed. – What a truly uncommercial and hideous shade of brown that is. It never looked that murky when we first saw it. Why, I swear it's almost slime coloured! Send them back, immediately.

   – Hey, Dovanna! cries Hymen. – Surely we didn't buy

skirts in that length, I mean just look at them, they're so *short*. Which kind of crazy customer is going to walk around with half her snatch showing? I'm afraid we can't accept them, *sorry*. So very very sorry.

And of course there is a reason for all this lack of confidence. It's called the Recession. It's been around a while and, you'd better believe it, it's here to stay.

All of a sudden you, the designer, realize you're in trouble. The bigger you get, the more sinister your cash flow begins to look. You've stood in the path of the juggernaut of loan, and now you are crippled with interest. The recession has sneaked up on you like a tidal wave, dragging the wads of dollars, the rustling lire, and the clanking yen from out of your pockets with the strength of its undertow, and in doing so has swept away your hard-won security.

Chapter Twenty-Seven

Kissing Crocodiles

Normally Deli loved cities under siege from the weather. She loved the way it made everyone so friendly, like in a heatwave: when the city was hot, when steam rose through the sewers and the pavements were as scorched as dry toast.

City folk leaning back in their convertibles would start dreaming of their August holiday. Their fantasy would be the Bacardi ad, and they would star in it. In the snow it was just the same. Nobody pumped their horns, nobody got aggressive, nobody took out a .22 Luger semi-automatic to shoot the pinhead who'd skidded into the buslane. No, the whole world was bound by the happy-go-lucky spirit of Extreme Conditions, the Cold War Effort, Weather Patriotism.

But not tonight, she thought, blowing her nose furiously. Tonight it was a billion degrees below zero. M had gone and she and Seb were alone in the office. There was a raging blizzard outside and she had a chest infection that would probably kill her before morning. It was pitch middle-of-winter dark and she wanted to go home to bed and to Rubin. But she couldn't.

She couldn't because she was getting ready to go to the Prime Minister's swanky party, but she was looking out the window at the Dr Zhivago landscape and wondering if they were ever going to make it alive. She had also begun wondering if maybe she'd been bad in her last life: maybe she had been so wicked that she'd been reborn as a tiny plastic figure trapped inside one of those glass bubble paperweight things you buy at the airport for your kid . . . the ones you shake upside down and the snow flies all around them.

It had been a year exactly since she had broken up with Ned. A year since she had been a single working parent and it didn't seem to her like she was making a very good job of it.

She didn't want to think about the conversation she'd just had again with M. Instead she pushed it to the special section at the back of her mind which she kept for unfilled tax returns, having her coil checked and getting the waste disposal fixed. She stared disconsolately out the window, watching the snow fall thickly past the sole of her shoe on the glass before it dissolved onto the iced surface of the canal below.

Shit, Deli muttered. Frustrated, she swung around and kicked the edge of the large cardboard box of clothes returned from one of their European stockists. The crumpled items lay jumbled one on top of the other. *Shit*, she said again louder to the empty room. Nothing was going right. Nothing was even selling at retail at the moment, boxes of clothes kept appearing accompanied by varying and ever weaker excuses. The recession had begun to hit hard.

The headlights of a car swung suddenly across the inky darkness of the ceiling. Deli peered back out the window, another car was turning warily out of the gates of the Blacknag.

—Deli! Seb was shouting from downstairs. —We should go, come on!

Hastily she got up and checked her outfit in the long mirror, hoiking up her tights to hide a ladder at the ankles. She couldn't believe there hadn't even been time to buy a new pair of tights in the last few weeks. It was truly pathetic. She thought again about what M had said, and she knew in her heart he was right.

M wanted to sell the business.

He reckoned they'd come as far as they could alone. It was tough to be independent, it was forever two steps forward and three steps back and now, with a shitty economic climate, they'd pretty much come to a standstill. And yes, Deli thought, of course it would be nice to get their hands on some money; sure it would be good to work a little less than eight days a week, spend some proper time with Rubin. All that quality of life stuff was pretty attractive but she still felt selling out was like giving your first-born child up for adoption because you couldn't take care of it yourself. Not to mention having to find decent, well meaning, God fearing and *rich* foster parents to look after it.

—Deli! Seb shouted again.

Deli took one last look in the mirror and sighed. She grabbed her bottle of antibiotics off the desk, turned off the computer and made her way to the front door.

—IT'S FREEZING, SEB, Deli had moaned. —Why don't you get the fucking heating mended?

The snow was still falling sideways across the windscreen of Seb's car in continuous lines, every so often the wind whipped the flakes up and whirled them into an angry frenzy in front of the headlights.

—I haven't had time, he said shortly.

Deli glanced at his profile, his face was pushed up over the steering wheel, eyes squinting at the road ahead through the windscreen wipers. His skin looked startling blue-white, alabaster.

Shocked, she looked at her hands, they were orangy, picking up the glow from the street lamps outside. She looked back at Seb.

His face was so familiar to her she scarcely noticed it any more. She studied him surreptitiously for a minute. Actually he looked more than tired, he looked ill.

—Hey, Seb, when are you going to take your holiday? You haven't been off for ages.

He shook his head. —Kevin's back in hospital.

—Oh. Deli was quiet. Kevin had been riding the roller coaster of full blown Aids for two years now. — Seb, you can't be expected to cope with it every time, what about his family? Why does it always have to be you?

Seb snorted. —Kevin's not exactly an easy patient, he won't see half his friends, and when they do turn up he's poisonous to them. He's so rude to the doctors, some of them won't even deal with him any more. Seb lit a cigarette, the tip gleamed, devil's-eye red in the dark. —It's me they ring when they can't get him to take his medicine, or when he's trying to discharge himself at four o'clock in the morning. He stopped short, his hands tight on the wheel.

Deli said nothing. Kevin had never been a big friend of hers, they had tiptoed round each other for years. She felt terrible now that she hadn't made more effort. —Do they think his brain's been affected?

—Who knows, said Seb, —but you can't expect someone who's dying to be completely stoic all the time. He's scared and frustrated, he needs someone to take it out on and I guess that someone is me . . .

—I worry about you. She hesitated. —Seb, when did you last take a test?

—Now, how did I know you were going to ask me that? he said with an empty smile. —Six months ago, and it was fine. And you?

—Ooh, tests, needles, unsexy idea.

Seb pulled sharply on the wheel as the car skidded on black ice. —I'll tell you something, Deli, he said quietly, —watching someone lying on a bed, their blood turning black, that's pretty fucking unsexy too. His face was tight and angry.

—I'm sorry, Seb, it was a stupid thing to say. She put her hand on his arm but he shrugged it off. Deli cursed herself silently. —Are you going to see Kevin tonight? You should have gone straight from the office. I could have got a cab.

—It's fine, it's on the way. Seb pressed in the car lighter again. Chain-smoking.

Deli rummaged in the compartment in front of her for Seb's emergency bottle. She unscrewed the lid and took a slug of vodka, feeling the white hot liquid zig-zag through her innards like a pinball in a slot machine. —Here. She passed the bottle over to Seb. Above the headlights of the crawling cars, a giant billboard of Origami was lit up. Her amazing tits with their black cherry nipples compressed into a designer one-piece, her neon cleavage surveying the moaning heave of traffic below. Her mouth, bright and swollen, was cradling a cigarette like she was about to suck it off. The caption at the top of the poster read:

Government Health Warning:
Smoking can seriously damage your health.

The quote at the bottom from Origami read:

You'd better believe it, baby, these are Killer.

—But, Jesus, shuddered Seb, his eyes widening. —Sometimes I thank God I'm gay. He handed her back the bottle.

Deli laughed, relieved that his black mood had passed.

Seb applied the brakes gingerly and the car swerved to a halt. —Will you be all right? It might be dangerous in there. He turned and grinned at her.

She gave him a quick hug and crunched out onto the snow.

—I'm armed with bullshit, she said. —Send Kevin my love.

Shivering, she watched him as he reversed, the snow clogging up the wipers of the car. —Good luck! he called, driving off. —And rape a few MPs for me.

DOWNING STREET. EVERYBODY'S number one choice for a rave.

Despite the weather most of the usual A-listers had already arrived, their hands hovering undecided over trays of roe eggs and aubergine dabs. Or should they have the flaked pike and chilli mayonnaise in filo parcels? So hard, so hard, they mused, the filo might crumble on their dress, awful, but then maybe a roe egg might wedge itself somewhere between their front teeth, too far in to be

BELLA POLLEN

dislodged with their tongue. God, no, not worth the risk. They resisted, trying instead to manoeuvre themselves in front of the *Nine o'clock News* cameras, smiling politely at the maids who tiptoed off in their black and white frilly uniforms.

The Prime Minister looked bored, everybody else looked smug to be invited. A speech was being made. Deli swallowed an hors-d'oeuvre off a passing silver tray, a small pastry basket filled with some tepid green substance that looked worryingly like phlegm. Deeply regretting it, she prowled around looking for someone to schmooze so she could go home without feeling guilty.

—Don't you dare leave till you've worked the room, M had instructed as his parting shot. She gulped down her drink nervously then skulked around the back of an impressive looking marble bust feeling bitter and twisted at the thought of him lying in bed with Tish, watching *North by Northwest* and eating Curry in a Hurry.

Thank God . . . there was a waiter within spitting distance. She lunged for another drink and smiled cheesily at him as she spilt half of it down his waistcoat. She drained the rest and put the glass back onto the silver tray.

—Sorry, she gurgled. And immediately took another one.

She downed it quickly and looked around the room. She wasn't remotely in the mood to do any schmoozing at all. Out of the corner of her eye she glimpsed Dovanna, her tiny but muscly mouth poised kiss-shaped near the cheek of the Chairman of the Fashion Council. Vernon was in the distance standing endearingly pigeon-toed as he regaled the *Guardian* with a description of his forthcoming collection. Deli knew she should be doing the same.

People milled around her yapping and pushing, she talked and talked, smiled and smiled until she had face-ache.

Suddenly, she was aware of a presence by her elbow.

She looked around. What seemed like a twelve-year-old choirboy was smiling engagingly at her.

—So pleased, he said, taking her hand. —So very, very pleased. Grant Teflon. I've been wanting to meet you for some time now.

—Oh, she said, momentarily confused by the brightness of his eyes. —Have you? Her voice sounded slurred, she realized she was drunk.

The choirboy smiled again, parading a line of warm milky teeth above a salmon-coloured lip. —Let's do lunch some time. Allow me to give you my card. Effortlessly he whipped it from out of his breast pocket and pressed it into her hand in one seamless movement. —I'll have my secretary call your secretary.

—Maybe they can have lunch together first, beamed Deli. She swallowed a burp, realizing her antibiotics had crashed with the vodka and written off the few social skills she still possessed.

—Sharp, said the man, —very sharp. I like that. He withdrew his teeth, smiled again with closed lips, then, as suddenly as he had appeared, floated off leaving faint whiffs of Paco Rabanne hanging heavy with promise in the air.

BACK HOME AND thoroughly plastered, she kicked her mules high into the air, watching them land with a thud on the other side of the room. The first stirrings of a headache began to hip hop around her skull. She turned the volume down on the CD player then unfastened her bra and allowed it to drop onto the floor. She motowned her way out of her dress, slinging it haphazardly onto the trunk at the foot of her bed and at that moment spotted the small white card as it spiralled like a giant snowflake out of the pocket and came to rest on the bedspread.

> Grant Teflon
> Chairman
> Ersatz Corporation

Grant Teflon. Why did bells ring so violently in her head? She reached for the telephone.

—Grant Teflon, Deli demanded.

—What? said M sleepily.

—Who is he?

—Deli?

—Grant Teflon, who is he? It's really annoying me.

There was a short silence then M groaned. —Jesus, Deli, it's one in the morning!

—Yeah, well some of us are forced to work late hours.

—Don't get snippy with me, bitch.

—Come on. She hiccuped impatiently.

—Oh, pardon me while I Roladex through my awesome memory bank, said M sarcastically. —Ersatz Corporation. He's the new chief executive or something, the one who's always on the cover of the Sunday supplements. I think he invented some sex aid. I'll tell you in the morning. He yawned. —Now, fuck off.

Of course! Now she remembered: the man was a fledgling legend, the newly appointed chairman of the vast but downmarket Ersatz Corporation. No one knew where he had come from, but suddenly there he was, a force to be reckoned with in the city. Rumours abounded. Some alleged that he'd been a humble merchant banker with a keen nose for a deal and an ability for assimilating good contacts. Other more obviously spurious reports claimed he'd managed the financial affairs of an evangelical bible thumper who had tried to scam billions on cable TV. Basically no one knew for sure.

The Ersatz Corporation housed forty different companies under its roof. Apart from being the largest producer of rubber goods for household use, including everything from non-stick kitchenware to candle-making kits, it had recently benefited from a highly lucrative spin-off, the DIY condom, a newly developed kit for making your own at home which used a liquid rubber substance patented at the beginning of the year by Ersatz. It was this brainwave that had been Grant's particular baby, and had resulted in many a snide paragraph by a cynical press speculating on his real reason for necessitating the invention, but all this had turned to grudging praise as the kits sold in their millions and put several pence on the share price. Recently it was rumoured that Grant intended to take the company into the lucrative area of upmarket branded goods.

—Hey ho, Deli murmured. Vaguely she'd wondered whether they would indeed hear from him. Switching out the light she sank into the empty bed. —Heigh ho for a corporate husband.

Chapter Twenty-Eight

Lunch with Grant Teflon. One p.m. said her diary. *Don't be late*, she had scrawled in brackets. Late leaving the office again. Damn. Now she'd arrive panting, sweat and indignation oozing from every pore, telling some appalling obstacle story with such conviction that her eyes would water. It was the Gratuitous Lying Syndrome, and, oh Lord, it had her in its grip. Finally Deli got herself into the car, and revved off. She looked at herself in the mirror. Ye Gods she looked a mess. But on three hours of sleep it was hardly surprising.

Depressed, she wondered whether she used to be pretty ever. Surely yes? Somewhere deep in the recesses of her memory she knew this had been so, maybe before Rubin, but today the black bags under her eyes were so big she could have prised them off her face and wholesaled them as bin-liners.

She reached over and opened the pocket in front of the passenger seat. Her car was her second home, make-up, spare knickers, mobile phone, hairbrush, Opal Fruits, bottles of water, everything a girl might need. Squalid but cosy.

On the Shepherd's Bush roundabout she tried to do some facial damage control. Balancing her make-up bag expertly between her thighs, she eased the zipper open with one hand, indicating left with the other. A car hooted as it drove past. Deli blew the infuriated driver a kiss. She identified the mascara brush and started to swipe it carefully on the lashes of one eye. *Bleep bleep*. Her mobile was ringing . . . aargh.

She fumbled the mascara, it fell onto the floor and wedged itself underneath the accelerator. The mobile bleeped again. She fished the telephone out from underneath the plastic carrier-bag full of tapeless boxes. It was Tish.

—You forgot to take the address, slag. Got a pen?

She found a lipstick. Holding the steering wheel against one knee, she balanced the mobile between her ear and right shoulder, and slowly eased the lid off.

She knew for a fact that one day she would die on the Shepherd's Bush roundabout. She'd be applying make-up and eating an egg sandwich when she'd finally lose control of her car and plough into a forty-foot cement mixer. She'd probably survive the impact but fate would have it that a large piece of mashed egg would lodge itself in her oesophagus and she'd choke to death.

★

THE RESTAURANT TURNED out to be a swanky West End Italian job and amazingly enough, Grant Teflon wasn't there yet. Deli breathed a sigh of relief as she was piloted to a table for two by the window.

She ordered some water, pulled a notebook out of her bag and started making lists, trying to look business-like and efficient, until from the back of her mind she suddenly remembered reading that compulsive list-making was the prelude to some unspeakable psychological disorder. She put down the pen and looked furtively around her.

She couldn't remember what Grant Teflon looked like. The PM's party had been two weeks ago and she'd been far too pissed to take him in. She could be eating with anyone from Groucho Marx to Darryl Strawberry, except of course she was reasonably sure he wasn't black and probably not so good at baseball, now she was on the subject.

Suddenly . . . an apparition, a hand shook hers, she looked up. A thinnish man smiled candidly down at her.

—Hello, I'm sorry, so very, very sorry to keep you waiting. Grant Teflon was zizzing with goodwill.

Deli felt an immediate warm glow ooze through her veins.

—It's so refreshing to see you again, Grant added. —and here, before we begin, this is for you. He produced from the folds of his raincoat a white envelope which he gave to Deli.

—Ooh, Deli murmured, —how kind. Two tickets for

Le Nozze di Figaro fell out of the envelope and into her hand.

—I thought you and your brother might enjoy them, he said smoothly.

An Italian with an enormous belly appeared, a stub of a pencil stuck behind his ear.

—Ah, Signor Merluzzo. *Buon giorno!* Grant bestowed on the oversized proprietor a generous smile.

Grant ordered more water for them both in perfectly accented Italian and asked about the dish of the day. Merluzzo, cockney born and bred, and clearly a stranger to his native tongue, shuffled off and returned erroneously with a couple of beers and two plastic-coated menus.

—Usually, I don't like to eat lunch, said Grant, generously ignoring the mix-up. —It's such a very post-modernist meal . . . But what will you have? he asked.

Deli studied him speculatively as he translated the entire menu for her. In the strong light from the window, he really didn't look so young after all. More like early fifties. A pale intelligent face, blackish hair so fine it looked like a draughtsman had painstakingly inscribed it on Grant's skull with a very sharp pencil. The shoulder pads of his beige suit hung down forlornly over his narrow shoulders.

—I'm sorry, what did you say? Deli realized she hadn't taken in a single word. She really must try not to make a fool of herself as usual. Grant was looking at her questioningly.

—You look like you're not quite on course, he observed. —What's diverting your mind?

—I'm having a mayonnaise day, Deli said limply.

—What's that?

—It's when getting a message from your brain to your mouth is like hitting a ping-pong ball through mayonnaise.

—Ah, he said, looking thoroughly mystified. —Enlightening. Now, he began forcefully as the waiter ambled over with their order, —I've been wanting to touch base with you for some time. Congratulations on your Award by the way. I've been impressed by how much publicity it has generated. Grant's eyes seemed to glaze over momentarily.

Deli tapped her fingernails nervously against the glass of water. —Oh, huh, thank you.

—My people have read the business plan you sent me and we feel very comfortable with it. I have the bones for a lot of ideas, but tell me where you're going? Tell me about your company, above all tell me about *you*.

Deli hated it when people wanted to know about the company as she was always forced to make a snap decision how much to exaggerate by. She told him briefly about Madison Ltd. Grant talked at length about Ersatz.

—We've long felt the need to radically change our product base, he explained. —We've flirted with the Retail Corridor with more than a little success, but we need to focus on erasing the downmarket image we have been labelled with for so long. He paused again. —You have a profile that is very attractive for us. We could exploit you.

—Exploit, Deli repeated perkily. —That word has an interesting fiscal ring to it.

—Well, in that case . . . Grant paused and eyeballed her something rotten, —I see this as a window of opportunity for the both of us.

It was three-thirty already. Deli started panicking about the time. She had a deadline for a project due in at five.

—So let me make myself plain, Grant was saying carefully. —We, Ersatz, are looking for a long-term investment. Ten years minimum. You, of course, will be suspicious of a partnership with a large business, nervous of being strangled in red tape, buried under corporate nonsense, and you have every reason to be, but the bottom line is not everything. We are not a Courtaulds, a Kaufmans, or Burton Group. We as a company do not have a bibs and brace approach to real talent. You on the other hand are cash starved, you lack a proper financial structure to grow with. You have the name Deli Madison, but we have the money. Think about this, talk to your brother, toss it round with your people, see if you have any unclaimed space in your diary so we can touch base before too long. We have the bones of something here, now let's try to put a little flesh on them.

Greedily, Deli's head began to digest the possibilities.

★

TEN DAYS LATER the smell of fresh lilies and fresias had permeated every corner of the office. Deli scrumpled up the Pullbrook and Gould paper and popped it into the bin. She picked the little white card off the floor and turned it over.

I so enjoyed meeting with you both again. Thank you for your time.
Grant

Deli lobbed it into her in-tray, resolving to write a thank-you note. It was the third bouquet that week. —Well? she asked, glancing over at M.

M sat at his desk, the letter of intent in his hands. —I've checked him out, he said. —He doesn't smoke, he doesn't drink, he's never had sex with any household pets, or at least any that have filed a complaint.

—It's like too good to be true, said Seb. —He's half-way between God and Man.

—Well, if he's willing to invest in us, he must be a damn saint, Deli said drily.

—I'M SO HAPPY, so very very deeply fundamentally happy at your decision, Grant said, his eyes luminous as an oilslick. —We must endeavour to keep things simple, let's let the lawyers handle this shall we?

BUT EIGHT MONTHS and a thousand legal meetings later found M and Deli climbing down the stairs from their lawyers' office in Oxford Street feeling drained and empty, a copy of the signed contract heavy in Deli's hand. It was dusk and they walked through Hyde Park arm in arm.

—Come on, Deli, lighten up, M said. —At least we got what we wanted.

—Maybe. But this . . .? She waved the wad of bound legal documents in his face.

—We always knew it would be hard to let go . . . Come on. He looked at her taut face. —At least we'll be hugely wealthy. You can have a pension now.

—Oh, sure, right, ha ha, that's great, she said.

—You can spend some proper time with Rubin.

—Oh, yeah, she said bitterly. —Quality Time, the child's toy of the eighties, every working mother's aspirational purchase.

—Whoah, sis, said M sharply. —What's happened to your sense of humour?

—I don't know, M, said Deli sadly. —I really don't know, but I reckon we may have just sold it.

LATER THAT NIGHT she lay in bed. She tossed, she turned, she wriggled. She watched the television for a bit, read a book, went to the loo eight times, kissed Rubin's sweaty forehead, crouched under the covers, lay on her stomach, executed three complicated yoga positions then finally lay on her back and stared at the ceiling, weeping.

She couldn't sleep. Again.

She hated her life. She hated herself, she hated

everybody else, everybody who was sleeping, she hated the night, with its crawling hours and threatening quiet. She checked the time, only two a.m. She closed her eyes. Her hand crept from the covers towards the bottle on the bedside table. Hastily she pulled it back.

It was there again, opening the bottle, beyond her control, shaking out the contents. The pill lay on top of the table, powerful, confident. It held the key to the night in its four quarters. Her hand broke off one of them. It looked very small, that quarter of one pill. She popped it into her mouth doubtfully, she could hardly feel it as it slipped down her throat. The remainder of the pill waited for her patiently on the bedside table.

It knew the score. She crumbled the second quarter . . . then the third.

DELI WOKE UP, still wired from the Valium, her thoughts loose and muddled with uncertainties for the future; only her head ached with appalling conviction. She'd stumbled downstairs to find a hand-written note plopped through the letterbox of the front door and a large bunch of red roses leaning outside against the steps.

So pleased, so very very terribly pleased that we have finally signed the contract.

Don't worry . . . your company will be safe in my hands.

Grant xxx

part two

Chapter Twenty-Nine Jellied Deals

NOTICE TO ALL ERSATZ EMPLOYEES
Date: 12 April 1991
Re: Toilet Visitation Guidelines (TVG)

It has come to our attention that the majority of our employees are spending too much time using the restroom facilities. Effective 01/5/92 each member of staff will be furnished with a Toilet Break Credit numbered at 18 for each week. Once an employee's quota is used up, the chain on the toilet will automatically cease to flush. Swipe cards and pin numbers are to be issued to employees within the next few days. If you have any special medical problems please notify the management.

Thank you for your co-operation.
Rachel Flat

Deli had been standing in the new office in Paris studying the latest piece of rule-mania pinned to the notice-board. Nestling on its right and left respectively were the CBRS (Coffee Break Rota System) and the even more controversial FACA (Fresh Air Credit Allowance).

In the last few months the office had become a motorway for memos. A total commonsense bypass. Giving in to a sudden wave of irritation she'd snorted and ripped all three off the green baize. The pin tacks dropped to the floor with a clatter.

So it had probably been naive, she'd admitted, as she scrumpled them in her hand and sat down at the desk, but after the contract had been signed, they'd been unprepared for any immediate changes.

—This is an inter-company marriage, Grant had articulated. —Our objective is to fertilize our obvious synergies and give birth to an embryonic strategy that with time and careful nurturing will grow to its full potential. We have a team of highly competent management people who will facilitate this relationship for you.

And they had been assigned Rachel Flat.

She was Grant's protégée. Cautiously M asked Grant for the low-down on her, watching him closely as he scanned through his backlist of facial expressions, eventually producing a half-smile that was at the same time both encouraging and respectful.

—I feel so warm, so very very warm about her capabilities, Grant had said.

Poor Rachel: suckled from birth on the milk of corporate speak, its teachings so firmly indoctrinated into her system that it was impossible to extract from her any opinion that hadn't been processed through her inner computer for controversy then ruthlessly purged before being aired. Oh, she was perfectly well meaning in her starched little suits and office politics hairstyle, but a sense of humour was not amongst her star qualities.

As soon as Rachel had opened the first board meeting, Deli and M realized that inter-company marriage or not, there was to be no honeymoon period.

—Ersatz, Rachel intoned, reading from her clipboard, —despite showing record highs on the stock markets for the last financial year is currently beset by inertia. We are determined like other companies to restructure our balance sheets and replace debt with equity, thus we have decided to radically alter our people base at the lowest level and downsize.

—Huh? whispered M to Deli. —Surely this woman needs a blood transfusion?

—We've decided to lay off ninety per cent of your staff, Rachel announced.

Grant was in his office having his photograph taken for *Business Weekly*. He leant back on his chair as Make-Up skilfully applied some cover to the reddening edges of his nose and surveyed the general air of controlled violence before him.

—You must understand, he said candidly, —that all we are doing is applying our classic Big Business formula for dealing with a small subsidiary. It's the back-end of the business that matters, let's concentrate on a bibs and brace approach to that first, shall we?

NEXT RACHEL HAD opened the summer board meeting.

—Unfortunately it transpires that we have no facilities in the construction sector for the manufacturing of your product in this country, she burbled, —therefore we have decided to transfer all current apparel assembly overseas.

Grant was hanging up on a telephone interview with the *Economist* as Deli and M stalked into his office.

Grant paused for a second while he considered the ugliness of their mood. He toyed with placating, threw it out, questioned conciliatory, thought better of it, then in a sudden move, took a surprise swipe at visionary.

—I have a vision, he cried, —about which I feel most quixotic and most visionary. Allow me to share it with you. I would like to buy one fashion house in every major capital city in the civilized world. With these I would like to form an umbrella under which you will all take shelter.

—With the greatest respect, Deli said carefully, I haven't quite grasped what you're suggesting.

We intend to integrate you into a company called Douche in Paris. You will move your operation there. They will help manufacture your product and form a *modus operandi* for the enhancement of your line and image.

—But Douche are our competitors, M had said, stunned.

—It's a direct conflict of interest, Deli said tersely. —Why on earth would they agree to help us?

—Well, actually they have no choice, confided Grant, —because, you see, Ersatz, as from yesterday ... he paused for dramatic effect, —have purchased the controlling interest.

There was a minutable silence.

—Trust me, he enthused, looking at their stony faces. —It is, after all, the home of fashion. It has glamour, romance, wonderful architecture, sumptuous food. You'll see. Paris, especially for you, Deli, will be Big Time.

BUT ON THE day of the introductory meeting with Douche, Paris had not even been visible from the air, shivering under a chemical-looking cloud. Deli pushed her face closer to the window of the taxi, the rain had washed the whole city with a polluted grey colour, only the uniformity of a thousand black umbrellas broke through the drizzle.

The cab finally drew up in front of a large eighteenth-century building inside which a less than cordial secretary in pinstripes motioned them into some wire seats in the reception on the second floor, where the President's offices were apparently to be found.

Dozens of girls in starched shirts click-clacked by, squawking frenetically and juggling folders while Deli tried in vain to dredge some O level French from the void of her memory. Just before an hour was up, the phone on the receptionist's desk blipped loudly, and with an airy wave of her hand she directed them down the corridor.

Monsieur Anchois, the President, stood in his office, back towards the door. After thirty seconds or so Deli coughed lightly to attract his attention.

—Monsieur Anchois?

—One moment, please, Anchois murmured. He flicked over a couple more pages of the file in his hand then slipped it back in the shelving in front of him and turned around. He appraised them with a quick glance before sitting down behind his desk, where he began crumbling a stale *petit pain au raisin* between his fingers, picking the currants out carefully one at a time and popping them into his mouth. Deli watched him uncomfortably. He must have once been a striking-looking man, but age or drink had covered his face with rubbery flesh and a little too much of it, the excess bagging heavily under his jawline like a Venetian blind.

—Allow me to introduce Léon, head of our Paris Division, said Anchois, indicating behind them.

Deli and M turned to see a man with a thatch of white hair sitting in an armchair in the smoky back corner of the room. The man lit up a Gitanes and inhaled the pale blue smoke deeply. He nodded in their general direction raising a pair of eyebrows grown so thick, it looked as if a couple of garden slugs had crawled across his forehead and were violently copulating on the bridge of his nose.

—It appears we have been instructed to offer you our assistance. Anchois spoke again.

Deli nodded, and attempted a smile of charming gratitude.

—We just hope you won't need too much of it, Léon murmured from his cancer corner.

—No, no, of course, stammered Deli, wiping the smile off her face.

—It is also fortunate that you speak French, Anchois continued, placing another raisin precisely on the tip of his tongue where it hovered as he spoke like a wounded fly. —As we as a company have no intention of speaking English. He stood up and placed his hands squarely on the leather surface of the desk.

There was the tiniest of pauses during which Léon stubbed his cigarette out in the ashtray beside him and let out a hacking cough.

—Wee, wee, byin sewer, Deli and M had said fervently as they crept out the door.

AND PARIS. AH, what a glamorous city! Ooh, the romance! My, the architecture. Mmm, the celeriac salad in the window of Fauchon. See the little crones inside with their fox-head fur collars crumbling *langues du chat* through trembling fingers, waiting to be blown up by the communists for the third time running that year.

Actually this said a lot about the French, Deli decided, as she had thrown the mangled memos in the bin and looked out the window of her tiny office in the Douche building. Their terrorists really knew how to hit where it hurts. Blow up government institutes? Naaa, who cares? Destroy National Monuments, who gives a flying fuck? But blow up a really swanky delicatessen? Now, that gets the good citizens *really* gritty.

But of course all that happened in the other Paris.

The Paris *she* worked in was a different one. It was called the Sentier, or if you were French it was called Le Premier Poubelle de Paris. Apparently Deli's city was quite near the other real one, but *not* near enough.

She'd been there six months.

She'd snapped shut the diary on her desk, put the docket sheets into her briefcase and tidied the filing. It wasn't as if Douche was the friendliest of companies either and although she had at least been able to employ Luc, a pattern cutter, who with his bobbing adam's apple was charm itself, it seemed amazing that after six months, all she'd managed to establish with the rest of the staff was a distant nodding acquaintance. Well, to be strictly truthful, she conceded, as she bolted the office door and ran down the corridor, she nodded whilst they were distant.

She crossed the road to the taxi rank and glanced at her watch. Rubin would be having a bath now and she was still five hours from home. It scared her how quickly London life had become removed. She'd looked at Rubin yesterday as she was leaving for Heathrow and suddenly realized he'd become shockingly grown-up. He'd recently developed a gap between his two front teeth like the Wife of Bath, and his eyes now had darker streaks running across the yellow pupils like tiger pelt. At first he hadn't liked her not being there for him. He'd look at her mournfully and say – but why? weeping into her crotch as the mini cab drew up in front of the house, and as she stepped into it, guilt would slice her in two like a cheese wire. But of late he'd become unnervingly blasé about her travel arrangements.

—It's okay, Mom, he would say, —it really doesn't matter, see ya when I see ya. Then he would make himself a BLT, crack open a Budweiser with his milk teeth and go back to watching the *Thundercats*. And guilt would slice her in two all over again.

And what had she swopped her so called Quality Time for? Paris Life: a series of never-ending airport traffic jams followed by a tedious day at work until such time as she was able to make her way to the luscious surrounds of the nearest Hotel Absolutely No-star, where she could finally relax amidst the splendrous decor of the brown carpeted walls, lie on the bed with its charming nylon-bobbled counterpane feeling her knickers flying with static whilst gazing in appreciation at the choice of Van Gogh artwork reproduced in coloured plasticene which inevitably adorned the room.

At first it had been only the odd overnight stay, but

now she flew to Paris three times a week. She wondered why she was feeling quite so disorientated – until of course it hit her. She was a commuter. My God, one of those eerie glazed-looking people anchored to their steering wheels on the M25 or sitting on the scratched plastic tube seats plugged into wild pornographic fantasies, dreaming of release from the sheer banality of everyday life.

Once upon a time, she used to sneer and feel pity as she raced to work against the flow of traffic. Ha ha, to be your own boss, to pitch up when you felt like it, to slope off at four o'clock to an afternoon movie, take two-month holidays to the Galapagos and live on bat dung.

She dumped her bag on the pavement and waved frantically at a passing cab. She thought about M as she wrenched open the door. His life seemed to be drifting even further away from hers. He was engaged to Tish, moving into a bigger flat, he was plotting his future as methodically as painting by numbers, whereas there she was, thundering in a directionless way round and round a foreign city, humbled by her own pornographic fantasies, lamenting the two-month trip she never took, the movies she never saw. And for the first time that she could ever remember, she felt completely pointless.

Chapter Thirty

Darling Aaron   21 June

Throughout the spring Paris has been hit by electrical storms; sheets of lightning, bolts of lightning, forked lightning, howling thunderstorms, grey polluted rain slanted against the wind like some kind of chronic interference on the television set.

End of the World Weather, Seb calls it.

Miserable grey Parisians are everywhere, slanted at the same angle as the rain. Sour eyes, sour expressions, noses wrinkled up, mouths turned down, complexions muggy. A nation of lemonswallowers . . .

Still, I'm having such a swell time here in the Marquis de Sade's favourite hidey-hole that I've decided to get a flat. This flat-renting decision caused a bit of eye-balling from the *Board*. 'There is a recession on you know,' Rachel said, darkly, as I put the idea to her, but eventually she gave way and I was sadly forced to remove the staple gun from around her genital area.

For some time now I have been fantasizing about

my new dwelling. When I wake up on my very first morning there will be that scene from *Oliver!* You know, '*Who will buy this wonderful morning*', da di da di da da di da, with all those flowers and milkmaids skipping and frolicking underneath my window.

At night I will return from another truly creative day at the office, buying my supper *en route* from any number of mouth-watering foodie shops, waving and exchanging pleasantries with the locals with whom I will have forged an exceptional and probably life-long bond, then I'll settle down to an evening sketching inspired designs and lightly flirting with my many Parisian admirers on the telephone.

In no time at all I will discover the apartment just above me is owned by a beautiful but tortured French poet who will have a name like Jean Luc Goddard le deuxieme, or Jean Paul Sartre Juvenile, who will write highly charged single verse poems like this:

> In the sand was a bone
> buried,
> Deep down washed over
> by salt water; my father
> I remember.

This desirable will immediately become my slave and be someone with whom I will enjoy great sex.

Feel free to come and stay any time.

**How is your son? Does he still have no penis? Rubin
(4 cms) is fine, but I miss him like hell.**

xxxxxxxxx Deli

Deli's cab had been jammed between two unloading
trucks. She peered out the window. Jesus! Where was she?
She was supposed to be on her way to the fabulous flat
she'd just rented, blind, from an architect friend of M's in
London. Dimly she remembered how pleased she'd been
that it was within walking distance from work and for the
first time felt a tiny quiver of misgiving. The cab squelched
to a stop in the middle of a shoe-shop street. Deli looked
through the splattered glass in dismay. Yup, here she was.
Right Bang Slap Dead Centre in the middle of the Sentier
still. *Fuck.*

Standing outside the giant doors of a courtyard, she
rummaged in the abyss of her knapsack for the scrap of
paper with the door code. She was keen to gain entry at
that point because an out-of-it-looking degenerate, his
face pockmarked as a pizza by bad acne scars had been
noisily disgorged from the bar next door and was swaying
gently behind her.

Inside the courtyard, on the right and left were two
outdoor staircases. A and B. Sheltering under B a Kurdish
flower seller was looking optimistic at her arrival. Deli
punched on the light at the bottom, puzzling fleetingly
about the lucrativeness of his passing trade before humping

her cases up the stairs. The flat was on the fourth floor. No lift.

As she put the key in the lock, *pam*! the corridor light gave out. Pitch dark everywhere. Deli groaned and fumbled around for the light switch, found it, jabbed it, but nothing happened. It was broken. Great. Exasperated she found her way down to the entrance again, socked the giant plastic nipple hard at the bottom and ran up the stairs. Now the key wasn't turning in the lock, it was jammed, the light went off. Down she went, headbutted the switch, and ran up again.

The Kurd was watching, puzzled. On her penultimate trip up the stairs he asked whether she would like to buy some gladioli.

—Do I look like Eliza Doolittle? she howled at him.

She marvelled at herself. She was not normally this aggressive but she'd had a tough day; creeping out of the house in London in time to catch the first flight, then when she was in the car she'd heard a banging noise. She looked up, and there at the bedroom window was Rubin, having recently regressed from his couldn't care less stance, fists clenched into knuckle-dusters crashing against the glass and calling her name. She couldn't go back or she'd have missed the flight, so tears pouring down her face she just reversed the car straight into the tree, making a hole in the back and smashing the brake lights.

Sorry, your Honour, driving without due care and attention, drunk on guilt.

Finally the door gave way. She looked around. There were three rooms and, it transpired, the same number of pieces of furniture. Exhausted she fell onto the sofa . . . and straight off again, as it had no back.

Okay, she got it. The flat was very much of the Comfort is for Wimps school of interior design. She plugged in the floor lamp. *Sput, crack*! The trip switch exploded the flat into darkness, fusing all the lights in the process. She gave in and sat in the kitchen sobbing messily, perched high on the apartment's third and last piece of furniture, a stool, its seat carved in the shape of an elephant's head, its wooden trunk sticking straight up through her legs like an engorged phallus.

BUT AFTER A month of Citron Jiffing, three visits from a disturbingly handsome electrician, the installation of a tiny TV set and some of the Kurd's gladioli, the place began to look more homely. Deli closed the door behind her. She padded down the stairs of the flat and sat at the bottom to pull on her blades, skated out down the hill of her street and swerved into Rue St Denis, mindlessly switching to the pavement.

She'd had to accept that Paris life had taken over now, London life had been all but buried. Rubin played in a house built of boarding cards, and Deli was scared one day the big bad wolf of her neglect would blow it down and eat him up . . .

She felt the city pollution hum against her cheek as

she worked up speed. God she missed M, worse, she missed Rubin, and, if it hadn't been for the constant reminders of his foul temper whenever he arrived to pick up his son in London, she might almost have missed Ned.

Seb flew over once a week when he would usually stay the night and take Deli out on a hot date to the movies. Their local cinema was in the Metro, and had that pungent smell of old urine that made Deli homesick for the Coronet in Notting Hill. Often she and Seb were the only two there, although this may well have been to do with Seb's obscure taste in cinematic greats rather than the theatre's heady perfume. Personally, Deli was always game to see something like *Seven Brides for Seven Brothers*. Seb wanted to see films where millions of tiny flesh-eating locusts crawled out of people's eyeballs and feasted on the nearest innocent baby during which he would blow his continually dripping nose and invariably fall fast asleep. His boyfriend Kevin had died several months before, finally giving up his meagre but stubborn hold on life and, although it seemed to Deli that he had taken much of Seb's colossal energy with him, Seb, gamely pretending everything was normal, called her without fail every evening.

The previous night his voice had sounded like someone had pulled out the aerial lead. —Hey, how drunk are you out of ten, Seb? Deli had asked.

—About twelve.

—You're lucky. She sighed. —You'll probably sleep. Personally, I'm considering an up all-nighter.

—Go ahead, he said, voice slurred, —treat yourself . . . Are you in bed?

—Mmm. Watching telly, she said. —You?

—Watching telly, eating ice-cream and reading mags, oh, and, he added, —by the way, I'm in love.

—No! So soon? Who? she shouted, flicking the channel changer.

—Someone whose picture's in *Time Out*, you wouldn't know him.

—I've probably already shagged him, Deli said. —I'm a world class celeb, remember.

—He's called Douglas Wilson.

—Sure, Deli said vaguely, channel surfing. —Ol Duggie, penis like a Black and Decker.

—The truth is, you should do yourself a favour and get a decent boyfriend, said Seb.

—I'm so sick of you and M telling me that, she said exasperated. —There isn't any decent boyfriend material around, it's like they've all gone to summer camp for the last year. They're all probably sitting around right now toasting the hearts of their ex-girlfriends over an open fire. Moodily she switched over to CNN, and listened to the news for a minute, not speaking.

—Deli? You there?

—Why aren't I tired Seb? she whined.

—Take a pill.

—I took one last night.

—Take Night Nurse then.

—Can't, I've just twelve-stepped for that.

—Then watch the porn channel or go manual, Seb chortled. —An overdose of sex kills insomnia. Bye bye for now.

Five minutes later the phone went. Seb again.

—Wank Patrol! he screamed. —Have I caught you in the middle of anything?

—Fuck off. Deli giggled.

—No, really, Deli, it pains me to see you like this, it's embarrassing, get a life, or even better still, get a date.

A date? Deli thought, as she bladed injury-free through the psychopathic traffic on the main road and crash-stopped into the wall of the Douche building. Now there was an obscure notion. No, that idea had gone to live in a far-flung corner somewhere with things like: bumping into Prince by the office photocopy machine and finding the other hoop of her favourite Billy Babe Hoover ear-rings she'd lost in the loo of Terminal 4 the previous month.

She squatted on the concrete slab by the industrial dustbins, velcroed off her wrist pads and a minute later found herself at her office at the end of the hall where Luc was waiting, the dregs of a fourth coffee sticky on his mouth. Luc, with his worried eyes and television set glasses, Deli's only friend and ally, and privy to an endless flow of Douche company gossip, scandal and rumour, which he always obligingly passed onto her.

And the rumour that he so obligingly passed on to her as she burst through the office door that particular morning was that Léon and Anchois were looking for a way, any way at all, to get rid of her.

IT HAD ONLY been five or six days after Luc's warning when he had called her at the London office. —Deli, his voice sounded guarded. —Deli, Luc had said, —the collection has been stolen. About twenty-five prototypes. You'd better come.

Both Seb and M had been out on appointments. She left a hurried message with Tish and called Sunshine Cabs. By the time she'd arrived late in the afternoon she'd managed to work herself into a horrible fury with Luc. Why the hell hadn't he locked up properly? Luc was indignant, he had been away, down at the factory. Léon had taken charge of the keys while he'd been gone.

Léon shrugged. —Perhaps, he said, making one of those irritating French gestures with his hands that denoted Bugger All, —perhaps the thieves have a copy of the key here, or they came during the day, when the door is not bolted. His voice crackled with the effort of sustaining genuine puzzlement.

But Deli looked into the blank spaces of his eyes, cushioned in their fleshy surround and she wondered just who was responsible.

★

SHE'D SAT AT the desk long after Luc had gone home, depressed and frustrated, still fruitlessly trying to get hold of M or Seb. Where were they for God's sake? She waited while the phone rang to an empty office in London. Outside the window, the sky was temporarily clear, a deep navy-blue. The stars looked platinum bright, washed shiny by the rains. She glanced at her watch, it was nine o'clock in the evening, she called Rubin to say goodnight and then decided to try Seb's flat once more before leaving, when suddenly the buzzer sounded. She started, then ran down the passage and opened the door.

Seb stood outside, shaky and unshaven, his white face contorted with the news that of course Deli instinctively knew before he even had a chance to open his mouth.

THEY HAD SAT in the local Bar de Truc, at a small corner table with worn brocade chairs and Deli had no idea what to say. Behind Seb the stained-glass window glowed red with the decorative blood of some past religious pageant. She looked around her at the other customers, their expressions broken by the flickering candlelight. What secrets of death and disease were they hiding behind the banal everyday function of drinking and with those secrets how was it they all looked so normal, so average, so fucking *calm*?

She felt she was already losing Seb, as though he was being dragged screaming across some borderline which she didn't have and wouldn't want the passport to. She

• 300 •

looked back at him. Actually he wasn't screaming at all, he looked as normal and average as everyone else around them, as if by retaining control, he thought to claim a pre-emptive strike over his enemy in the battle he was about to embark on.

—I don't understand, Seb, she asked him. —You had all those tests?

—I never took them, he said flatly.

—But why?

—Deli, Kevin dead, so many other friends dying . . . try to understand, I just didn't want to feel next in line. I'm sorry.

—For God's sake, she dug her nails into the flesh of her palm, feeling the ever threatening tears rise up and subside again.

—I got a rash two days ago, he said, —on my chest. I've seen it before. It's a prelude to full-blown Aids.

—But you don't know for certain? You haven't had the results? She suddenly had an insane hope – *he's wrong, it's a mistake, it's eczema, it's chicken pox, food poisoning, it's just a stupid rash. Nothing at all.*

—I'll get the result in a week's time, but it will be positive, there is no doubt about that, my health has been appalling this year, you know that.

Deli remembered the dripping nose in the cinema, the endless hacking cough. Oh God, she felt suffocated by remorse. *Why hadn't she noticed, made him take time off, helped him somehow? Selfish stupid bitch.*

—I kept telling myself it was stress, but, you know, he was saying, —the signs are pretty unmistakable. My body feels different, like it's not mine any longer. I can feel it in the grip of something stronger than me.

Appalled, she felt the hot fork of tears poking her eyes, she gouged round her sockets with her knuckles and bit her lip in an effort to stop them, but they came anyway. She jabbed at them with her shirt sleeve.

Seb lit a cigarette and took a deep drag. He put his chin up and exhaled loudly.

—Don't worry, it won't affect work, Deli. I won't let you down.

—For fuck's sake, she said angrily, —this is not about me, this is your *life* we're talking about.

—You don't get it, do you? I would really mind. We must make this show work, then we can get released from Douche . . .

—Seb, that just doesn't have to be your priority right now.

—We must get past the show, Seb said stubbornly. —It's only nine weeks and then we'll see. He finished his cigarette and ground it out in the ashtray with his thumb.

—What can I do? she asked him.

—Nothing.

—There must be something, she pressed.

—No, sweetheart, nothing, he said ruefully, —Well, maybe design me a new immune system maybe.

—Ha, bloody, ha. She wiped her eyes and put her

hand on his arm. She rubbed his skin, noticing suddenly how hairless it was. —I love you, Seb.

—I love you too, he said.

OUTSIDE, THE RAIN had begun falling again in heavy turbid drops from the sky, and despite the wind the greenish clouds overhead looked darkly obstinate in their refusal to move on.

—End of the world weather, said Seb, and smiled suddenly. He flung his arms out wide and spun around, whirling down the street, his head up to the sky, his mouth open.

—End of the world weather! he howled, and he hooted with laughter as the storm and the rain washed clean over him.

Chapter Thirty-One It's Raining, it's Pouring, my Love Life is Boring

Dear Aaron July, Paris

Seb's world is starting to shrink with frightening speed, and God knows Aaron I don't know how to stop it. I want him to give up work, find the sun, get some sleep, take a million vitamins. He wants to stay busy, do the show, and above all make out all is normal. So at the moment, we both spend all our time secretly watching each other's backs.

Meanwhile on occasions when I actually raise the issue of back watching to Grant he all but pats my head and says:

—You concentrate on press for your Paris show, my love, and leave the politics of big business to me.

Rachel, too, is understanding. —I'd like to be able to help, she says earnestly —but it bypasses my departmental field of remit. Let's agenda it for the forthcoming meeting. Silly anorexic bitch.

On a domestic front my direct neighbour has never heard of Jean-Paul Satre; he is old, ugly and doesn't seem to read much in the way of poetry. So far the two of us haven't had great sex together, but hey, maybe when I get desperate.

Call, fax, or send us some David's choc chip cookies, UPS.

Deli xxxxxxxx

Deli looked out of the window at the queue of cars ahead. The tailback on the motorway was so long, the cars at the top looked minuscule – God's dinky matchbox collection.

The whole world had been on strike: air traffic control was on strike because they were tired and planes kept crashing, the farmers were on strike because nobody liked their sheep. The buses were on strike, probably because there was a Y in the month, and the metro was on strike simply because they hated missing out on a good party, but now, to really curry the pot, the lemonswallowers had been banned from smoking in the streets of Paris.

A ludicrously hopeful law, thought the police, who had so far ostentatiously neglected to enforce such a measure. Even when they caught some angry Frenchman with ten cigarettes in each hand and a smoking Gitane stuck defiantly up his ass, they failed miserably to apprehend him.

Deli had been in a taxi, and to say inching could not adequately describe the lack of speed with which she was travelling. She had been *millimetering* her way across the capital trying to get to the airport. This was not going to be easy, the Brazilian driver had insisted on telling her for the umpteenth time.

It was two o'clock in the afternoon although from the colour of the sky overhead it might just as well have been midnight. She was trying to catch a flight several hours earlier than normal as she had to get to Rubin's birthday party that evening. Ned would be there, Mum and Dad would be there, M, Tish and Seb would be there – and she was buggered if she was going to miss it.

Getting to Rubin's party on time, despite the increasing pressure of the show deadline, despite Seb et al, was her new psychological resolve; she had decided that organizing this party at the conventional tea-time, making endless long lists, sending out the invitations, even buying the party bags and crappy toys then flying over and arriving before it began, would all prove, surely, that she had a life.

At the Air France check-in desk, the Ticket Lady told her the flight was delayed. Deli groaned. —Delayed, for how long?

—Indefinitely, the stewardess shrugged, applying some peach lipstick. —We don't know yet, come back in one hour.

Deli wandered around downstairs, weaving in and out of the shops and restaurants. After three quarters of an hour she was bored and fretful to get back to the check-in. —Any news on the 3.25? she asked vaguely.

—Of course, said the Ticket Lady. —It's boarding

now. She looked at the computer screen. —I can't check you in here now, it's far too late, you'll have to go straight to the gate.

Cursing, Deli ran for the escalator, scaling the rubber steps in the perspex tunnels, she felt like a miniaturized cyberpunk bouncing up and down on Charles de Gaulle's very own intestine. Panting, she arrived at the check-in. Thank God no one was boarding, but a lot of people were squashed round the orange upholstered seats of gate 14. She slapped the ticket down on the desk with relief.

An Air France person, his hair glistening like molten chocolate under his flight attendant's cap, picked it up. He made a small show of tapping into the computer then turned to her, pushing the ticket back over the desk as if it were a piece of radio-active litter.

—The flight is full, he said.

—What do you mean the flight is full? Deli eyeballed him suspiciously.

—There are no seats left. His mouth twitched.

—How can there be no seats left if I have a ticket?

—The flight is full, he repeated, undeterred by this logic. He looked at his watch and turned its face towards her, rapping the glass. —You're late, he added, looking somehow pleased.

—But I've been here for hours. I was told it was delayed indefinitely, she hissed.

—It is delayed indefinitely, yes, he agreed, —but we have sold the standby tickets. The flight is therefore full.

The tiny pause between therefore and full was clearly calculated to enrage her.

—Listen, you son of a bitch. Deli muscled up her voice to the consistency of cement. —I have been in the airport for over an hour, I was expressly told not to board by an Air France representative, and now you're telling me you've sold my seat?

The steward remained completely unimpressed but had adopted his How-To-Treat-An-Aggressive-Customer face. His eyes flickered with power.

—The flight is closed, he repeated finally. —I cannot help you, excuse me, I have other customers. He turned away to the queue forming alongside her and held his hand out for the next ticket.

—Don't you dare turn your back on me! Deli shouted, throwing pride to the wind. —You need to deal with this crisis *now*.

He completely ignored her, and the traveller he was serving shuffled and looked away.

A shot of rage surged through her like neat gin. Suddenly this faggoty French fucker epitomized her dislike of the nation in general, their rudeness and their misery, every stinking one of them. All her grievances and loathing of limbo life were suddenly distilled into a large globule of poison which landed neatly on the end of her tongue . . .

The other passengers were now openly staring, clutching their tickets, terrified they might be snatched away at any moment. Deli shoved the embarrassed traveller aside. The battle lasted five minutes. She had absolutely no recollection of whether it was a physical, or just a verbal attack, all she did know was that by the time it was over, she had a boarding card and a very sore throat.

Deli limped through the rope feeling like a victim of a particularly violent crime. Several frazzled looking business men were clapping half-heartedly. She smiled at them gratefully and sat down on the edge of the seat furthest away from the ticket desk, trembling with anger that frothed and boiled around her ears. She fished in her bag for something to read.

—Need a cigarette? a voice interrupted.

Deli glanced up suspiciously.

—An oddly familiar looking man was holding out a packet of Benson and Hedges.

She scowled. Great, just to cap a really bad day she was now going to be saddled with a talkative git for the journey. Still, she could certainly do with some nicotine. —I've given up, she said ungraciously, snatching one and wondering where she knew him from.

—Oh sure, he said, —another quit addict. He pulled a lighter out of his pocket and sat down next to her. He flicked on the tiny flame with his thumb. —That was quite a performance you gave up there, it had an interesting psychotic edge to it. You're not by any chance . . . an award-winning actress are you? He grinned, clearly hugely impressed by his own joke.

—No, Deli said. —Actually that's how I behave in normal life. She peered at him crossly. —Do I know you? I'm sure I've seen you before somewhere.

—Maybe, he shrugged, —probably here at the airport.

—Well, it's possible, considering I more or less live here at the moment, she said sourly.

—Here Paris? he murmured, lighting his own cigarette.

—No, here airport, she said with her unfaltering wit.

—Convenient for public transport I guess, he said, politely uncrushed.

—Mmmm. Deli flicked through her magazine restlessly.

—But you work in Paris? This guy showed no sign of shutting up.

—Yup.

—Doing?

—I used to be in fashion, but I guess I'm in politics at the moment.

—Hmm, he said, —I thought so.

Deli giggled, starting to relax. —Is this a very silly conversation?

—Yes, he said with a straight face, —idiotic. He had a good face, an interesting somewhat uneven face with eyes that turned down, a deep frown creased between them. —Mind you, politics sounds believable. After all, you handled that guy at the ticket counter like someone with diplomatic immunity.

—Yeah, well people say I have a cool predatory quality that drives men wild, Deli said, then startled by the sudden memory, —hey, now I know where I met you. It was on the plane, wasn't it?

—Yes. He smiled at her. —We sat next to each other, you were extremely aggressive; you ate the chocolate heart off my tray and then tried to pretend it was yours.

—Oh God, I do remember. Deli blushed. —And you knew all along. She looked at him again accusingly, he was amused at her, she realized. His eyes were dark blue, almost navy.

—Bill Lovell, he said and stuck out his hand.

—Deli Madison. She hesitated then shook it. —So you do this trip a lot too huh? Why? she added curiously. He didn't look like the average hassled and crumpled business oik on her flight.

—Oh well, I'm a psychiatrist. I have several berserk patients just like you in Paris.

—I just have the strangest feeling that's not true. Deli arched her eyebrows.

—Okay, just kidding.

—So, if you're not a psychiatrist then what do you do apart from telling lies?

—You're a girl which means you've lied at least three times today.

—You're right as it happens, she admitted. —I'm a gratuitous liar.

—Ah, but I'm a pathological liar, Bill said.

—No, wait, Deli said quickly, —maybe I'm a pathological liar too.

—Well, it's nice to meet you, Bill said, —however sick you are. Actually I own a magazine in London called *Have Your City and Eat It*. It's an entertainment guide like . . .

—I know exactly what it is, Deli interrupted. —The worst review I ever had my whole life was in *Eat It*. And you own it. She shook her head in disbelief. —I had to pay my friends to storm the shops and burn the fashion sections.

—I can't believe you're that neurotic. Bill paused. —Although I do remember circulation being particularly good that month.

—You know what this is, don't you, Deli told him solemnly. —This is cause and effect – nemesis. This is the point in the movie where we meet for the first time and I get to stick something long and sharp between your ribs for ruining my career.

—Doesn't seem to have done your career too much harm, he said, not looking even remotely repentant. —So, do you like Paris?

—Paris is like a war zone, a broken-down city which has stopped functioning. Deli, realizing she did indeed sound psychotic, stopped abruptly.

—That's a controversial view of the world's most romantic capital, Bill answered lightly.

—It's all these strikes. All this weather, she said lamely.

—Don't you find it weird all the storms and lightning and stuff?

—What storms? he asked and frowned.

Deli sighed. —So you live in London?

—Yup, but at the moment I'm setting *Eat* up in Paris and New York, so I'm feeling a bit out of a suitcasish.

—Huh, I know just what you mean. Deli looked at her watch. —This is ridiculous, we've been here an hour. It's 3.45 already.

—I'm starving. Bill looked at her. —Why don't we go downstairs again and get some tea? he said casually.

—Oh, no, no, no, Deli said, shaking her head. —It won't work, I've tried that before. It's all part of Air France's new game. They let you get to the restaurant, but just when your 2,000 franc steak arrives they call the flight, and so you have to abandon your food at a run, then they make you sit on the plane for a further three hours without giving you so much as a fucking fromage frais.

Bill was openly laughing at her now.

—I know, I sound really paranoid, Deli tailed off. —How desperate do I sound out of ten?

—Completely off your head. Anyway, look, he said, pointing at the gate, —they're boarding now, what's your seat number?

She looked at her boarding card. —4B, what's yours?

—I'm at the back.

They stood up and moved slowly through the queue down the umbilical chute and onto the plane.

Deli checked her boarding card. —Well, I'm here. She stalled by her seat, not wanting to stop the conversation.

—Too far away to steal my heart. Bill stood sideways to let another passenger past. —Of course I could lob it up the aisle if you're desperate.

—Oh, I never *ever* talk to people on planes, Deli gabbled, —so even if we were sitting together, I'd obviously have to ignore you.

—Your logic is admirable, Bill said wryly.

He made to move to his seat, but, just then, a middle-aged commuter in a rumpled linen suit pushed past.

—Deli, hello! he exclaimed. —How did the meeting go?

—Er, fine, she said, not looking at Bill.

—A girl across the aisle called, —Deli! There you are! Got your period yet?

Deli smiled sheepishly at Bill who was smirking in a particularly horrible way.

—Catch you later, he'd said, still laughing. He moved on down the aisle towards the rear of the plane. She kept the corner of her eye trained on him while she threw her bag up into the overhead locker. Just before sitting down, she'd risked a quick peep. Bill, looking round the side of his Air France magazine, caught her eye and smiled.

Chapter Thirty-Two

A week later, Anchois buzzed Deli to come upstairs.

—So, he announced in a jovial tone that immediately put the wind up her, —you've asked to see how the pre-season sales are progressing? He steered her by the elbow into Léon's office.

—I'd like to see all the figures, Deli said with as much authority as she could muster. The fact that she'd been asking for them for the last fortnight didn't appear to be weighing too heavily on his mind.

Léon sat at his desk behind a shield of smoke, toying with his lighter which rested on the red leather surface. Deli experienced an immediate desire to set fire to him, or at the very least his suit. Around the sides of the room, her precious collection hung sadly on rails, squashed together like well-dressed refugees. She picked up a jacket from the floor and put it back on its hanger. The cloth stank of ash.

—Léon, cooed Anchois, —I'd like to go over the results of the pre-sales with Deli. Do you have the figures?

—Ah, yes, indeed, my friend. I have them here, said Léon.

She wondered why they were both enunciating their words so carefully. Léon took the photocopied piece of paper off the top of his ashtray.

—Ah, yes, he said. Looking at the piece of paper he started to shake his head slowly from side to side. —Well, well, well. Tiens, tiens tiens tiens tiens. They are very disappointing, Monsieur Anchois.

Léon looked at Deli, and held both his hands out in despair.

—I have done everything, he said, his voice cracking raw. —Everything I can. I have shown the collection to hundreds of my customers but – he stopped, took a hit of his Gitanes and increased the breadth of his shrug, —nothing, no interest whatsoever. He exhaled loudly. —They just simply cannot stand the stuff.

—Oh dear, oh dear, do you have *any* sales for Europe, Léon? Anchois intervened.

—None, Léon responded sadly. —Perhaps had it been a third of the price . . . or looked completely different, been French, a blacker black . . . but it's a very sad tragic case of complete failure.

—Our sales everywhere else have been way over target, Deli said evenly. —You are aware of that, aren't you?

—Yes, perhaps . . . He smiled frigidly, leaning back and lighting another cigarette. —But it is not the same story here . . . and here is where it counts.

Speechless, she looked at the pair of them. Anchois, his face carefully enquiring, and Léon, his expression a mask of innocence. Fleetingly she allowed herself the heart-warming image of them bungy jumping from the Eiffel Tower using their intestines as ropes.

—I don't believe you, she said finally. She turned on her heel, and stalked out of the room.

The door shut behind her. There was silence. She walked stonily along the corridor, a poisonous fury spreading through her like the plague, and as she turned the corner to the stairs, she heard the low growl of Léon's chuckle. She made a call to Grant's office and headed straight for the airport.

So . . . AHA! THE flight is delayed. What an enormous surprise. A new experience, a novelty, a gimmick, a fad, yes indeedy, a situation with a certain newness, new-ew-ew-ew nessssssssssssss. *NEWwwwwneeeessssss*. Oh my God, she was talking to herself. Deli could see her lips moving in the glass reflection of the airport gift store on the lower ground floor. She was definitely losing it.

Through the moving tunnel, she could see the warm red glow of Gate 14's womb ahead.

He was already sitting on the cloth upholstery, those hated orange seats, drinking a Coke, book in hand. A

piece of serious trash she was pleased to note. She passed
through the rope, flashing her boarding card, then hesitated,
wondering whether to say hello or not. It wasn't like she
was exactly going to be riveting company this afternoon.

—Hello.

Bill looked up. His face creased into a smile. —Oh!
Hi yourself. He shut his book. —You on this flight? He
moved up a seat.

—Mm. Deli sat down next to him.

—So how was the party, did you make it on time?

—I made it for the cake. She winced, remembering
the triumphant look on Ned's face as she had run into the
kitchen more than an hour late. —How was your date?

—Gruesome. He made a face. —A witch on toast. So
what have you been up to since last time we were delayed?

—Oh this and that, she shrugged. *Fuck, those bastards,
what now?* She tried to think straight, make a plan, but
somebody was busy grinding coffee beans in her head.

—So what takes you over today?

—I'm on a mission to see Our Great Leader.

—Frankly, I'm surprised you're allowed to travel
without a member of hospital staff.

—Very funny.

—No, really, aren't the shows any minute from now?

—Three weeks from now. *Three weeks.* Oh my God.
Now a steamroller had appeared in her stomach and was
knocking down the walls to her spleen. She clearly was
going crazy.

—I might have to be in the States, but will you send me an invite anyway? Bill was saying.

Deli pulled herself together. —Only if you promise to cheer loudly, and give it a fabulous review.

—Seems reasonable.

They sat silent for a minute. Deli wondered whether Bill was longing to read his book.

—Travellers look just like their suitcases, don't they? he mused as she made a vague move to get up. You know, like pet owners look like their dogs? He nodded his head over to a man sitting on the far end of the gate. A wan-looking middle-aged woman sat next to him in bored marriage silence. —That one, for example, battered leathery face, lumpy overstuffed body, metal eyes . . . and take his lovely girlfriend. Zipper mouth, he continued. —Tourist class old bag stamped all over her.

Deli chuckled softly. —That's my ultimate fear in life. You know, to be with someone, like those two suitcases over there, and to have nothing to say to them at all.

Bill nodded. —Do you remember that story where a husband and wife lived in the same house, but hadn't spoken to each other in twenty years, they just left each other notes about milk bottles?

—Well, I've done that, Deli said. —Not the notes, but I've been in a restaurant with someone, and not spoken for the whole meal, not because we'd rowed, just because we couldn't think of anything to say.

—Who was it with?

—Ned, my ex-husband. Deli still felt uncomfortable saying the word ex. Almost as uncomfortable as she'd felt saying the word husband. —I was convinced everyone was watching us and whispering, 'Look over there, the Couple that have Nothing Left, the Empty Couple.'

—I didn't realize you were divorced.

—Mmm.

—So what went wrong?

Deli shrugged.

—You might as well tell me, Bill said, —because we could be here a long time. In fact, chances are, he looked at the departures screen, —we could decompose and become fossilized in this airport.

—Well, in a nutshell? Deli considered. —I suppose I'm an optimist. I always believe good things come to good people, fate rewards, that kind of stuff. Ned was a pessimist. It wasn't so much that he believed the worst was going to happen, he just didn't believe that the best existed.

—Ah, said Bill seriously, —but then negativity is the cancer of hope.

—Is that deep or just pretentious? she asked him, giggling.

—Who cares? I can never tell the difference, he said. —Personally, I am a closet double-bluff optimist. I always say the worst is going to happen just in case it does, so I can have the kudos of being right, but I always believe the best will win through in the end.

—Well, that's just being positive with a safety catch. Ned ruined so many things by being negative. She paused embarrassed. —You realize I'm only telling you because you have, you know, Stranger Status.

—I can be your travel shrink. He smiled at her, and for some reason that she couldn't quite make out, his smile unnerved her. She fiddled with her boarding card.

—How about doing something really controversial one of these days, Bill said. —How about meeting, like, not in an airport? Like how about supper this time next week?

—Oh no, she said immediately. —I'm not sure that's a good idea.

He eyed her. —Of course you're not sure, you didn't even think about it.

—Well, it's just maybe our relationship only works in an airport environment, you know, something to do with the thematic air control. Here we can have lots in common, we can confer about travelling, moan about the delays, discuss the colour of our boarding cards, maybe if we meet outside in the real world we won't have anything to talk about any more? She stopped burbling. He was laughing at her again. She felt idiotic.

—I see, he said thoughtfully. —How about I draw up a list of subjects we could safely discuss and fax them to you for approval. Would that help?

—Okay, it's a deal, she found herself saying. —Do you mind if I bring notes?

—Not at all, that would be fine, Bill said emphatically.
—Let's make this easy on the both of us. And hey, he said
as the last call of the flight sounded, —good luck with
your mission.

But three hours later in the oyster-coloured carpeted
offices of Ersatz Corporation, Grant's secretary had smiled
at Deli with dedicated sadness. —We're so very, very
sorry, she murmured, —we've had to cancel your appointment. Grant's having his hair styled for a programme on
Sky television right now, and there doesn't seem to be
any unclaimed space in his diary for at least six months.

Chapter Thirty-Three

                                    15 September

For the attention of Deli Madison:
Strictly private, confidential, and more than a little
personal

> Bestiality is the busy man's answer to
>   keeping pets. Discuss.
> Macramé.
> The enigma of the human heart.
> The enigma of my heart (just kidding).
> The death of post–abstract art.
> Alcoholic beverages beginning with the letter U.

> Will ring to confirm.
> Airport Bill

The fax had lain on top of the desk, where she'd been
stealing glances at it all day.

It had been nine-thirty in the evening, everybody had
still been at work, except for Seb who'd gone home early
looking tired and depressed. His T-cell count had been
very low when he'd finally got back the result. He must

be at home, the doctor warned, not in the office, not under stress. Seb obviously wouldn't listen. It would have been completely alien to his character to jump ship. But he had begun to change, though, in subtle ways, not physically, but certainly mentally. Gradually his priorities had started to shift around and regroup, his vision and expectation of his future inexorably altered. Deli watched him taking control of his life, as thin and fragile as a kite line in his hands and she wondered at him for it. He was dealing with it amazingly well.

To be honest, it was her who was having the problem. When he first told her she'd thought, well, it'll be okay, I'll look after him. We'll carry on as normal, things won't change. But, of course, how stupid to think that, because she knew they would, it was just that she couldn't equate the thought of Seb now with her fear of what might happen to him in the future. Like Kevin. Oh God.

The phone rang, the little red light winked teasingly at her.

—Bill Lovell for you, line 4, called Tish. —Sounds very charming, she sang.

Oh no. He was going to cancel her. Deli snatched up the phone.

—Hi, he said, —you frantic? Do you want to cancel me?

—Definitely not, she almost shouted.

—Good, so what would you like to do, where shall we go? How hungry are you?

—I haven't eaten all day, what would . . .?

—starved too –

—was thinking Japanese, they spluttered at the same time.

—Excuse me, are we both having the same conversation? Deli asked him. —Because, if so, why is it so difficult to understand?

—Maybe we're just both really difficult people, Bill said.

—Well, I try to be difficult, does it come naturally to you? *Will you please stop flirting.* She kicked herself, grinning.

—Actually, no, being an asshole comes naturally to me, said Bill, —being difficult takes more practice.

AND, OF COURSE, affairs always begin in restaurants, she remembered, pounding down Holland Park Avenue. But then this was no time for an affair.

—Whoah, said Bill, emerging from the shadow of Hiroko's entrance. —I thought I'd wait for you here.

—Sorry, sorry, she panted, startled not to have noticed him. —I had to come by tube. He kissed her lightly on the cheek and pushed open the wooden slatted door.

They sat down in the red bonkette furthest away from the entrance.

Deli whipped his crumpled fax out of her bag. —So, she said, pretending to consult the list, —I couldn't think of a single alcoholic beverage beginning with U, and I might be a bit flaky on the enigma of the human heart bit.

—The alcohol question was clearly a trick question, said Bill, —and, don't worry, we won't have to talk about anything personal.

—Uh, uh, she said. —No, tonight I thought I'd try out my Open Person act.

—Really, and how's it going so far? Bill looked amused.

—Only time I tried it before, the results were disastrous.

The waiter placed some bowls on the table. Deli prodded the green seaweed with her chopsticks.

—Lovely, said Bill, making a face as she lobbed it into her mouth. —Sperm of the Jolly Green Giant. So what happened before?

Deli dabbed her mouth with a napkin. —When Ned and I split up he accused me of being completely emotionally retarded, so the first guy who asked me out I thought, okay, how hard can it be? I'll be an open book to him, and I poured out my heart.

—And?

—Half-way through my monologue, I looked at him and he was sitting in his chair, rocking backwards and forwards, this eerie glazed look on his face.

Bill laughed. —I take it it was a somewhat short-lived romance then?

—It was over at the end of dinner, there was no need to have an affair with him. This guy, *BAM*! He knew everything before pudding. It was a shame though, Deli said wistfully, —because he had these fantastic hairy forearms.

—I was obsessed with a girl's beauty spot once, said Bill. She had this amazing 3D mole just below her nose, very sexy. It moved when she talked. I could never concentrate on what she was saying, I was always watching that mole morris dancing.

—So what happened?

—One day I noticed there was hair growing in it, this one thick long hair sprouting out the middle, and I was so frightened it put me off her.

—What? Deli was horrified. —Just for one lousy hair, you dumped her for that? That's terrifying.

—You think that's scary? Bill said, as a huge plate of sushi materialized between them. Listen I know this guy who was so obsessed with a girl that he drank her bath water. Bill picked some ginger off the board with his fingers.

Deli laughed. —So what's the most obsessive thing you've ever done for love?

—I've done a lot of minorly obsessive things, stuff that everyone does . . .

—Like . . . she prompted.

—Like convincing myself that Birmingham was on my way home from Camden Town to Kensal Rise . . . I had this one particular girl who I was crazy about. To think – an entire romance measured in Shell vouchers. He expertly chopsticked another bit of sushi into his mouth.

—So . . . this Ned thought you were emotionally dysfunctional, did he?

—Mm, yes. Deli hoped they weren't going to have to talk about Ned.

—Mmm, my ex-girlfriend was always calling me emotionally dysfunctional too. The minute you break up with someone they call you dysfunctional, makes them feel so much better.

—It might be kind of dangerous, Deli mused. —Two dysfunctional people at one table together, there might be some kind of atomic reaction or something. She paused. —How ex is your ex?

—About seven months ago, in practice; mentally, about two years ago. Bill glanced up at her ruefully. —Sometimes you want them to work so badly I guess you adapt to situations even if they're not ideal.

—We should have some kind of inner warning system, a loud burglar alarm that goes off to let you know when your life gets below a certain level of acceptability.

—Oh my God. Bill prodded the last bit of orange sushi goo with his chopstick. What is this *thing* you've ordered? he asked, looking horrified.

—Uni, Deli said. —It's yours, I've had mine.

He made a face. —Thanks, but I'm suddenly and mysteriously full. By the way, he added, —we're doing well. We're two thirds of the way through dinner and we haven't even started on that list yet.

—It's psychological, like keeping sleeping pills by your

bed, and not taking them. Knowing we have other subjects there to fall back on makes us feel safer.

—Now, said Bill, as two bowls of clear soup arrived, —I'm all done with small talk. Time to run me through your first three boyfriends.

—You can't be interested, she laughed.

—Believe me, this is strictly on a need-to-know basis.

—Oh, God, well, you know, rockers, bikers, obviously anyone with a police record for drugs and GBH . . . A boy called Adam made me go weak at the knees.

—I remember that stage too – Alice Cooper, acid. I went out with a whole line of girls who left me for rockers, bikers and boys called Adam.

—Most of that crowd are dead now, Deli said. —Overdoses, car crashes. Aids . . . she trailed off.

—You know, said Bill —the times when I was into the dirtiest living, I had the prissiest girlfriends. I had this one girl, Clean Pants, her nickname was, she was famous for douching between thrusts.

Deli grinned. —So how many times have you been in love?

—I suppose twice.

—Do you wish you were with either of them still? Immediately the words were out of her mouth she regretted them.

—No, said Bill. He shook his head slightly. —No, he repeated, taking her hand absent mindedly, —actually no, I can safely say I don't.

Change the subject now, screamed her good sense. Bill suddenly seemed to notice he had charge of her hand, and let go abruptly.

—When do you come back from America? Deli gulped down the rest of her sake.

—Sometime in the next week. I'm coming to your show, remember?

—Promise you'll bring me back some bacon, she said wistfully. —Jones, hickory smoked, four pounds.

—Pig products after a first date, he mused. —Well, that's certainly quite a commitment. He smiled, lit a cigarette and signalled for the bill.

Deli watched him. Sometimes in life, she thought, it was impossible not to feel clear, level, when you drive down a motorway hitting ninety, a hard blue sky ahead, lighting up the road to escape, and right then for a few seconds she felt overwhelmed with something. She had no idea what, but suddenly her head filled with Seb, Paris, the show . . . *Oh God*, she thought, *this time in a week, this time next week.*

—I'll drive you home, said Bill.

The passenger seat and most of the back of Bill's car was covered by a huge pile of *Have Your City and Eat It*.

—Sorry about the mess, he said, and swept them onto the floor. Deli climbed in and perched her feet on top of the magazines. —I need a daily for my car, he joked.

—What a coincidence, she said. —I need a car for my

daily. She shifted her knees to one side and rolled down the window.

The cold night air blew in over the glass and touched against her cheek. They drove up Holland Park Avenue, talking about whatever, careful only to give the right amount away. The car stopped at the traffic lights. As red changed to orange Bill pushed the car into gear, brushing accidentally against Deli's knee with his hand.

—I'm sorry, said Deli, quickly pulling them up. —Am I in your way?

—Not nearly enough, frankly, said Bill.

Deli choked back a laugh.

Bill turned and smiled at her. —So when will I see you again? How about you fax me your flight schedule? he said, half serious.

—I'm really stuck till the show's over. *Only seven days from now. Seven tiny days,* she obsessed.

—All right, but I'm coming to the show, Bill said, —and afterwards I'm going to take you for a drive round the city at night. I'll show you my Paris, and you will promise not to be cynical.

—I promise, she said meekly. —Left here, by the way, and it's just over there, the blue door by the motorcycle.

Bill slowed the car to a halt. —Okay, he sighed resignedly. He banged the top of the steering wheel lightly with his fist. —Here we are. He opened his door and stepped out.

Deli walked round to the kerb to meet him. She

stopped in front of him and fished in her back pack for the keys. —Um, you know I can't ask you up or anything, that would be completely against the rules.

—Perhaps you'd better send me the rule book as well. Bill leant down and kissed her suddenly. —So I know what I'm up against. He kissed her again. His mouth was cool against hers. —Goodnight, beautiful girl, he added softly.

—Goodnight, she said, her heart jumping. —Thank you for dinner, thank you for my lift. Her voice sounded more and more distant. She dashed up the steps and shoved the entire bunch of keys somewhere near the lock.

As the key finally opened the door she turned around. —Don't forget my bacon, she told him.

—Screw the bacon, Bill had said from the bottom of the steps. —Don't forget *me*.

fashion tips n° 8

Press

Fashion, as everybody knows, is a soup of rock and pop stirred by the grittiness of world events, and then flavoured with just an essence of youth ideology and imagination.

And fashion people, as everybody also knows, are people who make a difference. Their purpose in the scheme of things? To save the world from drabness, which is why every six months fashion people are seized with the impulse to travel the entire world, to search out the radically different, to discover a talent, a hero, and above all, to proclaim a Saviour of the Season.

So it's the collections in Paris and the city is stuffed full to bursting of these Important People. Thousands of journalists wearing this season's *au naturel* suits so God-Almighty-organic they look like they've been woven out of Alpen.

And every night the parties, the openings. Who's got an invitation and who hasn't.

—Thank God! squawks Hymen. —The invitations to the TIL Radar party. Relief courses through her body, a river of confidence, nourishing her ego, and trickling down the twin tributaries of inadequacy and insecurity, filling her pool of self-importance until it is brimming over.

And you, the designer, sweats. Buckets. Just to think! It was only a decade ago that you had to snort eight grams of cocaine to get this high.

Man, how old fashioned! How naive.

Chapter Thirty-Four

Scrambled Legs

Deli arrived at the theatre. Inside it was as cold as doom. A single industrial heater blew vainly against the elements. Hair and Make-up arrived shivering and mute and switched on the electricity. One hundred light bulbs pinged into life around thirty feet of mirror.

—Six a.m. Four hours to go.

Huey the producer arrived with Thug his pit bull terrier in tow.

—We'll be doing a music run-through at six-thirty, he announced. Thug positioned himself by the sandwich table and farted contentedly.

Backstage it was beginning to warm up. Three models arrived and perched near the blow heater, their hair in curlers, moaning good-naturedly about the early start.

—Hey, girls! Deli crossed them off on her running order.

—Hi, they chorused, —betchya nervous? They screamed with laughter and offered Deli a Silk Cut.

The first cigarette of the morning sent her racing to the loo. By the time she got back the dressers had arrived and were unfolding ironing boards.

—Your names will be on the model cards, Deli intoned numbly. —*Please* cut out all hanging labels.

The dressers broke ranks and headed for the rails.

It was 6.50. Deli lit another cigarette. More girls were arriving. High buns, centre partings, leggings, flares, long suede boots, platform loafers, skinny rib polos and so on. The early lot were now sitting in front of the make-up mirrors, in varying stages of paint work. Deli put her face next to one of theirs and reeled back in disgust.

The shoe crisis began. Pulse had feet the size of a skateboard. Denim was refusing to wear hers at all and Origami's seemed to be missing altogether. *Oh God.* Deli fucking hated the shoe crisis.

It was 6.59. M had arrived. He gave her a hug.

They watched the huge polystyrene letters being hoisted up at the front of the stage. Deli felt another volcanic wave of nerves. —Amoebic dysentery, she muttered, and rushed to the loo.

At 7.15 Vince and Freebie, the PRs, arrived waving the seating plan.

—One misinterpretation of the pecking order, and we're sunk, panicked Freebie.

—*You* work it out, said Deli backing away.

At 8.30 the gorgeous Solo walked through the front entrance wearing a black leather bouf hat. Solo was beautiful, well beautiful, anorexic, and temporarily a junkie, but on the catwalk she left a trail of sex appeal behind her like a snail, drawing tongues out of the mouths of even the terminally celibate.

Deli jumped on her and sent her to Make-up.

8.40 bleep bleep. Huey's mobile.

—It's the agency he said, snapping the phone back onto his belt, Soda's got her period, her thighs are fat. He's sending over 'Sleeps with Young Artists'.

Suddenly a microphone appeared almost inside Deli's nose, then a claw, then the unmistakable gravelly voice of Donna Chubb – The mood of the collection? Donna demanded.

Deli grinned wantonly into the camera and began to burble . . .

—Colours? Donna interrupted.

—Waterlily, eau de nil, tangerine, glassy white, mutant silver, lovelip red . . .

—Supermodels? she demanded.

—There's Katy, Lark, Pale, Water. Solo has just arrived and of course, Deli paused for dramatic effect, —there's Origami.

Deli escaped, looked at her watch. Gasped. 9.45 a.m. Jesus wept! Four girls short still.

Outside hundreds of people were queuing up, waving the de-luxe Andy Warhol meets Star Trek invitations.

—*All girls into their first outfits, please*! Huey shouted.

Dozens of photographers were now camping along

the edge of the catwalk aggressively holding their elbows rigid to keep their space.

—The limo's here! screamed Freebie. The last four girls had arrived.

Origami, Katy, Lark and Water strolled by and were ushered into Make-up. Deli hugged Katy.

A fight was going on in Hair. —I'm not going to even try to put those extensions in Origami's hair, thank you, moaned Claude feebly, —last time I tried to do something with her hair, the bitch hit me. I don't care how famous she is, she gives off the worst bad vibes.

Where was Origami anyway? Deli looked frantically around, she'd disappeared already. There she was, phoning her stockbroker on Huey's mobile. Deli sidled up.

—Hi, so glad you could make it, she quavered. —Thank you so much for being here before the show started, it was real important to me . . .

Stop it, stop it, goddammit, stop being so obsequious for Christ's sake. Inwardly Deli resolved to be a bitch.

Origami nearly kissed her.

—Hi, Doll, collection looks fab, I love my outfits, can I keep the shoes?

—Sure, Deli groveled. —Anything, keep the outfits too. Keep the whole collection. Can I just get Claude to put this one teeny little thing in your hair? You know, because you're the first girl out? Because you're the bestest and the most famous, and your ankles are so slim . . .

Origami's eyes were the colour of sloe gin, purply blue, she looked at Deli for a tiny mesmeric second.

—Honey, you can do anything you like . . . after all it's your show.

Deli caught Claude's eye and tried not to laugh.

The theatre had become stiflingly hot, the annoyed rustling of programmes fanning people's faces and a light coughing could be heard.

Huey flicked the fizzing screen of the monitor with his fingernail. —We've got to start like *now*! he shouted. —Or people will begin to leave.

Deli hauled Origami out of Make-up and coerced her into her first outfit, and now Origami stood at the monitor ready, Hair were coifing her, dressers smoothing her, Make-up painting her, a blushing student was at her feet shoe-horning her into spangled platform wedges.

The lights flashed on . . . the music started . . . This was it! Deli's mouth was full of dust.

Origami pouted her collagen into the mirror, blew herself a kiss, took the cigarette out of her mouth, gave it to Deli to hold, waited for the correct beat of music, then stalked out on stage and stood under the arc of light at the top of the catwalk. There was absolute silence now save for the single thud of a drum.

The show began.

Deli was in focus now, she could feel concentration cutting through the dough in her head, sharp as a bread knife, oblivious to the mayhem around.

Origami was off stage already, snatching the fag out of Deli's hand for a quick puff. She was closely followed by girls two to five. As the pace hotted up, pandemonium broke loose backstage. Deli and Seb ran from girl to girl, straightening skirts, ripping labels, yanking zips, jerking off earrings.

The shoe runner was lobbing shoes over their heads, Huey was shouting out the names of the girls on next: Katy, Lark, Solo, Moon.

Solo! Where is Solo, we need you now!

Solo was stoned, fuck! There she was by the mirror fiddling aimlessly with her hair, Deli pushed her on, and watched her nervously on the monitor where Katy was obediently stalling.

Deli couldn't hear anything from out front, no clapping, nothing. Oh God, they hated it. Katy was off again hot and flushed, excited.

—Fucking fantastic music, Deli, they're loving it!

—They hate it, Deli whimpered. —They hate it.

—Go look out front, Katy said.

Deli peered through a crack in the wooden partitioning from the back to front stage. Five girls were on the catwalk, the extensions looked sensational, Deli got momentarily lost in the thudding of the music, then scanned the audience intently for signs of scorn.

Front row, she spied a chain of asbestos faces, devoid of expression of any kind, their knees and shoulders pressed tightly together, their eyes hidden with large black sunglasses.

Sunglasses? What? For Christ's sake! Don't you get it?

She'd put six months of sweat and tears, spent days, weeks even, ensuring the exact shade of the print, the subtle collusion of colours, and they were wearing tinted sunglasses. *You bastards!* she wanted to shout but just as she opened her mouth she realized they were clapping. Christ Alive they liked it, they liked it. Deli was suddenly filled with an overwhelming fondness for each and every one of them.

Back to the monitor, the final scene, thousands of tiny, multi coloured, hand sewn, sand washed pebbles reflecting the light in spots around the audience. Lark's dress was so short they'd had to make her special knickers that were only half-finished, maybe they won't notice, Deli prayed wildly . . . obsess, obsess, obsess.

Oh my God, it was over. Hair and Make-up were advancing on her threateningly with a hairbrush and assorted cover-ups. Deli backed off, *I know, I don't look human. I don't care, I don't care.*

Elbows were being grabbed and hustled on stage, everyone was grinning, Deli's eyes felt sunken and scratchy. Desperately she looked around for Seb, he was sitting on the steps up to the stage, exhausted, a thin film of sweat on his forehead. He touched her hand faintly with his fingertips as she was hustled by. Deli grabbed his hand and squeezed it quickly.

Katy, Origami and Lark relentlessly dragged her closer to the end of the catwalk, lipstick everywhere, maniacally she thanked everyone, the lights shone painfully in her eyes.

Out there on the catwalk at the end of the line with the models, wishing she could drop through the stage, the world whited out by the millions of camera flashes, Deli could just make out Mom and even Dad still in his bear coat. She cast wildly around then suddenly saw her little Rubin, M's hands around his waist, holding him up, his face scowling with love, his thuggy arms outstretched. Rubin coming closer and closer now through the ranks of photographers, coming straight at her. She grabbed him with both hands, pulled him on to the stage and squished him to her for dear life, sucking in his hot boy smell, and thinking: If for nothing else, what had she missed so much of his life for, for what reason could she possibly justify endlessly pontificating about quality not quantity of time with him, if there were not an end to it all, some kind of ultimate destination that she could give him to slate her guilt and say, well, there was always a reason, a purpose, an aim, and here it is, it's tangible and you can hold it, see it, touch it, feel it, and it's yours to keep. But in the same flash she knew that the question was unanswerable, because there was only one thing she could give him, only one thing he wanted to hold, see, touch, and feel . . . and that was her.

Clutching Rubin, Deli had backed off down the end of the catwalk, feeling hollow and deflated, on the edge of tears.

—Phew, thank you Hair, thank you Make-up. She

hugged Seb, hugged Huey, hugged a hideous video technician by accident and looked for a hiding place.

But there had been no escape. The dark glasses were picking their way over the wiring and cables on the ground, advancing backstage. Donna Chubb approached with her crew again and behind her Noleen Banjax, wearing a bronze sheared fake-beaver coat, even Benevolent from American *Vogue* was smiling in her hip distressed mini hobo dress.

—Congratulations, congratulations, kissed one.

—Tell us about the inspiration, enthused another.

—Your best collection yet, screeched a third waving her crocodile handbag.

Deli felt faint, dizzy, feverish. She put a hand out to steady herself. Rubin's mouth was still firmly suctioned to her cheek.

—What's wrong, dear? asked Donna, her microphone so far down Deli's throat you'd think she was interviewing her tonsils.

> mumps said the doctor
> measles said the nurse
> nothing said the lady with the alligator purse . . .

Freebie and Vince were holding the TV crews at bay. Deli cast around wildly for Bill, praying he'd come, but knowing he hadn't, the plastic of his security pass cold in her pocket. *He promised,* she thought, *he promised.*

—Come on, Deli, Freebie whispered urgently . . .
—Get it together. Give me the boy. She prised Rubin
from Deli's grip.

The flames in Deli's stomach had been smothered
with damp waves of depression, the beginnings of the
great all-time low.

It was 10.38. She had lit the fiftieth cigarette of the
morning, mouth too dry to smoke, took a deep breath
. . . and smiled into the waiting camera.

THAT SAME NIGHT it had been the hot party of fashion
week; the opening of the new Til Radar emporium.
This season, the Slavic-born designer, whose time after
twenty years of comparative obscurity had finally come,
had been proclaimed the Saviour, the Queen of the
Season.

Following the show, Deli and Seb were suddenly and
miraculously A-listed, their invitation hastily hand-deliv-
ered to the office earlier that afternoon. As they drew up
on the corner of Rue Rivoli, a huge mushroom of
ruthlessly determined partygoers could be seen heaving
one against the other outside the double doors. A brightly
coloured explosion of dismembered legs, arms and satin
handbags bottle-necked at the entrance, until every few
minutes a fortunate guest was sucked from the crowd at
random and shot through the magnetic force-field of the
doorway where once safely inside, they quickly shook
themselves out, smoothed their outfits and recharged their

egos with a quick pitying glance at the mob, shrieking and demented outside.

Inside, stars were everywhere, cooing and gurgling, each of them wearing their own little red Aids bows, which the most serious amongst them had had the foresight to reproduce in rubies and diamonds.

—How sweet, Seb said, as a woman pushed by, a glittering red badge pinned to her bosom. —Yes, I do care, he mimicked. —I really do care about homosexuals with nasty anti-social diseases. I just hope none of them come to live next door to me on Rue Du Seine.

Everywhere Deli and Seb turned, the Great, the Talented and Important were either snubbing or kissing each other, everyone playing their own complicated hierarchy-led games of 'I recognize you, I recognize you not.'

—Ayo, Deli cried, seeing one of her buddies from New York who had just been promoted to style director of *Charisma* magazine.

Ayo paused, momentarily losing the journalist he'd been tailing, and looked wary.

I recognize you not, said his eyes, looking straight through her.

Deli kneed him gently in the balls. —It's me you little fucker, don't get snooty.

Ayo's head snapped back to rejoin his mouth which suddenly widened and twitched with recognition.

—Deli, he says, —Jesus, I wouldn't have known you!

Look at you, why, you cute thing. You look fabulous and I hear from Gawdy the collection's *Di*-vine.

Already running out of conversation, Ayo held his smile fixedly towards her while his eyes darted feverishly from one person to the next eventually spotting Beppe from Bergdorfs. Relief flashed across his features as he moved swiftly off.

Seb was back at Deli's elbow.

—Hey, isn't that Billy-Babe Hoover over there? he exclaimed.

—Where?

—Over there, that guy in the hessian whip-me shirt and the hair.

—Hey, Billy-Babe!

But dark bars were radiating from Billy-Babe's eyes, he slithered by, ignoring them, his tongue flicking in and out as he spied a crowd of quality journalists and loosely buried himself in their midst with a wriggling and shuffling motion.

—Uh oh, said Seb watching him glide by. —He's hunting.

—Who's the prey?

—Looks like it's Joan from *Herpes Bazaar*, she's talking to Gawdy Wolff.

—It's the notorious nocturnal strike, watch! There he goes. Deli observed him, fascinated.

Billy Babe was indeed patiently awaiting his moment of ambush. His victims, talking animatedly to one another were still ignorant of the danger, but suddenly after a burst of laboured laughter there was a slight pause. Billy's neck coiled, his body inflated with hot air, his chest puffed out, he hissed loudly and struck, kissing them both on the cheek.

—Yup, told ya, said Seb. —Double fucking whammy.

—I'm going to get us a drink, said Deli grimly. —Stay right here.

Behind Deli at the drinks table, Dovanna and Hymen were fingering Til's merchandise. Hymen eased a cigarette out of the little pink velvet pouch she was wearing round her neck, clamped it between her dazzling caps, lit it, sucked in the precious smoke and exhaled high over Dovanna's head.

—Oh! We just love this particular shade of earth, gurgled Hymen. Hey Dovanna! Don't we just love it? It's so subtle, it's so Winter. It's so utterly clean, fresh and modern.

Deli fought her way back to Seb, pinned prisoner against the circular staircase. They hung over the balcony down to the ground floor and watched their world go by.

Maybe Bill will walk in now, Deli thought.

Bill had called her from the States a couple of days after their dinner. Checking in, he'd said. When she'd recognized him on the other end of the line, she found herself holding the receiver close, hunched around his voice. He'd be there, he had promised, at the show, definitely. And after she'd hung up she'd thought, no, this can't be happening, where's the angst? What happened to the rules, why aren't we playing the game properly? And she'd been right, she thought hollowly. It wasn't happening. Because he hadn't come. She looked down again. *Of course he could just walk through the glass doors, look up and it would all still be okay.*

But through the glass doors, the mushroom had now reached its full nuclear potential. The store was too full, nobody could come in, a human explosion threatened.

Surrounded by TV crews and photographers, but with guests pushing ruthlessly past her, stood Til herself, a tiny figure in a neat trouser suit the colour of the dawn mist. Her mouth was puckered with stress. She was completely alone amongst hundreds of people.

—Look, Deli, the face of success, said Seb.

—She looks miserable, said Deli.

—Listen, Seb took her hand suddenly, —you know this is where I bow out, for good, don't you?

Deli stared at him for a second. —Seb!

—I haven't any more time to waste on things that don't matter, Deli, he pleaded.

—I know, I know, she said sadly. She squeezed his hand. —Maybe you and me alike, Seb.

—No, Deli, you've earned your future. You take everything you can and make damn sure you enjoy it.

fashion tips **n° 9**

The Cycle

After the last and final night of parties/awards/brown-nosing dinners, you are suddenly aware that your head is slowly turning to cement. Even your scalp starts to feel heavy and strange; this is because your brain has pulped itself into the consistency of grape jelly and you are now entering your own private dream world.

The After Show Stupour has set in. The condition can be diagnosed by two symptoms:

1) mentally you deteriorate
2) physically you deteriorate.

Depression enters through an unattended crack and blithely takes up residence. The devil takes off for a well-earned holiday leaving a band of toads in his wake who jump up and down on your damaged spleen making you feel queasy and apathetic.

Physically all your features drop by half a centimetre, your skin dries up and threatens to self-combust, your eyes become rheumy and doggish. Your shoulders slump. By day you continue to work, but by night, you sit on your bed, eating microwaved rice-pudding, watching TV and praying you don't succumb to one of the fatal post-collection diseases that often strike at this point.

It goes without saying that you don't look attractive during this period, and naturally you dispense with the following beauty routines: washing (hair and body), exercising, make-up, teeth-cleaning and flossing, waxing, shaving, nail cutting and other forms of personal hygiene.

There is no cure for the above disease, but that's okay, because you know it will pass, it's just a matter of time, and when it does you will normally emerge, re-born in fact, with an almost pathetically keen desire to get back into work, ideas for new collections zipping round your head like fireflies, your fingers dancing with lust to get at the drawing pad. It's a cycle so you can count on it always happening.

Most of the time, that is . . .

Chapter Thirty-Five Face Ache

It was four days after the show, eleven o'clock at night.

Deli had been lying on her bed in Talbot Road, eating microwaved rice pudding and watching TV. On the table next to her, Aaron's flowers sagged low over the side of their vase, their stems wedged into the syphilitic green slime that used to be water.

They'd arrived in Paris, the day after the show, a bunch of flowers with no card, but a fax lay on the table beside them. She had prayed they were from Bill and had opened the envelope with shaky fingers, but the fax was from Aaron.

Deli   **6 October**

Followed your progress in the papers this week, and, by the way, even Adelaide saw an interview that you gave for NBC. She said you looked like a crackhead.

She also liked when all the girls tried to drag you out at the end of the show, how timid you tried to be, but I know this was just an act.

Big Kiss, and congratulations,
your number one USA fan with the family membership.

Aaron xxxxxxxxxxxxxxxxxxx

Deli had nearly cried with disappointment. She hadn't heard from Bill again since that first phone call. She cursed herself for misjudging it so badly, for imagining something was there, a phantom beginning of something that was not to be.

Rubin was asleep beside her. She'd been beyond playing Killer on the Run games with his Duplo which required too much intellectual commitment even at the best of times. So they had agreed on a video which Deli got to choose, being the eldest.

As they lay on the bed watching *The Scarlet Pimpernel*, she clasped Rubin to her bosom, weeping at the mere sight of Lesley Howard, and mumbling Percy, Percy! into his baby locks.

> Is he in heaven?
> Is he in hell?
> That demned elusive
> Bill Lov-ell

Oh shit, you idiot. She cursed herself again.

Rubin had fallen asleep after the first five minutes and was now lying on his stomach, most of one hand stuck firmly up his nose, the other clasping his balls in protective embrace. Deli was now so veggied out that she was lying completely horizontal, and the rice pudding, still in its semi-molten plastic dish, the edges brownish and contorted from being zapped for a minute too long, was lying on top of her just below her chin, so that with the minimum degree of exertion, she could spoon it up to her mouth with one hand.

Feeling comfortably sick, she tried to think of any one thing to look forward to in the next few months, anything at all to relieve the dead weight of depression that had sunk to the pit of her insides. *If there's any one thing out there, could it please make itself known at reception . . .*

Rubin was snoring, short sharp staccato noises that half blew his fingers out of his nose before he plugged them in again. Deli rolled him over. His heavy-lidded detective eyes stared at her disconcertingly. She decided to move him to his own bed. She picked him up, rescuing from underneath him the semi-chewed fax she'd finally received from Grant, still on his regional TV tour for *Finance Today*.

So concerned, so truly, truly concerned to learn of your problems with Douche. The Extraordinary

Shareholders' Meeting is confirmed, 16 October. I will be there.

Grant

She would use this meeting to grab hold of the future, she thought, echoing Seb's words to herself. She smoothed the piece of paper out and putting it carefully in her briefcase, carried Rubin to his room upstairs and tucked him into bed.

Back in front of the TV, she channel surfed, licking the empty carton of rice pudding vaguely, suddenly starving. She experienced an urgent need for Ben and Gerry's double-chocolate fudge brownie. Well, too bad she hadn't been shopping for about a year. What else could she eat?

Her mind locked onto the fridge, opening it with extreme psychic powers, and zeroed in on the top shelf. Empty. With extraordinary mental flexibility, she started to open the food cupboards . . .

Suddenly a loud buzzing noise interrupted her concentration. Deli jumped with fright, the plastic dish fell off her chest and onto the floor. It was past midnight. She sidled to the window nervously, pulling her T-shirt down as far as it would go below her waist, naked there below. The doorbell rang again, this time more insistently.

She looked out. A dark-coloured car, its headlights full on and shining, had stopped in the middle of the road.

It didn't look familiar. Maybe Léon had taken out a contract on her. Nervously she stood on the radiator and craned out further to see the front door. The radiator burned the soles of her feet, she yanked her T-shirt down again, and opened the top half of the window.

—Who is it? she yelped.

She could see a pair of heavy boots and the bottom half of a pair of jeans, but just as she was about to spring for the panic button, the legs stepped back into view, and, oh Holy Christ – it was Bill.

Bill, looking up at her from the doorstep. Bill's face breaking into a smile.

—Hey, did I wake you? Were you up? he asked, talking much too fast. —Look, I've brought you some bacon. He whisked a package wrapped tightly in silver foil from behind his back.

—Jones hickory smoked, four pounds, his voice trailed off. —Hello, he said lamely.

She grinned back, her heart racing, nerves boiling.

—Would you like to come in? she asked him, bending double with the effort of hiding her crotch and hopping up and down on the radiator.

—Actually, that would be very nice, he said politely. —Maybe I'd better park. He smiled again and walked back to his car. Depression flew out into the night, and Deli closed the window after it. She hopped off the radiator feeling absurdly happy, he was there, he was actually there.

Then her eyes swept the room. *Shit shit shit*, the grunge gold star award of the decade. Clothes all over the floor, bits of food on the carpet, four mugs, still with the herbal tea bag, its string stiff with rigor mortis hanging out, cartons of dead food, press cuttings, and shredded newspapers stockpiled by the bed.

She caught sight of herself in the mirror. *Oh shit shit shit shit*, even worse. Hair matted, eyes piggy, face pasty and white, mouth, Christ, she rushed to the basin.

Dad always used to say halitosis was better than no breath at all. Ha Ha Ha, Dad, she thought wildly, as she attempted to brush her teeth with a tube of Nair, realized her mistake and started again.

No one could park in under ten minutes in the Talbot Road. If you tried to part even vaguely within the limits of the law, you'd be talking quarter of an hour minimum. Most people just double-parked, but she prayed that Bill was diligently looking for a meter. She pulled a hairbrush through her hair, noticing her T-shirt had virtually disintegrated on her body. She ripped it off, jumped naked into the empty bath and sprayed every orifice spiritedly with the power shower head.

She could hear the engine of a car being switched off outside as it double-parked and seconds later the doorbell went again. She scrambled into a dressing gown and ran downstairs, hyperventilating, shaking her head trying to exorcise hysteria.

Deli opened the door, calm, collected, totally cool.

—Welcome to my hovel, she said.

Bill stood outside with his suitcase in one hand and the bacon in the other, extended like a bouquet of flowers. She looked at his suitcase.

—How long will you be staying then? she asked, only half joking.

Bill looked at her quizzically, his face in shadow hid whatever might have been going on behind his eyes.

—If I come in now, he said easily, —I might not leave.

—What? Ever? She laughed again. Even to her it sounded fake and high-pitched.

—Well, he paused, —certainly not before morning anyway. He threw the spinning thread of promise flying through the air, straight at her.

There was a tiny pause while it hung suspended before she caught it and stowed it down the front of her dressing gown. —I guess you'd better come in then, she said, stepping back and closing the door behind him.

He followed her inside leaving his suitcase in the front hall. She felt his eyes on her back.

—So this is the sitting room, she said, going in and slumping on the sofa for want of anything better to do. —I don't expect you're much interested in a tour of the house? She jumped up again.

He leant in the doorway. —Maybe some other time thanks. He was looking at her, staring her out. Speak, speak, she ordered him, say something, anything to break the tension. But he was silent.

—What? she asked softly. He didn't answer, just stood in the doorway, his arms crossed looking like he didn't dare come any closer.

—Bill, you're making me nervous.

He straightened up quickly. —Hmm. Does your hovel stretch to a bathroom? I'd kill for a shower.

She showed him upstairs, and gave him a none too clean towel. *What am I doing, she thought. Just what am I doing?*

FOR ABOUT TWO unnerving minutes she sat on the bed paralysed with fear.

Fear at him being there, fear at her letting him be there, inwardly cursing. She wanted him to go away, to go home, leave her to amass some self-control, but more than that she wanted him to stay, to finish his bath, to come into the bedroom to . . .

The sound of the plug being pulled, fuck it, she remembered the state of the room, thought suddenly what the hell, and with a precision born of desperation, ruthlessly kicked all evidence of coma life under the bed in thirty seconds flat.

He reappeared, leaning again in the doorway, towel around his waist. Deli stood in the middle of the bedroom, grungy tracksuit bottom in one hand, empty glass in another, trying frantically to turn down the volume of her heartbeat.

—You look beautiful, he said.

—I look like shit, she muttered, not meeting his eyes, —but thanks anyway.

—Do you mind that I'm here? he asked.

—No, no, I'm glad that you're here. I'm just not sure I should be here too ... she trailed off feeling self-conscious.

—It's just that you didn't return any of my calls, said Bill. —I just thought maybe you ... He stopped.

Deli gaped at him.

—I left you three messages, Deli. —Is this a chick revenge thing?

—I didn't get any message. I thought you ... You didn't come to the show.

—And I sent you flowers.

—Flowers? Deli twigged suddenly and glanced at her bedside table.

—I've practically qualified as a boy scout, I've behaved so well, Bill was saying.

Deli said nothing, rubbing her foot against the matting. Inside her head she was smiling.

—Well, I'm sorry, Bill said, pulling his towel tighter round him, —I suppose coming in person is definitely against the rules.

—Oh, it's out of the rule book altogether, she said and beamed at him.

—So, he asked lightly, —got anything clean I can wear?

She jumped up and rummaged for an old T-shirt

which he took back into the bathroom to put on over some boxers he'd extracted from his suitcase.

—Are you tired? Bill re-emerged and slung the towel on the chair.

—Ha! There should be a prize for how tired I am right now, she answered, completely unsure of her next move.

—Well, if you can stay awake, I could really do with a sandwich. I didn't eat on the plane.

—Let's go downstairs, she said, relieved that the awkwardness had passed.

They slouched in the kitchen, talked, smoked a joint and fried a whole packet of bacon. Deli perched up on the sideboard feeling much less jumpy, but the air crackled with tension and the bacon spat in the pan beside her. Bill leant against the sink opposite, arms crossed, watching her, still with that same oblique look in his eyes.

—Well? she asked him smiling.

—Well, what?

—You're staring at me again, you know, it's no good, you're going to have to stop.

He came closer still looking at her, then closer still. He untied the cord of her dressing gown. It dropped open. He touched the side of her cheek lightly, Deli rubbed against his hand with her face, closing her eyes, and opening them again as she felt his fingers move from her cheek and fall, tracing up the side of her waist, and circling round her nipples. He was still looking at her, not letting her go. She hooked her legs behind his back and pulled him closer.

—Deli, he whispered, not really as a question.

—What, she whispered, not really as an answer.

His hand was at the back of her neck, his fingers pushing into her scalp, through her hair, drawing her head down towards him. He touched her lips with his mouth, they kissed. Deli's hands pushed down inside the elastic at the back of his shorts, her legs pulling him deeper and deeper into trouble, pulling him up close as he could go. They kissed and didn't stop kissing till her neck was sore and the bacon had shrunk and burned into tiny strips and only then when they stopped, they noticed the smell of burnt fat and saw the smoke swirling round under the lights.

They detached, giggling at the smoke, relieved by physical touch, and hankering after more. Deli put another ten slices in the pan. Neither of them were hungry. Deli stood in front of the cooker swaying slightly, her legs juddering, trying to pay attention, but failing. Bill stood behind her, hard and impatient, his arms wrapped around her waist, pushing against her, his chin buried into the back of her neck. She couldn't concentrate on the bacon and it cooked lopsided, one side blackened the other side still raw, but they ate it anyway, straight out of the pan, dripping grease on the floor.

Upstairs she made him sit on the bed, kneeling beside him. It was still and quiet outside. Black black beautiful night. Slowly she pulled off his T-shirt, rubbed the palm of her hand against his chest. She licked his mouth and holding his arms pinned against the bed, she moved down his body feeling him jerk and shudder.

They made love slowly, grindingly, stoned. Half-sleepy, half-aroused. Time flew out of the window and the night seemed to grow darker and lighter by turn. She only dimly remembered coming, hovering on the pinnacle right at the top just for an instant in suspension before tumbling down, all the way down to the bottom. And just before Bill let go, she watched his face above her, holding him tight, his body burning, she watched as his eyes closed and his face screwed up and he looked about twelve-years-old, his face momentarily clear, devoid of the complicated expressions that get stamped on it as you get older.

They lay in bed, semi-conscious, minds hazy, skin dreamy, it was much less dark suddenly and the birds were beginning to screech outside. Oh boy, insomnia hour, Deli thought vaguely, and fell instantly asleep.

Later she stirred, the lamp was still on and she leant over Bill to switch it off, but he caught her wrist, wide awake. His eyes were inky black against the light.

—Don't, he said softly, —leave it on. I'm on guard. He put her hand against his cheek. —Deli, come with me, he whispered, —just for a week, come back with me in the morning.

—Don't try to pretend you came over just for tonight, she mumbled sleepily, curling around him.

—I told you I did, he said simply.

—Bill! Deli lifted her head onto one elbow. —Bill, I can't, she said seriously. —I have to be in Paris . . . on the 16th . . .

—Seems to me, Bill interrupted, putting his finger on her lips, —that you've been working non-stop for the last few months. Surely you can take a break now?

—I really can't, Bill, she pleaded. —There's so much to do. And she had listened to herself saying it. 'So much to do.' The echo that followed her everywhere, her own hopeless shadow of an excuse.

—Uhuh, said Bill. His hold on her arm relaxed.

—Maybe in a few weeks, she faltered. But even as the words came out, she knew they were a lie. She thought of the meeting, of Seb, Rubin, the inevitable cycle of the next season and the rattle of panic started.

Bill turned and lay on his back. —Sometimes you have to have the guts to take what you want without asking anybody's permission, he said softly and stroked her arm almost absent-mindedly.

—I'm sorry, she said bleakly, but she hadn't been sure whether he'd been talking about himself or her. She hooked her leg back around his warmth, trying to mend the hole beginning to yawn in their bubble of promise.

—It doesn't matter, Bill said roughly. —I have no claim on you. He pulled her to him again and stroked the inside of her thigh with the back of his fingers, pressing hard against her. Breathing softly by her ear, kissing the back of her neck.

Later when the haziness had returned Deli had felt him push himself inside her, still hugging her tight from behind, as if she was about to jump up and start packing a suitcase in the middle of making love to him. And even later still she had wondered why it was that she had come and started crying at almost exactly the same moment.

—It's okay, go back to sleep. He kissed her and put her face against his neck, wrapping himself around her again until she was cocooned.

But when she woke up in the morning, Bill had gone. His telephone number, scribbled on the empty pack of bacon, lay on the pillow beside her.

DELI FINALLY SNAPPED to and pushed open the door into Le Moule Debonair. Inside and immediately enveloped by the central heating her cheeks began to tingle and her eyes run. Her regulation puffa was slicked with water, rain dripped from the zip as she pulled it off and handed it to the hat-check girl. Pocketing the ticket in return she suddenly caught sight of her reflection in the shiny brass plaque on the wall.

—Oh, shit, she muttered in dismay. Her hair was a sodden mass of tangles and her nose bright red.

—Hot date? enquired the hat checkeress sympathetically. She pulled out a comb from behind the counter and directed Deli to the loo. Lips too she suggested after her, running an imaginary Chanel stick over her own Permanent Pink mouth as Deli turned around.

In front of the mirror, Deli swept her hair into a high bun and stabbed at it with a couple of silver grips. She quick-dabbed some Kiehl's spot cover-up on the traffic light of her nose, swiped her mouth with Vampire lip gel and made for the exit.

Well, it would have to not matter about Bill. It would have to not matter about anything except this, the company, the future . . . Thank God at least Léon and Anchois hadn't got wind of tonight.

The patron of Le Moule Debonair had a natty toupee hair flick which was gelled with Gallic precision over his otherwise bald head. He met Deli as she came out of the loo, his hands working each other over in unctuous caress and showed her up the stairs, clucking behind her in genuine concern at her wet feet.

The meeting was in a private room. Deli stood in front of the baize-pinned door and felt her stomach squirm, an oyster in anticipation of the lemon. She took a deep breath to shoo away her nerves. She was determined to handle herself carefully, cleverly, impartially . . .

—Mademoiselle? The patron was eyeing her questioningly. He stepped in front of her and pushed against the green cloth. Immediately a leaden cloud of emphysemic smoke billowed straight into her face and flew past her through the open door. And as the pollution cleared to reveal the table in front of her, Deli's heart flat-lined for two non-existent beats.

Anchois was sitting at the head of the table sucking on

the scummy end of a chewed cigar, and, next to him, Léon, already three parts drunk, slobbed back against the blue velvet chair, his obligatory Gitanes dangling out of his slack mouth. Both were looking at her with the deadly combination of smugness and aggression.

Frantically her eyes searched out M on the opposite side of the room. He looked at her steadily, a muscle pounded away, a tiny hand grenade in his cheek. Next to him Rachel perched frigidly on the end of her chair, her eyes watering from the smoke of his Marlboro.

Deli realized she was still holding her breath. She exhaled incisively, trying to pull herself together. There was only one person who could have told them about the meeting.

She looked around for Grant but to her amazement he wasn't there. Instead a man on the other side of the table whom she didn't recognize, stood up, his hand outstretched to greet her.

—Hello, he said pleasantly, —we haven't met, but I am in fact in charge of your brand at Ersatz . . . Clive Roth. Grant Teflon sent apologies for absence . . .

Deli gaped at Clive Roth as he shook her hand. She'd never even heard his name before. She looked over at M, who raised his eyebrows at her in return. Clive motioned her to the one remaining seat at the end of the table where, feeling completely retarded, she gulped down two glasses of Badoit to steady her nerves. All right so they knew, they were here, it was better to have a direct confrontation, there was still a fight to be had.

The atmosphere was murky. Everyone was silent. In her stomach now, the Devil had osmotically ingested the bad vibes and was tossing them around her guts with gay abandon.

There was a tiny pause while she tried to empty the porridge from her head and assemble her thoughts in order to address the meeting, but she was far too slow. Clive Roth cleared his throat and began to talk.

—Blah, blah, blah, blah, he said, —blah, blah, blah, blah, blah, blah, blah, blah, blah, blah, blah, blah, blah, blah, blah, blah, blah, blah, blah . . .

The words continued to march out of his mouth, an army of well-trained platitudes and at first she didn't hear them but they continued to come, rising and huddling next to one another in ranks of jumbled sentences above her head. She felt dazed until finally the letters and words forming in front of her eyes read loud and clear, and gradually it began to seep into her brain that it was not a question of having to fight a battle, it was the simple fact that the war was already lost.

—We called this meeting to discuss the future, M stated flatly to their assorted allies.

Future? asked Léon pleasantly, lighting another cigarette off the stub of his old one.

Deli looked at M.

There was another slight pause. Clive Roth cleared his throat for the second round.

—Douche as a company has done everything it can to

help you, he said. —Extended their hand in friendship – tried their very best.

—Tried everything, corrected Anchois sadly.

—However they do not believe that you have any potential. Therefore there is no incentive for them to continue helping you. They are no longer willing to have you integrated into their operation. They are of course very distressed about this situation.

—It's heartbreaking, *certainment*, agreed Anchois, surreptitiously wiping a tear from his face.

—Furthermore, said Clive, —I would like to point out we at Ersatz are not a charity. The purpose of us owning a subsidiary is to make a profit. This is called the bottom line and since we have had financial control of your company we have lost considerable sums of money.

—Don't think we hadn't noticed, M said, his voice was even but the muscles in his neck were bolted rigidly to his shoulders.

The porridge in Deli's head started to turn cold and congeal around the edges of her brain. She thought about speaking, she knew she should be shouting, attacking, fighting back, but her throat had swelled to closing and her mouth had turned to metal.

—We're simply not interested in long-term projects, Clive continued. —We have now consulted *everyone* that matters in this—

—Except for us, M interrupted.

—We have even done a national survey, said Clive,

blithely ignoring him, —and eight out of ten housewives consulted believe yours is not a viable business . . .

Deli looked at Clive, watched as his mouth opened fire and spat out iron pellets.

—So we have looked at the choices available to us. Clive was still droning on. —Which are as follows: shooting ourselves in the foot, or slitting your throat, and I think we can all agree with the exception of a very small minority present that the latter is a more attractive option. We have therefore decided to close the business. He paused, looked up, the lower half of his mouth moved over his teeth in what under the circumstances passed for a smile.

—As from now.

He had finished. The corporate crocodiles swivelled their eyes collectively in M and Deli's direction. Rachel's embarrassed and shameful, the tops of her eyelids glistening with sweat, Clive's hard and satisfied, lit by a tiny ray of curiosity. I wonder, Deli could see he was thinking, will she cry? swear? faint? Instantaneously combust?

M was already out of his chair. —Well, you bastards, he said pleasantly, —it's been a real pleasure doing business with you – you'll hear from us.

He held out his hand —Deli?

Deli rose as well and managed to negotiate her way towards the exit mercifully without knocking into the hat rack blocking the door.

—Oh, said Clive Roth, —just one more little thing

which I would like to share with you. If you open your mouth and talk to the press, you may well find the result is that your company ends up bankrupted, in which case you will retain nothing. If you keep quiet, however, you will be paid a substantial amount of money. Thank you for your time.

Downstairs in the restaurant, just before they made it to the street, Deli caught sight of a waiter hurrying towards her carrying a bundle which he shoved into her arms.

She looked down to find herself holding a bunch of drooping flowers, wrapped in cheap pink paper. She took out the card as she pushed through the restaurant door and into the street.

> *My lines are open*
> *My thoughts are with you at this so very very*
> *difficult of times.*
> *Grant xx*

Outside it had stopped raining. Deli took a deep breath, sucking the cold air into her throat as the shock began to set in. A slight wind rustled the note in her hands. M snatched the flowers from her abruptly and threw them in the gutter. Then he took her arm and walked her up the street to the taxi rank on the corner.

THEY CROUCHED AROUND a bar table in Charles de Gaulle.

—Okay, we have a choice, M had said.

—Yeah, sure, she'd said tightly.

—Come on, Deli. We'd be out of business for what? A year minimum, maybe eighteen months, but then we start again, plenty of other people have done it. This is classic fashion business sob story stuff. It really is not the end of the world.

Deli was silent. A hard look had come into her face.

—Or you let it go, take the opportunity to break out, M said gently.

She shook her head.

—Deli, there was always going to come a time when you had to say what you wanted, and the time has come now.

But the total abortion of her life at this point was an operation too bloody to even contemplate. An undefinable taste hung in her mouth, the bad breath of failure perhaps. She pulled herself sharply together, lit another cigarette and swiped the smoke deep into her lungs.

—Some day soon I must give up smoking, she said. *Never deal with today what you can bury till tomorrow.*

—You seem to think you have to either pig out on success, or blow out on failure, M went on. He took her hand. —There's life in between, you know. He glanced at her, but she was staring into space.

—Where's Bill? he asked abruptly.

—How did you know? she asked him accusingly.

—I am your brother. We're related. You and I have met before. Remember?

—New York, she said and looked away. *I suppose I blew that one, just like I blew the rest* . . . She conjured up the image of Bill's face, heard his voice, felt his touch.

—Deli! She realized M was calling her name. For just a few seconds the memory of that night had wiped her mind clean, but now the devil was back, scribbling his eternal list in red hot ink across her forehead. Gerard, Aaron, Ned, Seb, now even Bill. *Yes baby, he confirmed*, hooting with laughter, *you certainly sent him packing*.

Maybe it was true, maybe she just didn't have the guts to take what she really wanted. She felt oddly distant as the realization crept up on her. Of course her life was shitty, because sooner or later she managed to fuck up most things she cared about.

—Hey, Deli. M was pointing at the departure board in front of them where the flight details blinked their invitation. —Fate? he asked hopefully.

Deli looked scornfully at him. —Maybe I don't believe in fate.

—Well, if it's not up to fate, then maybe it's your move, M said emphatically. —There's nothing we can do tonight, tomorrow's Saturday. We can't get in touch with any lawyers until Monday. Stop feeling so bloody sorry for yourself. He raised his hands in question. —Come on, why not?

She thought of Bill, of Rubin endlessly waiting for her, she thought of the old tramp, going round and round the Paris Metro on his interminable circuit to nowhere.

Her face began a slow crumple towards tears, one welled to the surface but there was no relief of the flow behind. The river had frozen. A hard cold emptiness inside her.

—Bill's not a knight in shining armour, you know. She sniffed and wiped her eye with the palm of her hand.

—Here, said M giving her a tissue, —it wouldn't be uncool or anything.

—What wouldn't?

—Crying, sobbing, wailing, whatever the hell it is you'd like to do right now.

—I feel completely numb actually. She mashed the tissue between her hands.

Overhead the loudspeaker droned the flight details. M flashed his Visa card at her.

—Come on, he grinned. —Company credit card after all. I feel sure, just this once, they'd want you to go first class.

Deli gazed at the board in front of them for a long time. —You know something M? It's twenty years since we've been home together. She paused. —So I'll go if you come too.

M looked at her for a second then gave a short laugh. —Christ, why not . . . I sure as hell haven't got any work to do.

A GARGANTUAN BLACK man with a heavy bunch of keys dangling from his trousers' belt loops sat down next to her in Central Park and began reading the sports section of the *New York Post*.

—Yeah, he growled, looking at the results of the Nicks Match. —Oh *yeah*.

—*Hello there, Mr Basketball Fan,* Deli wanted to say, —*I grew up here. Yes, right here in this bumpy oval scraggy bit of Central Park with its stained concrete road. And, guess what? In case you're interested, which I know you are, that's where I got bitten by the dog scared by my roller-skates.*

In front of her bench about forty yards away, a father pushed his daughter up into the branches of the tree.

Dad in his red jumper, whistling Rita Coolidge songs, Mom in her huge tortoiseshell glasses. M in his orange fairisles, making a face at her, his tongue stained red from cherry-pop ice.

Fragments of memories only. She tried to dredge up the rest, but they were locked away somewhere too distant to find.

A white frisbee sailed by on the afternoon breeze, a boy in a blue T-shirt with the letters 18 printed in yellow raced around the path on his bicycle, standing up high on the pedals. He eyeballed her to see if she was watching.

The old life was there, the one left behind, the one lost and forgotten – the new life was broken and lying in pieces somewhere across the Atlantic.

The boy in the blue T-shirt re-appeared on his second circuit round the park.

—Heya, babe, he said, and flashed her a grin. He

couldn't have been more than seven. The sun was warm on her back.

She hadn't called Bill yet. Three days and she hadn't called him. She hadn't even called Aaron. She'd spent her time mostly in the hotel watching re-runs of *Rosanne* and speaking long distance to Rubin, or inside the Angelika Cinema staring at the surprisingly popular lesbian double-bill titles that were playing as part of Gay Celebration month.

M had flown back to London the day before. —Let me know what you want to do, he'd said. But how the hell did she know? She was a mental paraplegic. A gigantic sticky mess of confusion and indecision had lodged itself in her head. For so long she'd envied people with choices. Now a dizzying number of jumps had opened up, all of which gave her vertigo.

Restless, she wandered round the park from 98th street down. A few rollerbladers whizzed past, splitting ranks to skate around her. A thousand Styrofoam cups, printed with ADVIL lay in tidy piles of trash by the side of the reservoir, left over from yesterday's marathon. The cups looked curiously decorative, but then probably, she conceded, vaguely, you needed to admire ugliness on a deep level to fully appreciate the aesthetics of this city.

At the exit to the Met she left the park and walked along Fifth Avenue for a while, passing several telephone booths on the way.

Call him, you dorkess, she ordered herself. *Call him, you stupid cowardly bitch.*

But she couldn't call him. She felt too brittle and mean; emotionally defunct. She was also disturbed to discover that what was left of the soup of white hot anger had boiled down into what now resembled some kind of burnt pride.

On 65th she went back into the park again, trying to remember what it was she was searching for when suddenly she found herself standing in front of it. The Alice in Wonderland Statue. Alice with her hands stretched upwards, the March Hare holding out the clock . . . the mouse on the top of the mushroom. Memories of thirteen years of afternoons.

She walked round it, then climbed the steps. She touched the ears of the March Hare, laying her hand on the edge of the mushroom; the metal was warm, its ridges smoothed and melted by a million hot hands. *It used to be big enough to slide down, when on earth did it get so small?* She sat down on the step, aware suddenly that here she was, once again waiting for a sign, an omen, anything to tip the scales of indecision.

The sun had lost its warmth now, and the park was getting empty, the schoolchildren all on their way back home for supper. Deli stood stiffly and looked up at the statue again; and as she stared up at it, she felt her ribs squeeze painfully in on her chest and suddenly without warning, she was bawling like an idiot, all her memories prised painfully loose. And then she couldn't stop them coming, every tuft of grass, every lump of dogshit, every squashed soda can brought them flooding to the surface. On and out they poured, completely out of reach of her self control.

When her face was blotched and puffy, hagged out beyond redemption, she found she could stop and suddenly inside her head there was a potent coolness. She walked back to Fifth Avenue, bought two chocolate ice-creams, took a deep breath and called Bill.

THE PARK WAS almost deserted when she spied the tall figure lolloping in by the entrance at the far end of the boat pond. She narrowed her eyes and squinted out over the water. He hesitated for a second while he weighed up which was the shorter route to Alice in Wonderland, East or West of the pond? He plumped for West, and hurried towards her.

Epilogue

Deli could hear the telephone ringing as she put the key to the lock of the brownstone. Transferring the bag of shopping to her last two fingers, she gritted her teeth trying to make the key turn. The book she'd just bought dropped out of its paper bag and fell to the ground.

Fuck.

She put all the bags on the stone steps, and tried the key again, but the plastic handle had cut off the circulation in her fingers. As she finally heaved the shopping through the front door, she heard the remainder of a message playing out on Bill's answering machine.

Okay, yes. She'd finally admitted to herself that Bill was her boyfriend. After all, it seemed churlish not to after a year and a bit, and particularly so, given she and Rubin had moved in with him. She didn't know quite how this had happened, but it had. And it was great, she was happy, it was working.

Oh, sure, they argued sometimes, after all Bill was no pushover when it came to getting his own way, but they weren't the scary kind of arguments, the ones without a beginning or an end, the ones plucked out of thin air with the poisonous barbs that stuck in your flesh and stayed there.

She kept waiting for Bill to go off her but he didn't. Sometimes she asked him if he was bored of her yet, suggested he might like to get another girlfriend, like maybe one with slimmer ankles and a current career option, but he just looked at her as if she was retarded and threatened to give her a good thrashing.

What she found even more scary was that he went on digging himself deeper and deeper towards her heart. For a while she was worried he was going to get there only to find nothing, and that that nothing would gradually turn their relationship sour. But it hadn't happened.

She'd tried hard not to like him too much but recently she'd found it almost impossible to remember what it was like to wake up in the morning without some part of him in her arms. So she supposed now she didn't have a whole lot left in the way of defences and the weird thing was she was getting used to that too.

Odd how fast life could turn a somersault.

On the mat inside the front door, a postcard lay on top of the afternoon mail, picture side up.

Dikes on Bikes, Gay Mardi Gras, Sydney Australia. She picked it up and turned it over. It was from Seb.

Hi Sexy,
Love Seb

Typical Seb. Mr Verbose, the world's most hopeless correspondent.

Deli smiled. God she missed him.

He'd left London, just before Bill's financing came through and they had moved to New York. He'd rented his flat, bequeathed her his favourite CDs, then bought a round the world ticket and become a traveller.

She'd driven him to the airport.

—I wish to God you weren't going. She hugged him at the departure gate.

—You'll have to fax me. I'm a useless correspondent.

—You were a useless assistant as well, but that didn't stop me employing you.

—Bitch.

—Fag.

—Just promise me one thing? Seb said, taking her hand and putting it against his cheek.

—Maybe.

—Promise? He smiled wickedly.

—You're making me suspicious, what?

—Don't let Bill go, will you?

—Give me a break, she said, snatching her hand away.

—He's given you back everything Ned took from you, Seb went on. —Don't make the mistake of throwing it away.

—Seb, you're making me nauseous.

The loudspeaker crackled.

—There's the final call, Seb said. They both looked at the screen. She hugged Seb again, gripping him tight to her.

—Don't go, don't go, don't go, don't go. She released him. —All right, fuck off then.

—I'll be back in a year.

—I'll be here if you need me, she said, embarrassed suddenly. —And I'll be wherever you want me to be if anything happens.

—Deli, don't make it so hard on yourself to admit you're an okay person. Not a great one but perfectly okay and stop snivelling onto my one good jacket.

—I love you, Seb, look after yourself, watch out for snakes, watch out for air stewards . . .

He hugged her again and then walked backwards through the gate, smiling and waving before he bumped into a group of howling Australian tourists wearing psychedelic shell suits. She watched him till long after he disappeared, then with tears streaming down her face, spent three quarters of an hour in the short-term car park searching for her car.

DELI PUT THE postcard in her teeth and carried the bags downstairs, thinking how much life had changed for everyone.

So there was Seb: then there was M, married to Tish, expecting his first child. And of course there was Rubin, her little slug with his giant earlobes; this strange three-dimensional boy that had emerged rather than just the sore reminder of her guilt. In Rubin now, she saw Ned, all those parts of Ned that she'd loved, his charm and his childishness, his originality, but luckily not his frightening blackness. And sometimes, first thing in the morning when Rubin wormed his way into their bed, squeezing his hot body between them, she found she could just hold him tight and lie on top of Bill to feel surprisingly whole again . . .

She put the shopping in the kitchen, and made herself a banana, fungus and wheatgerm milkshake . . .

After the lawyers got finished, Bill took her and Rubin away, and for a month they wandered around South America, went to subtitled U certificates at 4 o'clock in the afternoon, slept under the sun and burnt away all the stuff that didn't matter any more.

Deli walked slowly upstairs clutching the filthy yellow concoction in her hand.

In the sitting room the answering machine flashed provocatively: four messages.

Absent-mindedly she pressed the button, it clicked into life.

—Hi, stupid, it's M. Don't pretend to be out and busy, because I know you've got nothing to do. Give me a call when you get through painting your toe-nails. Tish and I are coming over next week. The line clicked and beeped, then clicked again.

—Hi, Deli, it's Adelaide. Aaron wants to know whether you're both coming to Shelter Island next weekend or not, call us when you get in.

Another click.

—Hello, where are you? I need to talk to you in the next ten minutes or I'll be forced to go to the local S & M sex show. She smiled at Bill's message. Ironic really that the high point of her day was giving Bill a hard-on in his office.

Suddenly the fourth call came on. A stranger's voice.

—This is a message for Deli Madison. I hope this is the right number. This is John Mosley speaking, we have met once, in Paris, although you may or may not remember. I'd like very much if you could give me a call. I'm staying at the Carlyle, room 104. I'll be here until Wednesday. I know all about you, and I have a proposition I think you might very well be interested in.

The line clicked dead. Deli looked at the machine. John Mosley, he of the desperate cab ride. She probably still had his card somewhere. A pin-prick of curiosity started.

Uh uh, she squished it hurriedly. No, no, no. Stick to the policy, ignore any call that might conceivably be work oriented. After all she'd managed to do just that for a whole year now, and the lingering sense of guilt at doing nothing had only just faded into a delicious feeling of luxury . . . except that recently, if she was very honest, that feeling sometimes had the browning edges of bore-dom around it. But she pushed the thought away, jabbed at the machine and wiped off the messages.

She took the empty glass downstairs again and washed it up, making sure she got all the stubborn flecks of bran from around the curve of the bottom rim. She looked at her watch, another couple of hours before Rubin got out of school and had supper.

Supper, yes, well . . . Rubin's early life would pass in a haze of good things to eat: Twinkies, Ring Ding Donuts, Lucky Charms, Jell-O, Cheesedoodles, Baloney . . .

She pulled the book out of its Doubleday bag and brushed the dirt from its front cover.

'Twenty ways to make Organic Bread' was printed onto a subdued photograph. Recycled Paper, boasted the back cover.

She put it on the shelf with the others, scanning the titles vaguely.

How to Cook Your First Boiled Egg
Butter Me with Pride
Love Your Everyday Household Objects
Juice Joy

She frowned, looking at the titles again and suddenly shook her head angrily.

Juice Joy? Butter Me with Pride? Fucking hell, what's going on here? Who did she think she was kidding?

She stood still for a split second, looking around the neat kitchen, indecisive, then bolted upstairs, grabbed the telephone and dialled information for the number of the Carlyle.

Impatiently she stabbed at the buttons. —Room 104, please, she squeaked.

It picked up on the fourth ring. A voice answered:
—John Mosley, speaking.

—Yes . . . of course I remember you, she babbled. —The man that got me to the most obscure restaurant in Paris. What kind of proposition? she said. —Sounds interesting. What? Can I meet? *Oh!*

Oh shit no, she thought suddenly. What am I doing?

The thing was, she had this life now, this great big enormous life stuffed full of solid things, she had friends she actually met with, a brother she didn't have to talk budgets to. She had a small boy with yellow eyes and huge ears. And on top of all that, she had a man who said he loved her. In fact she had a man who said he loved her even when she had lain catatonic on the floor blowing bubbles out of her mouth for three months, and she guessed it didn't get much better than that.

—Oh yes, I'm still here, she said to John Mosley.

Her stomach cramped, she felt the familiar stab of the fork, heard the cackle of laughter.

But, hell, she thought, so she had this great life now . . .

—Sure, she said into the receiver. —Sure I can meet. When would be convenient for me? Oh, um, tomorrow would be just fine.